Death By Peppermint

Tim Randle

Published 2007 by arima publishing

www.arimapublishing.com

ISBN 978 1 84549 228 1

© Tim Randle 2007

All rights reserved

This book is copyright. Subject to statutory exception and to provisions of relevant collective licensing agreements, no part of this publication may be reproduced, stored in a retrieval system, or transmitted in any form or by any means, without the prior written permission of the author.

Printed and bound in the United Kingdom

Typeset in Garamond 11/14

This book is sold subject to the conditions that it shall not, by way of trade or otherwise, be lent, re-sold, hired out, or otherwise circulated without the publisher's prior consent in any form of binding or cover other than that which it is published and without a similar condition including this condition being imposed on the subsequent purchaser.

In this work of fiction, the characters, places and events are either the product of the author's imagination or they are used entirely fictitiously. Any resemblance to actual persons, living or dead, is purely coincidental

Swirl is an imprint of arima publishing.

arima publishing
ASK House, Northgate Avenue
Bury St Edmunds, Suffolk IP32 6BB
t: (+44) 01284 700321

www.arimapublishing.com

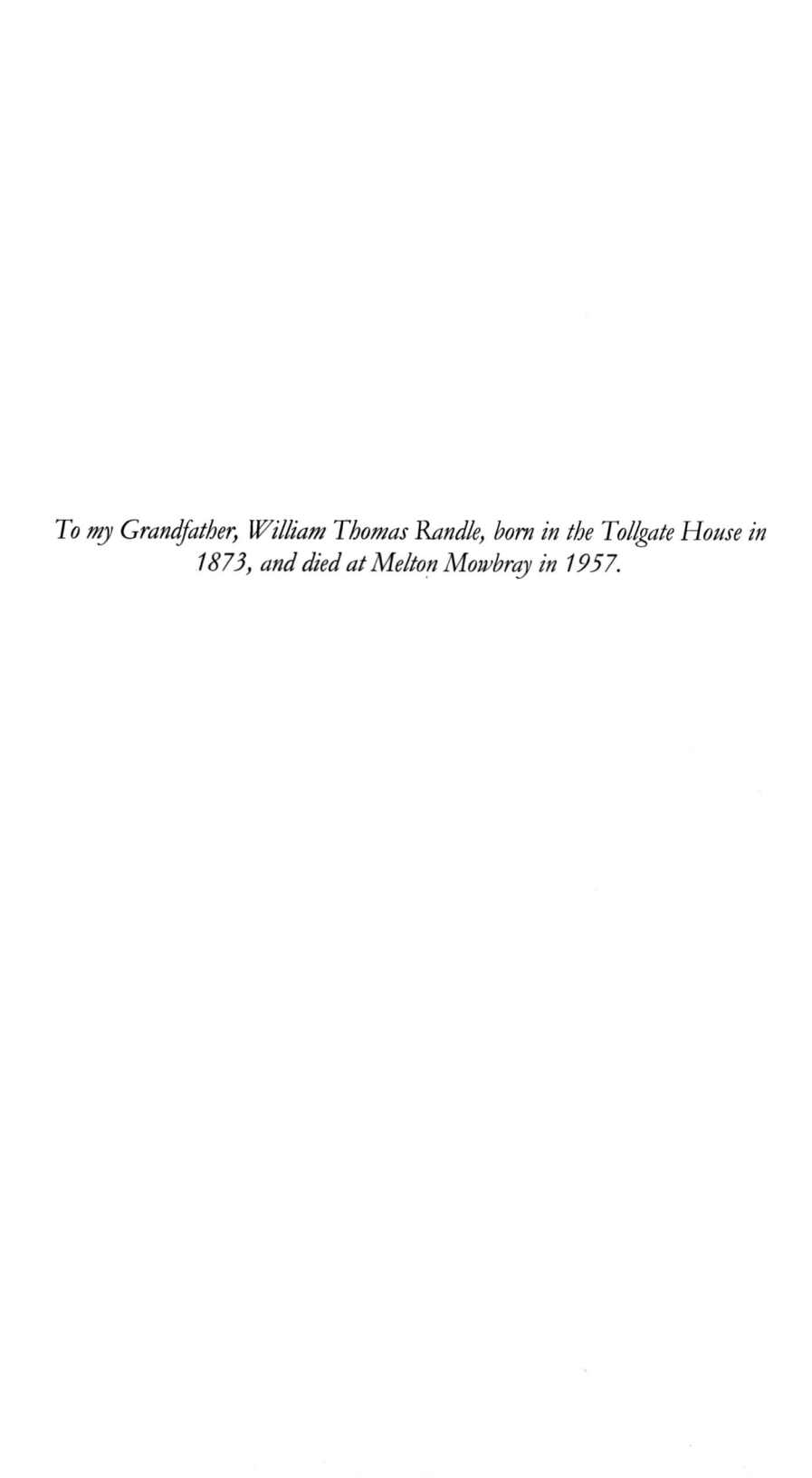

To my Grandfather, William Thomas Randle, born in the Tollgate House in 1873, and died at Melton Mowbray in 1957.

My thanks are due to Dick and Jo Winters of Melton Mowbray who share my interest in Peppermint Billy and who have been sources of great encouragement and support. I also wish to thank Josie Brewster of Radcliffe on Trent who provided interesting notes on the history of that great river. The Leicestershire author, David Bell, has also been very encouraging and helpful. In Australia, Steve Shattuck of the National Insect Collection was very helpful and provided the facts about soldier ants in Tasmania. As usual, my wife Ann has been very supportive throughout all my writing projects, and especially through this story of Peppermint Billy.

Tim Randle

Prologue

August 1835

Billy was restless. For the fourth night in a row, his sleep, indeed the whole household's sleep had been disturbed by a group of ruffians banging tin lids together, some blew on whistles and others rang bells. Billy was too young to really understand, but his parents knew the meaning of this familiar demonstration. They were no longer acceptable in the village, and should make a move to leave it. Billy was not too young to remember hearing his mother and father quarrelling about the ritual and its meaning. Both of them believed the instigator to be the Bailiff Woodcock. His father, a blustering Peppermint Jack, had crossed swords with the Bailiff many times in the past. Then, that fifth disturbed night, Billy heard his mother crying before dawn. Her husband realised there was only one course of action left,

"We'll leave in the morning, gel. It'll be alright, me' duck".

The next morning, Billy could see packages littering the lane-side in Scalford Village. The activity became more urgent because young hotheads were in evidence, already itching to dive in to do damage. One of their would-be assailants, thinking the coast was clear, tried to enter the cottage but was repulsed by his father, an exasperated Peppermint Jack, who threw him back.

"Hold yer 'orses, yer blackguard!"

The blackguard stumbled to one side, half falling but steadying himself as Jack emerged from the erstwhile family home. It was a warm morning, and Jack was clearly already feeling hot. Yet, his wife, Ann, worried about her children, especially young Billy, assailed him,

"Jack, tell'em! Jack, where's Billy?"

"Billy! Come out of it!" Peppermint Jack's voice was urgent and demanding, "Your mother's worrying herself sick".

There were shouts heard, and the few bits of crockery smashed loudly within, as figures raced through the cottage. The acrid dust of a broken home filled the air. Billy appeared in a doorway,

"I'll do for that toss-pot Woodcock", he said with a show of bravado that belied his fourteen years.

"Come out, I say, Billy come here!"

"Billy, Billy" called his mother plaintively.

At her call, Billy acquiesced and picked his way over debris back to the point where his family was standing. Jim, his older brother, pulled him to himself and told him,

"You're better out of it, Bill". He added, "Take care not to upset the young'uns".

Billy nestled into Jim's always-protective arm.

A crowd of people were approaching, clamouring and vengeful, like a threatening cloud. The sun was up and a slight breeze: not enough to do any damage unless you had a mind to. This crowd had a firm and crazy purpose that was announced loud and clear.

"Smash them!" cried a passionate hothead.

"At 'em, lads!" answered several voices in sharp unison.

Billy's sister Elizabeth was a bit younger than him, and prone to sulks. She sobbed in her Mother's arms. Peppermint Jack and his wife had plenty of warning. With all legal avenues exhausted, the villagers had finally taken the law into their own hands. Jack and his wife struggled with their lads to stop them resisting with some force,

"Hold still, lads!" appealed Jack.

"I don't want broken heads", cried Mother.

"It's those boggers the Woodcock boys, Pa," yelled young Peppermint Billy, "Let's get 'em!"

A sod of earth and grass flew through the air. The window shattered. These villagers, including old man Woodcock and his sons, were on the rampage, inflamed by facts and fictions, many woven by them around the activities of the Brown family.

"Let's get rid of the thieving lot!" shouted old man Woodcock. His sons set up a chant of "Get rid, get rid", and this was picked up and many shouts were heard. Men and women cussed, and the crush of people grew. Their feet trampled through, driving rats before them. The table and the chairs, broken and splintered were discarded through the gaping holes. Billy saw figures moving noisily through the hovel, so at least the children knew they were not ghosts. One hothead lit a faggot of wood and threw it onto the roof. The dry thatch crackled into life amid the hubbub. Soon, smoke also filled the air and those closest found it choking and dense.

"Stay together" urged Jack, with a protective arm around his wife and as many of the boys as he could manage. They went to stand in the road as more men tackled the burning roof, and others took cudgels and rakes to the walls themselves.

"Pull 'em down!" was the cry.

"Get rid, get rid!" was the answer.

Shard by shard, the clay hovel tumbled down in a cacophony of staccato sound. Pots smashed at their feet. Clouds of dust, smoke and ash enveloped the moving figures that suggested to Billy's fertile imagination some dreadful shadow drama. They meant to eradicate all trace of them, good and proper.

ONE

Michaelmas 1833
The Brown family eked a living like many others. The father Jack had earned his soubriquet through the making of peppermint sweets, and it had been passed on to his son Billy. Children loved these sweets; it was part of folklore that the children of his Grace liked these candies. His Grace, however, did not like the firebrand Jack, the radical Jack, who many times had been a thorn in his side. Billy was of course too young to understand this animosity. Where did Jack earn this reputation? In Scalford Village, the Bailiff occupied a room at *The Plough* to hold 'court'. Here, he took in rents, noted down - grudgingly - the need for repairs. He was particularly harsh with short-changers, or those with rent owing. The Parish Constable was usually in attendance. He kept order; if necessary, he made arrests. Peppermint Jack arrived to pay his rent. He had no problem paying rent; even though he had scant opinion of recent rent rises.

"Huh! That's five pounds for Midsummer, and six pounds for Michaelmas, Brown!" Woodcock, the Bailiff spoke sharply.

"There's the eleven pounds you ask for, sir", said Peppermint Jack, placing a tightly tied bag of coins on the table.

"I'd like to be able to charge you for your lads and their thieving ways!"

"This is your rents meeting, sir, not the Quarter Sessions".

The clerk was scribbling furiously. Woodcock was stung by this unexpected remark. He was quick to anger,

"What I say, Brown, is that you keep them on reins, or we shall resort to harsher methods to stop their scandalous behaviour".

"The only scandalous behaviour here, sir, is the raising of rents twice since Lady Day".

"You dare to question his Grace's management of his estate!" thundered Woodcock, now reddened and wild-eyed.

"All I question is the reasonableness of these rents for the farmers, the journeymen", he looked slowly around the room, "the farriers, the blacksmiths, for example; and, lastly but not least, householder tenants such as myself".

This reply rendered the Bailiff speechless; he collapsed into his chair, banging his fist upon the table. John Lumpage and his wife, Kathleen were present. Whilst Kathleen made sure the two dogs behaved, John took the opportunity to press home his ideas for there to be some sort of insurance against unemployment –

"Say a man is crippled or killed on his farm, who would look after those left behind?"

The Bailiff expressed his astonishment that His Grace should be expected to look after the widows and orphans as well!

"What's your sick club at your local for? What does that provide?" he sneered.

"It's not to provide comfort to his Grace, I reckon".

The Bailiff could hardly contain himself - he was so cross. Indeed, the whole room was taken aback by the ferocity of the exchanges. The murmurs of agreement with these ideas were quickly stifled by the glare of their Bailiff. The firebrand Jack, the Radical, took his leave and walked from the room. The consequences of his personal now public feud, two years later, were evidently at crisis point. John Lumpage and his wife, Kathleen caught up with him outside the building. As the two dogs fussed about Jack's legs, John Lumpage said,

"You gave him what for, in there! Well done, lad, well done".

Jack the Radical beamed in pleasure,

"That's good of you to say so. Not many would!"

Jack was still beaming at John Lumpage's compliments, when his wife Ann arrived with two of her children in tow. Jim and young Billy were enjoying the walk.

"Hello, me' duck!" he said in welcome.

Ann was keen to find out how well the meeting went,

"Hello, dear. Did you have a good meeting?"

Ann nodded to John and Kathleen, whilst the two boys began to play tag around the group, adding whoops of joy. This strategy soon affected the two dogs that began to yap in excitement, so that Kathleen began to worry about them.

"Stop that boys, you'll upset my dogs!"

"That's right, boys", added Ann, "Move away a little – go and play round that tree".

Jim and Billy needed no second bidding and bounded off towards the welcoming tree. Kathleen relaxed as the boys moved away. So did the dogs.

"By all accounts, the men had a lively meeting".

"You didn't upset the Bailiff?" asked Ann in mock horror.

The men laughed in reply, remembering how flustered the Bailiff had become.

"We made him uncomfortable, I think", said John.

"We did that, especially when he tried to turn the rent meeting into a Quarter Sessions", answered Jack the Radical.

"How could he do that?" asked Ann.

"By publicly criticising our children and their behaviour".

"What! The cheek of the man!" exclaimed Ann, just as the Bailiff emerged from the building to walk to the stables at the rear. Woodcock studiously ignored the group. It wasn't clear that he'd heard Ann's comment, but nothing happened, other than the Bailiff rode out on a chestnut gelding and turned towards Belvoir. The watchers had had enough, and turned themselves towards home. Ann called for the children, and Jim and Billy dutifully joined their parents for the walk back. Jack made his way home reflecting with some humour that his family had been a thorn in the Bailiff's side.

August 1835

The sons of the Brown family were a handful - tearaways, all of them. They had plagued the villagers of Scalford and the farming community around, usually by horse rustling, or the stealing of livestock. Once a brace of pheasant was taken just as it had ripened for a family feast; the wrong family enjoyed it! The question of the family's right of settlement in the Parish had proved a problem after weeks of argument involving the Vicar and the Church Wardens. Even proof that some of the children were baptised in the church was not enough. And then, a year after the Great Reform Act, the community had, with one voice - encouraged by Woodcock - determined to get rid of this nuisance and were in a maddened rage. Where their cottage stood, all was chaos. Peppermint Jack and his wife and family walked slowly away from the mayhem, shepherded for the most part by the Vicar and his Verger, who had thoughtfully provided a carriage and pair to take them and their few belongings to their relatives.

They moved on to Frisby, on the way to Leicester, and not far from Melton Mowbray, where Ann Brown's sister and brother in law had a smallholding. Evelyn and Richard felt able to support them after their appalling experience in Scalford. But would Radical Jack begin to mellow; would his sons be any more manageable? Even young Billy wondered,

"Have they seen the last of Bailiff Woodcock, sometime local Magistrate?"

TWO

"Come in, my dears and settle down", was Evelyn's warm greeting.

"I'll put the kettle on," said Richard, disappearing into the kitchen. He noticed Ann close to tears, so decided to move to the other room so as not to embarrass her. Jack and Ann sat down looking quite exhausted, while their four – three boys and a girl – made friends with their cousins – four younger children who confidently took them on a tour of the farm and showed them their responsibilities with the chickens and geese. As the chatter of the children faded, so Ann sobbed. Jack was attentive but felt helpless. Richard returned with the tray of tea, so Evelyn plied her with sweet tea and her spirits began to revive.

"Don't fret, me duck," said Evelyn, "You can stay here as long as you need".

"This is very good of you, sis," replied Ann, with another fit of sobbing.

"There, there, stop your worrying".

As the lioness protects, so Evelyn was a powerful defender.

"This isn't Scalford!" Evelyn swore, "so settle down here for a while".

Ann felt much better and asked about the children,

"Surely, we are too many for your family".

"Kids," said Evelyn, "kids can take care of themselves and each other. They won't bother us! It'll be good to have a bigger family living here. And you can take all the time you need!"

Ann relaxed. She recognised Evelyn as the good mother she was, with strong feelings for their welfare and well being,

"Sis, I can obviously help with the kids, and in the kitchen too if you need."

"Well," replied Evelyn, "an extra pair of hands in the kitchen would be very welcome and that's a fact! Stop worrying about the kids, will you? You know I've raised four and buried one as an infant".

Evelyn spoke from tried and tested experience. Family was as important to her as life itself, so to take her own sister in with all her troubles was actually no trouble at all. Evelyn stood up, wrapping herself in her voluminous apron,

"Come along, and help me get dinner ready. You can do the vegetables while I see to the meat".

The two sisters moved to the kitchen, while Jack went with Richard to help with the livestock. The 'farm' was, in reality, a smallholding – enough to keep one man busy. Richard was particularly pleased to have an extra pair of hands with the cattle, the sheep and goats. Evelyn and the children looked after the chickens and the geese.

As the two sisters worked, Evelyn's smile got warmer,

"Do you remember Ann, how we helped our Mam in the kitchen? How we used all that sugar in the butterfly cakes?! How cross she used to get?" and the sisters collapsed in laughter. There was no problem in Evelyn's kitchen. It was her common-sense approach that stocked the meal table; their own livestock provided the meat and milk. Evelyn was generous in her actions. She found small amounts of cash regularly for her sister. Neither of them saw fit to tell the men-folk. Evelyn's home was God-fearing,

"Now Ann, we are all in church on Sunday morning, but you don't have to feel obliged".

"Oh", replied Ann, "if it's all the same with you, Sis, we'll stay here and mind the baby".

Richard and Jack, now recovered from his worrying time, were in the cowshed, sweeping and sluicing. Jim, Jack's eldest helped them. Richard explained the good arrangement they had with neighbouring farms,

"Cooperation is very useful to provide a good stock of fruit and vegetables at fair prices. We sell our own apples and potatoes".

Richard liked talking about the farm, and the two brothers-in-law had an easy-going relationship. Each enjoyed the other's company. Richard appreciated the hard work put in by young Jim.

It wasn't long before Jim was eighteen; he was often working away from home from that time on. He didn't explain his work to Billy, but their father Jack was convinced,

"His business is risky, that it is! He's fallen in with a rum lot!"

Jack knew it was criminal work. To be exact, Jim was cattle rustling. This sort of work, by its very nature, meant that he was often away for a long time. In effect, this meant that Billy had to grow up quickly. He was already shouldering responsibilities for the younger kids of both families. Billy enjoyed the work, because young kids paid no heed whatsoever to Billy's disabilities of eye and leg. His blinking face held no terror for those children, as they played tag in and out of the hay bales; as they swung in the barn to a lofty perch. There was much shouting and laughter as they encountered each other. There was nothing better they liked doing than sitting on a fallen tree in the bottom field to watch the trains rattle past. They often merited a whistle!

In his turn, Billy never questioned Jim about his nefarious activities – not even when Jim returned home, white and frightened. There were no questions when Jim returned his horse to the stable late at night – nor, when he did not return home at all for three or maybe four nights. Jim immediately began to learn the 'trade' of horse and cattle rustling with a gang that was led by a ruddy-faced ruffian, Heathlighter.

They rode far and wide, to the Trent valley to the north, and Grantham in the northeast; and then roamed south towards Northampton and west towards Leicester and the Wreake. Jim learned the likely places for a herd of cattle or a dozen horses; as well as the likely markets for the beasts. Heathlighter was also known for his use of the new train services, then networking across the entire country, which served as arteries for markets even further away. He kept a half dozen of trusty 'generals', like Tommy Beattie, to oversee the operations and to gather intelligence of cattle and horses. Rail junctions such as at Radcliffe, near Nottingham, were very significant in Heathlighter's planning when he hoped to get rid of his booty very quickly. Jim realised that the 'game' could be very dangerous. Whilst his younger brothers and his sister gambolled and frolicked on the farm and its fields, he was on the wing, far and wide across Leicestershire and Nottinghamshire. Sometimes, he was one of up to twenty riders, when he fancied himself in the Wild West. He thumped his trousered thigh with a flat hand, but could not quite manage a "Yahoo!" He listened to the 'chink – chink' of the reins as the horses walked quietly through a sleepy hamlet in the Wreake valley – he was not far from home, but it would have to wait a while longer.

The riders were heading for Barrow upon Soar and then on to Woodthorpe for a prime herd of cattle, about forty head. Heathlighter had received this intelligence just the day before and already had plans to mount a raid. It was a big undertaking, if only because the distance to Radcliffe rail junction was getting on for fifteen miles. Getting the cattle moving was easy enough, with a deft swish of a cap here and a gentle shove with a horse there. The bridge at Cotes was managed well, and Jim as usual was the rearguard for stragglers. Heathlighter was business-like in his management of the team. Everyone knew their place and felt an important member of the exercise. At Burton on the Wolds, the team turned north towards Wymeswold and Keyworth. The last stretch through Cotgrave to Radcliffe would be a dangerous one, because by then the alarm must have been raised, and single riders, unencumbered with cattle, were speeding across the wolds to spread the news of the raid.

At Cotgrave crossroads, a makeshift barrier was erected with an old dray slewed across the road, and empty beer casks were rolled in front and stood up as silent sentinels. The Bailiff Woodcock was fairly new in post, so his deputy, Joseph Goodson was efficiently placing up to fifteen, may be sixteen men about the barrier. The outriders had done their work well, passing news of the cattle raid across the Vale and over the Wolds. Now one was sent south to see if any signs of the herd could be noticed.
"There's no sign of 'em!" said the scout, breathlessly.
It seemed from his report that the herd had vanished into thin air

Jim realised that Heathlighter, in fact, also had his own outriders and depended on their fresh information. So by the time he and his men had brought the herd as far as Wysall, Heathlighter had received word of the barricade from Tommy. Now, he made a strategic decision that showed how sharp he was, and such an effective leader.
"We'll turn 'em to Widmerpool and Kinoulton, then north through Owthorpe and the Cropwells".
He made his plans very clear to his other 'generals', and the herd moved forward accordingly. There were no loud noises, nor foul language. Everyone simply followed the lead, and made their part in it efficient. Jim learnt quickly and he was already wondering if the work would suit his brother, Billy. So the herd walked on willingly through the Cropwells to Radcliffe, thus neatly outflanking the barricade at Cotgrave crossroads. Woodcock, the new Bailiff had been thwarted – not for the first time!
With the beasts sold and already on the train wagons in the sidings, Heathlighter paid off his men as he always did at the end of a raid.
"Here you are Jim. Good work tonight!"
"Thanks, boss. I'll be off now then".
Jim reined his horse about and headed off following the drovers' road back towards Owthorpe, through the Cropwells. He reckoned it was an

half hour ride to Frisby. It was a lonely ride and it was late. The moon was playing tag with wispy clouds. The fox called to its mate with strident voice. As Jim approached Kinoulton, he wondered about following through to Hickling and the Broughtons, possibly saving him time. He was not as attentive as usual to his surroundings, so was unprepared for what happened next. Suddenly, a mounted figure emerged from a gateway on his left and grabbed his reins by the horse's head. A second mounted rider moved to his side on his right.

"You're under arrest. Come with us!"

This felony cost Jim dear. Quarter Sessions sent him to Leicester jail for twelve month's hard labour. It was his first count! But wait! It could have been his second count! Billy was unsure, and afraid for his brother.

THREE

Billy missed Jim's company, but since the family had moved to Frisby he had been busy growing up and taking some responsibility. At that time, Billy was fourteen going on eighteen. He wanted to be older in order to take part in men's 'games'; especially he wanted to take part in the feud with the Woodcocks. His father's attitude to them and to the Bailiff made a great impression on Billy. He saw Jim ride off and yearned to be with him, but at the same time he loved to help with the littl'uns.

He soon had a useful routine of games and feeding, the changing of clothes, even to the washing of baby's napkins. He received ample praise from his Aunty Evelyn,

"Billy, you are so good with these little ones! You'll make someone a good husband, one day, you mark my words!"

All the children settled well to playing together; a band of happy cousins. Jack and Ann were pleased that their children were enjoying their new home. Billy, in common with the others, particularly liked Aunt Evelyn's homemade jam, full of delicious strawberries or blackcurrants, served on homemade bread as thick as, well – doorsteps.

Aunty Evelyn and Uncle Richard also had a couple of farm dogs. One in particular, Jock a black cocker spaniel, became Billy's shadow. They went everywhere together and all the children loved him too. Many an afternoon, four children and a dog could be seen in the fields below Frisby Top. Billy with his brother Dick, Sam aged nine and Tom aged seven, and Jock enjoyed a good romp. They were always cautioned about the railway. The children's love of railways was well known, so it was not surprising to learn of their game known as 'flat penny'. Sam and Tom filled their pockets full of copper pennies, and the game was to place one on the rail and wait until the train had passed by. Needless to say, the image of Queen Victoria's head was flattened and squeezed into an unrecognisable disk that amused the children so much they raced to put another penny on the line. Billy was the oldest and was concerned for the children's safety, but he needn't have worried because these children were very competent and careful. Or perhaps, it was Jock, the spaniel that was very careful. When the corn was stacked and drying, for example, the quintet built a 'house' by pulling together the bales, and of course disturbing the farmer's careful work. Whoops of joy and the falling of bodies through the 'windows' or through the 'door' occupied the youngsters for a long time. Jock enjoyed dodging the falling bales, first from one 'window', then from another. He yelped and danced about, his happy eyes glistening and his red tongue lolling about his mouth. As completely absorbed, as the children were, Jock, however, noticed the figures gathering at the foot of the field and gave a low growl that Billy found arresting. As when the fox trails the scent of man and horse and is wary, Billy looked down the field and saw the approaching danger.

"Come on!" he shouted, "Make for home!"

The quintet scampered up the hill and through the stile, with Jock frolicking along and finding a hole in the hedge to squeeze through. Billy could see the shaking fists of the farmer, but the chase had been abandoned, and the men began to tidy up the stack.

Aunt Evelyn was always telling the children not to go to the river, the 'Big River',

"It's too dangerous, the water will suck you under in a trice – you keep away from it, you hear?"

Her admonitions to stay away from the 'Big River' were of course ignored. A number of afternoons, four children and a dog could be seen on the banks of the River Wreake. Jock chased in and out of the shallows,

"Here boy! Fetch!" called Billy, and Jock willingly raced off to fetch the thrown stick.

Children gambolled happily in the shallow water.

"Catch this, Jock!"

Billy stripped off his shirt, kicked off his shoes, his trousers and his pants. Dick gathered them up and followed him along the riverbank. Billy enjoyed a swim in warm weather, wearing only his skin! Jock paddled beside him, trusting the lad, adventurous in the deeper part of the River Wreake, and coping well with the rushing currents.

Danger has a habit of lying in wait and snapping at you when you least expect it. Tom and Sam were Evelyn's children, cousins to Billy and Dick. Tom, Sam's brother, was shadowing Dick along the bank, and suddenly he was laughing and bundling Dick along so that he dropped Billy's clothes.

"Hey, you stop that horsing around, Tom!"

"Don't be mardy – only having fun!"

Dick managed to rescue the clothes, but Tom was again very overbearing,

"Ah, ah!" he yelled, and tripped up Dick. This spat meant that neither of them noticed the difficulties in the water for Billy and Jock.

A tree trunk came floating downstream. It had gathered speed in the currents and then bore down on Jock who got entangled in the spreading limbs. He was soon being swept away, barking and struggling all the time to free himself.

"Good boy, Jock – I'm coming!" Billy urgently swam after him and tried to grab a branch but it slipped through his fingers.

"Damn and blast! I've got to get hold of it!"

He tried again and managed to hold on fast; his body acting as a kind of rudder, the whole stump slew toward the bank and shallower water, eventually grounding in the gravel. Jock was now able to leap over to the safety of the bank,

"Jock – good boy. Come here lad!" and the dog jumped into the waiting arms of the naked Billy. As Billy climbed out of the water, he allowed Jock to run on ahead and shake himself dry in the field. Tom had reached this point and started to act the fool,

"Ha! Show the girls, Billy. Oh dear, not much to show the girls!"

Billy could see that Dick had his clothes and looked upset. Billy took his clothes from his brother,

"A fool is he, Dick? What's up?"

"He's a bully, Billy, plain and simple. I had no idea he was like this".

Billy turned menacingly to Tom,

"You'd better choose someone your own size, Tom".

Billy hurried to put on his clothes – he would dry in what was left of the sunshine. He donned his shoes, slowly and deliberately – the last items, and then Billy launched himself at Tom,

"Throwing your weight about, Tom? You leave my brother alone or you'll be sorry!"

Billy reined down blow after blow as Tom shouted,

"Alright, Billy, I was only fooling about!"

"Well, fool about with someone else".

Billy deemed the spat to be over as Tom shrank away with his brother Sam.

Billy did not engage any more in these romps with the younger kids. He considered himself to be 'grown up', ready to play men's' games. The reason probably had more to do with his developing manhood than his official age.

Talking of official ages, there was nothing Billy enjoyed more than a mug of tea in a warm kitchen and the gossip of the grown ups.

"She's a stuck up cow!" said his mother, of some unknown villager

"Don't be heartless, Ann" replied Evelyn, "She's had a lot to put up with since her man went off".

"Well, you'd think to say 'good morning' to anyone you meet, wouldn't you?"

"She's got a lot to think about without troubling to bid you a 'good morning'!"

He was a good listener, but increasingly, as he grew older, felt the need to add his own thoughts.

"Hasn't she got kids?" he asked, pushing aside a now empty plate of bread and jam.

"What's that? You've been listening!" scolded his Mother, but smiling merrily.

"He's got head on 'is shoulders, gel" added Evelyn.

"Well, he thinks too much, grows up too quickly".

"If she's got kids, she's had it rough, then?" Billy carried on. His words found their mark with both women. He was only repeating the words he had heard from a few days before. His talk sounded challenging, but it was his own lack of experience that spoke. His father cautioned him more than once to stop interfering in the women's talk and to temper his language.

It was a few days later, after an evening meal of mutton, potatoes, cabbage and gravy, that matters came to a head. The grown-ups were relaxing and small talk developed.

"I reckon the milking cow could be worth a bob or two – thought we might sell it and buy two others," reckoned Richard.

"You sure," replied Evelyn, "Will market be good enough?"

"Market's fine. That milking cow is better than two weeks' rent, so we can buy two young 'uns and soon be better off".

Billy tried to interrupt at the words 'better off', felt able to add his own thinking to the discussion. He didn't waste much time before he got talking, his squint emphasising the wildness of his remarks, about the big houses in the neighbouring Parish. With father still cautioning him,

"Watch it, son, take care now. Remember we are guests here" advised Jack.

Billy wondered aloud, imagining the rich pickings these houses might hold, speaking longingly of the silver and gold, the coins or plate. Young, impressionable ears were listening and Peppermint Jack stepped forward to stop Billy's mouth physically with an open hand raised threateningly.

"Will you stop? There are little 'uns here".

Billy at last fell quiet, sullen and deflated. He sought solace with Jock the cocker spaniel, but Jock was beneath his master's chair and spurned Billy with a snarl.

Twelve months later, Jim returned to find his younger brother sullen and quiet.

"It's not like you, Billy. What's up?"

"It's just me and my big mouth, Jim".

The brothers laughed and joked. They went off towards the river for a gossip.

"How would it be if you were to help me a'times?"

"Really, Jim, help you. I'd like that!"

"Say nowt to Mother and Pa, now!"

Imagine the excitement Billy felt as, after a few days, Jim asked for his help. Jim had horses for them both that afternoon; they rode off into the gathering dusk. Dick fretted for a while, but settled down. Jim and Billy joined a group of riders so that the whole group was now sixteen horsemen. They rendezvoused at the Broughtons, to enable them to take the lane to Long Clawson, then to Harby. Why Harby? The target was a herd of cattle and horses at Harby in the Vale of Belvoir. Jim smiled at the mention of their old hunting ground,

"That's alright, Billy. We know where that is!"

"Sure, Jim".

Heathlighter made a fuss of Jim, now that he had returned from his enforced absence,

"Good to have you back, Jim! Who's this?" pointing to Billy.

"This is Billy, my younger brother".

"Pleased to welcome you to the gang".

Billy beamed. He was accepted!

"Right, lads, we are away – but quietly!"

The men reined their horses to the lane leading to Long Clawson, ambling along, no great rush. It was a dark night, so horsemen in dark clothes seemed almost invisible. The occasional whinny or whiffle by the horses were the only indication that riders were there.

At Long Clawson, the men dismounted and walked their horses through the village. At their approach, an owl began to call insistently. A dog crossed their path, and ignored them. After the crossroads formed by the junction with Waltham Lane, the men remounted and soon picked up a cracking pace towards Hose and Harby. They soon found the field earmarked and labelled for a new chapel. The goal they sought was in the field at the back of that one! Their prize was disappointing – little more than a beast per man. Total, twenty animals – sixteen cattle and four horses.

Heathlighter, ever efficient, with two of his 'generals', including Tommy Beattie, on duty, soon had this retinue on the road, leading them to the bridge over the canal and thence north towards Langar and Bingham. The animals gave no trouble, trotting on gamely, so that the crossing was achieved within twenty minutes. Heathlighter was pleased,

"Well done, lads. We can move them along sharply from here!"

They covered the ground well, so that by eight in the evening they had passed Langar and were just before Bingham, swinging left into the lane that led to Radcliffe and the rail junction.

"We have a meet at Radcliffe by nine!" called Heathlighter.

The column of riders and cattle turned into the rail yard at quarter to nine. Heathlighter led them to a penning yard where the animals were tethered. Heathlighter's contact emerged from the shadows and paid the gang leader; they shook hands and separated. As was his rule, Heathlighter paid off his men and the group split up their various ways. Before he left, one of the 'generals' had a kind word for the brothers,

"You were very useful tonight. You drive cattle well. It's a pleasure to see you work".

The general was, of course, Tommy Beattie, and he invited himself to ride with them. Billy and Jim, with their new companion, turned due south through the Cropwells and the Broughtons. Tommy was in a reflective mood,

"Do you remember Thomas Plunkett?"

"Young Tom who couldn't hold his water?" said Jim, laughing.

"Yes, him. He was only seventeen and hadn't learned to be a team player. We were driving cattle through Pickwell along the drovers' road, when we realised we'd lost him. I rode back and found him following on – it seems he needed a pee".

Billy chortled,

"Yes. I remember saying he'd have to tie a knot in it!"

"That's it, he couldn't hold his water", said Tommy, and the three of them chuckled loudly as they rode,

"Thomas Plunkett – and he was bloody useless!"

It was at the top of Broughton hill that Tommy Beattie bid them goodnight with a cheery wave and cantered off to the northwest. The lads planned to ride to Asfordby, but Jim had to admit to another plan, because he was seeing a girl in Asfordby. Billy knew nothing more yet of this budding romance, but it set him thinking as he left Jim and rode home. He stabled his horse and let himself into the farmhouse at about half past ten o'clock.

Earlier in the afternoon, around four, Bailiff Woodcock reported to his Grace that the Brown family had been successfully ejected from Scalford and were now received by Frisby-on-the-Wreake.

"They have kin there, so that should be the end of the trouble we've had in the recent past".

"If you say so, Bailiff", observed his Grace, "Are you confident our troubles are at an end?"

"As certain as I can be, your Grace".

"Good".

FOUR

Edward Woodcock, Bailiff to his Grace, returned to his Scalford home, where his wife Sarah had finished her baking. As he walked into the lounge, he breathed in deeply to savour the warm, sweet smell that pervaded the house. Woodcock lived well on his earnings as bailiff. He relaxed with his late morning cup of tea and the toasted buttered scones and strawberry jam. He scraped his chin with his index finger to coax the dripping butter back into his mouth; he licked the heavenly sweetness adhering to his fingers. He gave no mind to the family he had recently usurped and sent packing to the other side of Melton Mowbray.

"Sarah, my love, your baking is superb! This is splendid!"

"There's more", she replied, pushing the plate further towards her husband.

The barking of their little white Scottie, Ben, signalled the arrival of a visitor. It was the Sexton, the Cambridge man, come to check that Edward was well after his recent ordeal.

"I'm fine, Sexton – thank you for asking. You're just in time for scones!"

"Oh, Mrs Woodcock, you have been busy. I don't mind if I do", sitting down in a commodious armchair.

Sarah was the good hostess,

"May I pass you something?"

"Just the one scone and jam please, I must take care of my figure!" he said, patting his ample middle.

"Would you like a cup of tea with it?"

"Oh yes, if you please".

Sarah went off into the kitchen to refresh the teapot, while the two men tucked into the cooking. They heard the noise of the two sons of the house, who had decided to get up after a late night the night before. They tumbled down the stairs and into the kitchen. Samuel swept his mother into his arms,

"Come here, beautiful girl!"

"Enough of the girl, my boy, really!"

Philip laughed,

"We smelled the cooking", he sighed as he saw the empty plates.

"It's all gone", said Sarah, in mock horror. Then she saved the situation by whipping out a Barn Brack Loaf and cutting two generous slices for the boys, and serving this with two cups of fresh tea. Sarah left her boys enjoying the baking, and took the teapot back into the sitting room. The Sexton was pleased to partake of another cup of tea, but then explained,

"That was lovely, but I really must be going as I have other calls to make".

He stood and began to move towards the hall. Edward saw him to the door and bad him well, the Sexton left with a quick blessing for the household. The rest of the day was quiet, apart from the two brothers occasionally arguing or coming and going at odd times. Edward and Sarah liked to spend the time reading. Sarah had some knitting to finish. The measured ticking of the English floral mantelpiece clock and its gentle striking of the quarter hours mirrored their contentment. Their home was comfortable; she was a world away from her husband's troubles, such as his recent disappointment at losing a herd of cattle from Woodthorpe. There was no room for thoughts of broken homes and ejected families; neither was there any discussion of his work in general.

Bailiff Woodcock left home in the morning after a hearty breakfast. His first call was to the blacksmith, Hewerfield, simply to pass the time of day – a sort of oblique reminder to him that rent would soon be due. Hewerfield was respectful of his Grace's representative, but soon returned to his forge where the heat and noise were not conducive to small talk. The Bailiff left, turning his mare of twelve hands away to the north of the Vale of Belvoir, the road to Stathern. As he rode, his two sons, Sam and Phil joined him, and decided to ride with him as far as the village,. It was a bright morning for a ride, with impressive views across the escarpment followed by the exhilarating descent of the hill at Stathern village. This descent was made more memorable as the father and his two sons made it a race,

"First to the water trough!" shouted Sam.

"On girl!" shouted his father.

Phil struggled to turn his stallion to the task, but soon he too was going pell mell down into the village. The three were virtually abreast, but Edward's mare, nostrils wide and eyes ablaze, just got its nose ahead to reach the stone water trough first.

The boys admitted defeat bravely and happily. The three pulled up and cantered over to the *Red Lion Inn*, where Edward was well known. The three horses were tied to a rail in the yard. Sam and Phil began to rub them down, while Edward went into the bar by the back door. There were two or three drinkers and Woodcock joined them.

"Three scotches, landlord, if you please".

"Mornin' bailiff – all in order?" asked one of the drinkers.

"Good morning to you; yes, all is in order".

These few words were exchanged, before Sam and Phil made their noisy entrance, laughing and joking and slapping each other on the back. To their surprise, and everyone else's, there was an even noisier entrance close behind them - of his Grace! Those that were seated, jumped to their feet in deference.

"Woodcock! There you are!"

"Your Grace – whatever's the matter?"

"I want you to get over to Harby. I have reports of some rustling going on. I must say this, our troubles are certainly not at an end!"

"I'm sorry, your Grace. I'll leave immediately".

The Bailiff turned to his two lads who had seated themselves,

"When you get home, tell your mother where I have to go".

"We will, father", answered Sam, "Take care!"

Woodcock was soon at the gallop heading for Harby. Farmer Matthews showed him the broken fences.

"Forty head of cattle and twenty horses are gone. Two nights ago".

"Any idea which direction?"

"It's an open road to Nottingham through the Cropwells and on to Hurstpierrepoint".

"You don't mean they'd be marketed there?"

"Rather sold on and no questions asked, and possibly on train at Radcliffe".

Woodcock realised the trail was almost cold, but still worth a look. He turned towards the Cropwells and again was soon at the gallop. At Nottingham, Woodcock questioned the staff at Radcliffe station, where he discovered that both cattle and horses were sold there that morning and entrained to the north. There was no way of knowing where the cattle and horses came from, or indeed who sold them. Those were long gone, as witnessed by the empty cattle pens. Woodcock turned his mare towards the Cropwells and was about to leave the station yard, when a man ran forward and grabbed the reins.

"Your beasts, sir. I saw them this morning".

Woodcock halted immediately and asked,

"What did you see, man?"

"Sixteen riders, I think, all on horseback. Two in the rear seemed to be brothers, I reckon. One had a squint and a gammy leg".

"The Brown brothers!"

Woodcock tossed a crown piece to the man.

"I'm obliged, man!"

Not exact proof, he thought as he rode off, but near enough.

"That description fits Billy, and his brother Richard not far behind, eh?" he said aloud triumphantly, "Or could he be the older one, Jim?"

*

Billy was pleased with the fuss of his return. Dick, his younger brother by that time sixteen turning seventeen, was overjoyed to see Billy home again. They briefly laughed and joked together, but the older Jim did not stay long as he needed to disappear again in the direction of Asfordby Valley. At least now, Billy knew the name of Jim's girl. She was Mary, a twin to Michael, son and daughter of a middle-aged couple. Their father worked with Michael; they were both labourers. Mary was a pleasant girl, the same age as Jim – perhaps only a month difference in birthdays. She was easy with Billy when they met. Billy took to her as quickly, she was fun to be with. On occasion, the two had taken Billy on a walk into Holwell Mouth with its wooded valley – where the boys used to roam from their former home in Scalford. Billy enjoyed these times, but was careful to leave the lovers to themselves when appropriate.

Dick soon began to ask Billy about the times with Jim, but Billy was firm in refusing to talk about them. Dick, always full of questions, tried another tack, and quizzed Billy about the big houses Billy used to want to look at. Billy was at first diffident and non-committal, but this time the ploy worked. A few nights later, Billy began planning a raid on a big house in the next parish. Dick insisted he was now old enough to trail him to the big houses with his horse and wagon. Billy agreed.

The evenings were still short when they walked close by Rotherby. The gloom found no-one moving about. As the moon skirted the scudding clouds; as the young fox weaved through the thicket, in and out, Billy skirted the rambling farmhouse and found at last a wicket gate ajar at the side. He reckoned there was only one dweller – a fact determined on an earlier evening walk. Just one, but one he hadn't reckoned on. Dick brought the wagon close by in the leafy lane and waited, calming the horses with his hands and making a whiffling noise through his cheeks as if to imitate the horses' blowing. His was a particular skill and he was good at it. The kitchen door was firmly resistant but full of glass. Billy wrapped his hand in a piece of sacking that lay near by and set to. One pane, two panes and the key was on the other side. A quick turn and he was in. The interior was quiet enough and he found the dining room and then the parlour. On a finely worked small table lay a watch with its key and a couple of seals – the sort he thought that might be affixed to a sale of land. Watch, key and all he slipped into a deep pocket. What was that? He thought a board had creaked. He listened intently but put it down to the old house groaning, or maybe Dick's horse snuffling. Billy thought,

"Soon, will I be groaning?"

He was right as right could be. By the time he reached the kitchen garden, just past the large barn, the owner had him in his musket sights. Billy let out a low whistle for Dick – the agreed signal for him to take off. He could hear the lad racing for the bobby. He might have run straight by Dick, who urged the horse forward urgently, and soon proceeded into the night at a great pace.

That burglary cost Billy a year's hard labour in Leicester prison yard. Quarter Sessions sent him down. The work in prison served him well. It was not designed to but Billy made the most of it. For example, he was used to farm work so prison farming was not such a burden. Again, his older brother Jim survived this work, so Billy determined that he would also. He did find beating hemp tedious, it made his fingers ache. He was particularly good at the crank – completing the winding and earning his supper. His preference was the open air, if he was ever allowed to exercise it.

Billy thrived however. He became firm in health and agile despite his gammy leg. Billy was released a fitter man than before, so that he could again take an active part in the activities of his older brother Jim, who had fallen in with a gang of rustlers that was terrorising the Leicestershire countryside. Through these activities, it was not long before his family experienced the first of a number of tragedies.

FIVE

Billy watched in excitement as Jim, his older brother, called at the Frisby farmhouse. This was going to be the day he rides with Jim to meet up with the 'gang', to be one of their trusted workers again! The rendezvous was at the stocks in Grimston where agreement was nodded through after a brief discussion, and the small group of riders headed northeast through Holwell to Croxton Kerrial. Clattering through Main Street, they arrived at *The Peacock Inn*. The riders surprised a few locals in the place; they took a quick but curious look at the six riders and made a hurried exit. The self-appointed leader of the gang was a short, squat ruddy-faced man, obviously used to the outdoor life. He chatted briefly with the publican who seemed to recognise him as 'Heathlighter'. One of his 'generals', Tommy Beattie, engaged the publican in conversation and quickly received the information Heathlighter was after – the numbers of a herd of cattle in the field next to the Mill. Billy learned all he could by watching Jim; he marvelled at the way Jim understood the 'game', especially how difficult it was with only six men,

"We can drive'em to Grantham easily tonight".

The six worked as one, immediately driving the cattle to the road and urging them on towards Denton Hill – a major barrier between them and Grantham market. This barrier they took in their stride – the ruddy-faced Heathlighter tying the leading cattle together in pairs and these had the effect of steadying those following and the hill was safely negotiated. Within the hour, the market was reached, and the cattle were herded into the pens, their backs steaming from the drive. After the count, the cash changed hands and the six riders disappeared into the night.

Bailiff Woodcock was out riding that evening, with other employees of his Grace.

"I have heard that there is a body of riders roaming to the northeast of the Vale", said the Bailiff.

"We think the news is accurate - a herd of cattle rustled from Croxton Kerrial", answered his companion.

The Bailiff reined in his horse,

"They will have sold the beasts in Grantham".

There were voices in agreement, and Woodcock thought aloud,

"They may already be riding back into the Vale".

Woodcock ordered a change of direction. They were now close to Waltham, and turned to the drovers' road leading to Harby and Colston Bassett. The men spurred their horses into action, and the animals were steaming as they arrived in Colston. They had no time to stand and stare. Approaching through the gloom were five riders heading south from Bottesford. Woodcock correctly guessed they had made a large circle – approaching Grantham from the south and leaving it going west. By switching their route to Colston from Waltham, Woodcock and his men had effectively intercepted the rustlers.

Billy did everything he could to keep up with Jim and the other four during the drive back into the Vale. A successful evening so far, with two-dozen head of cattle sold in Grantham and then the ride home a little richer. Their detour through Bottesford was quiet; very few people were abroad. They ambled quietly into the plain stretching in front of the castle, and picked up speed between Granby and Langar. It was at Langar that their sharp-eyed leader, Heathlighter, noticed a cloud of dust in the far distance and cautiously assumed it to represent riders – in force. He passed the word along. Immediately, Billy was spoken to by Jim, who said,

"Not a word Billy, head for Harby and Melton from here", he pointed to the lane on their left, "Go and see your friend the baker. Go home tomorrow".

Billy thought of protesting, but Jim's voice told him this was urgent. So without a word, he turned his mare into the lane and was gone. Billy was sure that Jim and the four were then preparing for the encounter ahead of them. Heathlighter, Beattie and one other primed their pistols and ensured they were comfortable in their waistbands. Fearlessly, they urged their horses forward towards Colston, aiming to reach the Broughtons and through them to Asfordby. Billy hoped that Jim would then be able to ride on to Frisby.

Fetlocks flashed and nostrils flared. As the riders entered Colston, pistols fired, battle was engaged. Woodcock and his men were not armed, but had rakes and hoes with which to hinder the riders' passage through the village. One was particularly careless as he moved forward to toss his rake. He was felled by a well-aimed pistol shot by Heathlighter. Three horses and their riders swept through the streets followed at an interval by Jim and another. This interval afforded

Woodcock the opportunity to make another strike. The last two riders were attacked by men as they leapt out from their cover, wielding sticks and staves. Jim's horse reared up in sudden desperation to avoid the hazard. Jim found it almost impossible to control her, and the horse stopped at the point where Jim's friend was already fallen. Jim jumped down to see if he was alright. In the same instance, Woodcock's men threw themselves on the both of them and hauled them to their feet. Their two horses were shooed away. Jim's horse was at first reluctant, but then the two turned away to follow their group riding ahead out of Colston.

*

Billy reined in his horse at the rise of the hill leading up to Harby. His vantage point enabled him to witness the 'Battle of Colston', but not to guess at the outcome. He saw the dust, heard the gunshots and the shouts. Anxiously, he spurred on his horse towards Harby and Melton. He was a solitary figure riding along the drovers' road. It was a cloudy evening on the high ground, and a drizzle set in as he descended into Melton from the Scalford Road. He made his way to the stables at the top of Rutland Street and lodged the horse with water; a feed and a good rub down. Then he walked round to Timber Hill and the home of his friend Will Moore, the baker. William was surprised, but being the good friend he was, he invited Billy in and offered refreshment of pork pie and a slice of Stilton washed down with ale.

"I'm sorry to be a nuisance, and so late. Can I be really awkward and ask if I can stay the night?"

"Sure, that's easy enough – except we start early in the morning".

"That'll be alright – I need to collect my horse at Rutland Street early and then I can make an early start back to Mam and Dad".

The next morning, Billy was riding out of Melton as St Mary's bells rang eight o'clock. His ride along the Leicester Road was uneventful and he soon reached Frisby top and swung down to the farm. The jolly impromptu party to celebrate having Billy home again got underway. A turkey freshly plucked and dressed, courtesy of a night walk by Dick enriched it. Billy's aunt did a mountain of potatoes and vegetables to go with it.

"You'd think it were Christmas!" observed Dick.

A chorus of squeals from the younger children answered him. It was wonderful, thought Billy, the way these two families had joined forces. His aunt and uncle took them in after the debacle at Scalford, and now the two families looked like one. Everyone relished their lunch. Afterwards, Billy and Dick went to the stables to check on Billy's horse. The younger ones raced off to the field and enjoyed a chasing game. Dick and Billy could hear their squeals of delight and merry laughter. The grown ups were pleased to settle, some smoked, all chattered.

The following morning was a lazy one it seemed. Even Billy had not stirred by nine. Playfully, the younger children went in search of Billy and Dick, and wakened them with a whoop and a whistle, and a well-aimed pillow. Billy and Dick joined in the revelry and wrestled with the youngsters; all was laughter and good humour. The appearance of Jack and the children's father brought instant silence. The children were ushered away by their father, and Jack spoke to Billy and Dick,

"Your brother's horse has found its way home alone. Jim is arrested for rustling. He's at the next Assizes, and it will be his third count".

The two of them were stunned. Billy was fearful of the rule of three counts. It was unspoken, but the third count meant certain transportation to the other side of the world. Billy shivered. Dick fell back into the bedclothes and was very quiet. Jack left them both to think things over. Billy lay down next to Dick and put his face close to his brother's. He spoke softly,

"Don't worry, Dick. Jim's made of good stuff – he'll be alright".

Dick turned towards his brother, always full of questions,

"Are you sure, Billy? Won't he be sent away?"

"I am sure. Yes, he will likely be sent away".

Billy threw his arms round Dick and held him tight. The warmth and emotion of the moment brought the two brothers together. Dick groaned a lot. Billy stroked Dick's hair and whispered,

"Shush, shush, lad".

Dick was consumed by tension, but it was released in a warm, moist moment, hidden within the mountainous bedclothes. They washed and dressed and went down to the large breakfast room arm in arm. After breakfast, Billy went out to the stable to check on Jim's horse. It was none the worse for its trek home. He saddled up his own horse to lead him into the yard. Dick rushed out to ask,

"Where are you going, Billy? Can I come too?"

"I'm off to find Mary, she'll have to know. I want to go on my own this time, Dick. Sorry!"

Dick was crestfallen as Billy left, cantering round the yard and out the gate. Dick heard the horse break into a trot and then a gallop. Billy took five minutes to reach Mary's home in Asfordby Valley. He found her in the garden with her Mam. Mary looked up from her fragrant flowerbed and recognised Billy at the edge of the garden as he tethered his horse at the gate.

"Hello, Billy, what are you doing here?"

Her Mam was cheerful,

"Hello Billy, George is at work, and Michael. They will be sorry to have missed you".

"What is it, Billy?" asked Mary again, slightly worried, "Is it about Jim?"

"Yes Mary, it is", said Billy, stepping forward.

Mary was very sensible. She clearly understood the nature of Jim's work – how dangerous it was, and risky. She and her Mam linked arms; there was no need for secrecy between them. Anyway, Mam was interested in Billy's news. The two of them were impatient for him to tell them what he knew,

"C'mon, Billy, what is wrong?" asked Mary.

"He's been arrested and will have to go to the Assizes next month".

Mary was shocked, and her Mam clung to her in her distress. Billy could only look on feeling helpless. At last, Mary freed herself and hugged Billy,

"Thanks, Billy, for taking the trouble to find me and to let me know. Will it be his count of three?"

"I'm afraid it is, Mary, it'll be transportation".

The next Assizes came quicker than they had all imagined. The working of the court was well understood. There was no surprise at the outcome – transportation for fifteen years! Mary was there with her Mam, and they were a great comfort to the Brown family, especially to Billy.

A month later, and Jim was already on his way to the other side of the world – transported for horse rustling. Billy believed Woodcock had caught up with him for that job at Harby, as well as the job at Croxton Kerrial.

SIX

Billy had gone in search of Bedford Street in the city, where his brother John lived with his wife Ann. After the adventure with Jim and the unfortunate outcome, he wanted time to himself to think things through. He spent a while with them because later he would be returning to Mother and Father and Dick. They had a good jaw about what had happened to Jim, and how shocking it was for Mary.

"Crying shame that Jim was caught" said John.

"Yes, it was shocking – especially the working of the three count rule", answered Billy.

"Is that what was inevitable about his transportation, the third offence?"

"Yes it was. We understand it but it is a cruel shame".

Billy wanted to stay longer; his heart had already noticed Ann, how lovely she was.

"Yes, John. I've now had two spells in Leicester prison, so I have to be careful in future. I expect Mother is cut up about Jim. I'd best get back".

Billy wondered what Ann thought of him - her brother-in-law with his squint and a gammy leg. It was far from clear; she was no Juliet and he certainly was not her Romeo. But Billy held her picture in his mind through everything that followed. A great deal followed.

Billy returned to Frisby where the family made him very welcome. Jock the cocker spaniel made a fuss of him. Billy was comfortable with the younger children, even though he was now older and wiser. Nevertheless, five children and a dog could be seen in the Parish most afternoons; Billy and Dick, their cousins Sam, thirteen, Tom then eleven and the young Evelyn, boisterous and all of nine years old. Billy and Dick were cautious with Tom, a known bully, but he seemed then to be respectful and apparently chastened. They rambled through the village and up the chalk hill towards Frisby Top. They met no one, but always imagined that villagers saw them and retreated indoors; that even the curtains twitched a little. Even Jock met no new acquaintances. Billy and Dick were often in close conversation, but the others paid no heed and were quite capable of occupying and amusing themselves. Jock preferred to walk with Billy, confident, nose twitching, ears pricked and those happy eyes very watchful. They resembled two brown pearls shining as lamps in his skull.

So it was a surprise to all to meet a group of village kids halfway up the chalk hill. There was no antagonism whatsoever, but friendly 'hellos' and immediate interest in each other. Evelyn was delighted to meet young Mary. Sam and Tom sat down on the grass with James and John, two brothers like themselves and about their own age. Billy and Dick stood to one side, still their own masters and observed the children happily engaged. As the afternoon progressed comfortably, young Mary's parents came to ask her in for her tea. The parents of James and John with a similar request closely followed. The children made their farewells and the sextet wandered home.

Neither was it a surprise that village children often called to see if Jock was able to come out and play. He usually was, after checking with Billy's Uncle Richard. The dog recognised the Uncle as his master. Indeed, if Jock was installed beneath the Uncle's chair, the dog was unapproachable. Billy tried it once and Jock almost nipped his hand. So, often Jock was out to play, if not with the family, then with the village children. When Jock was with the family, then, of course, he shadowed Billy. What happened next affected Billy the most. Young Mary's mother called a few days later, during the morning whilst Billy was walking in the fields with his father looking for game. Billy returned to the farm in time to witness his Uncle leading Jock on a tether to the barn. His Uncle was carrying his rifle. Billy knew something was wrong and his fears were confirmed as he heard the single shot.

"No!" he cried. The shot ripped through his body as surely as if it had been aimed at him. Billy began to blub, then quickly to sob. He could not be consoled. His father spoke to his sister-in-law and got the story. Apparently,

"Young Mary's mother came to complain, Jack, and showed me the wound, that Jock had nipped her daughter's ankle. There was little I could say to her, except make out Jock was getting old and we'd do something about it".

Jack and Ann had no grounds to quarrel with Evelyn and her husband. The decision was taken to put Jock down that same day. Billy missed his dinner. He slept in the barn for several nights, and was rarely in for meals. His mother Ann became concerned, but Jack thought,

"He'll get over it".

Billy probably never got over it, even went a bit too far!

It was Sunday morning; Richard and Evelyn were in church with their children, Sam, Tom and young Evelyn. The baby was at home with Ann and Jack. Mary was there with her mother. James and John were with their parents. The children looked around for their friends Sam and Tom, and wondered where Billy and Dick might be.

A distraught Billy arrived as the second hymn 'How Great Thou Art' sent crashing harmonies around the small cruciform church. He was carrying a rifle! Indeed, he aimed it at Mary and her mother and began to yell,

"This is for Jock, you murderer!"

A shot rang out, striking the masonry pillar above their heads. The service and the organ ground to a stop. Billy sank to his knees, sobbing.

Richard was the first to move, feeling mortified that the lad had found the rifle, and even more sorry that he'd brought it to church to use. Richard and the Vicar pulled Billy to his feet and began to lead him from the hushed and shocked church. Richard took the rifle from Billy gently and calmly. The Vicar turned and indicated to the organist and the strains of 'How Great Thou Art' again began to fill the church. Evelyn shepherded the children from the pew and followed the Vicar with Richard and Billy to the door.

The mood in the farmhouse that Sunday lunch was glum. Billy was in the barn as usual. Richard and Jack held earnest discussions,

"I'm so sorry the lad was able to find my rifle. I should have kept it under lock and key," said Richard.

"Don't blame yourself," replied Jack, "The lad would have found something to threaten the world with!"

Ann helped Evelyn in the kitchen to prepare and serve lunch. The kids went to the farmyard and mooched around.

"Short of tying Billy to a post, I don't know what to do with him," said Ann, "He just lashes out, doesn't he".

"Well, he does seem to be going off the rails. There's so little here to occupy him," replied Evelyn.

The sisters could not have guessed how Billy was to occupy his time in the following days. Dick arrived and wondered what's up,

"Why all the glum faces, kids? What's up?"

"Its Billy," Sam and Tom replied together, "He's gone too far, this time!"

"Billy aimed the rifle at Mary and her mother", said Sam.

"He was wild with anger", added Tom.

Death By Peppermint

"The silly clod!" observed Dick, who immediately sympathised when he was told what happened to Jock, "That's tough and no mistake!"

Evelyn and Ann announced that dinner was ready and called them in. The meal was served around one o'clock and Dick volunteered to take Billy's plate to the barn. Evelyn almost protested, but Ann handed him the plate,

"Dick, thanks," said Ann, "Please see if you can have a word with him".

Dick opened the barn door slowly and carefully. He stepped inside not sure what he would find, and discovered Billy sitting woefully on a hay bale. Billy accepted the plate and began to eat. Dick sat beside him. Billy picked at his food. He was disconsolate and emotion began to well up. Suddenly, Billy threw himself into Dick's arms and began to sob. Dick held him firmly and eventually asked him to talk. Billy spoke of his love for Jock, and the shock of his Uncle's reaction,

"Jock must have been tormented to actually nip someone. Mary must have hurt him. So on her word, Jock has to be put down, it doesn't seem fair – it doesn't make sense!"

Actually talking about it was the best medicine, and helped Billy better to come to terms with this tragedy. However, circumstances had conspired to drive Billy to a reckless life. This unfolded in the following days with dreadful consequences.

In a neighbouring parish Billy had seen a stable yard flanked by a stone walled country house. His newfound freedom gave him and Dick the chance to delve a little deeper. It was full summer, early August, and all was draped in a shining silvery light for a long time into the evening. They discussed the best move and when to make it,

"We shall have to move at night", said Billy.

Dick made his usual commitment,

"I'll have the wagon parked in a nearby lane, but in a shadowy part".

Billy determined to sleep in the daytime and moved about the stables night time, but wide-awake. This he practiced three days prior to the taking of the prize. The stable lads slept above the horseboxes, whilst the Master and Mistress were in the main house but at the farthest end. The house servants likewise were in the main house, but in the boxlike rooms in the eaves.

On the fourth evening all was set. Dick and Billy watched as a few carriages left the property and after an interval the house fell quiet.

"Dick, wait in the lane, but listen out for my whistle," urged Billy.

"I'll be there in the darkness".

Billy approached the stables and Dick moved the wagon and horses to a shady part of the adjacent lane, but it was raining steadily. Good planning ensured that by ten of the clock, he was in the stables. The horses knew him by now. He blew loosely through his cheeks and patted the heavy mare. He was not so good at whiffling as was Dick, but horse and intruder both settled down amicably. The place was quiet, save one slight disturbance as the cries above momentarily indicated that one of the older boys was clearly taking his pleasure with a younger lad. All settled as quickly.

By two in the morning, Billy moved into the spacious kitchen of the main house, where the embers of the last evening were still warm. This surprised Billy who knew it was the height of summer, until he recognised the spit above, still greasy from the cooking. It must have been quite a party. Someone had obligingly left a cloth dressed out with shekels of the Manning silver cutlery and serving spoons. It was awkward wrapping the silver, but he did not want to leave any! It was awkward still to make for the door, and the stable yard beyond. He was being very careful. The wet flagstones did not help. Slowly, the bundle and Billy crept across the stable yard. He could picture it still. The bundle moved. He snatched thin air as a dozen spoons fell to the floor with ringing tones that would have wakened the dead! The house and stable quarters immediately sprang into life and several hefty lads threw themselves at him. The bundle now abandoned, Billy raced off into the dark, hoping vehemently that Dick had heard the commotion and vanished. His flight was no use.

"Grab 'im, Joe," said a gruff voice.

"Gotcha!" was the reply, panting through heavy exertion.

He felt their warm breath on the back of his neck as first one pair of hands grabbed an arm, and then another flung him to the ground.

The prison van delivered Billy to Leicester again, after the due processes of the law. He was thrown into a familiar cell, where he met some recognisable inmates. They exchanged greetings gruffly, fleetingly, as guards chained them and led them to the work yard. Billy had seen this yard before. It was the place where stones were broken into smaller pieces – for road building. The stone was the hard core. He'd seen men falter under the weight of the hammers. It helped to have a rhythm – Billy developed a rhythm when he swung the hammer. This helped him to survive where others all but perished. A stripling of a boy, caught and jailed for stealing a loaf, chained like a wild animal, fell foul of a swinging hammer that struck him full in the chest. He collapsed and died on the spot. Just breaking stones. An older man swung his hammer high and let it slip from his grasp. It crashed down on his shin and the bones shattered in several places. A month later he reappeared with a wooden leg, was chained and set to work. Just breaking stones. This Billy endured for nigh on two months, and then he stood before the Quarter Sessions in October. The panelled room echoed a bit as his bungling was explained. How he'd taken the silver, but could not get it to a fining pot before discovery. He had not then the cunning to work in silver that he later learned on the other side of the world. He could hear the spoons clanging on the stones, as the Magistrate, following the instructions of the jury and its foreman, Woodcock, uttered those fateful well-remembered words,

"The sentence of this court is transportation for ten years". His Mam and Dad wept.

SEVEN

In Scalford Village, near Melton Mowbray in Leicestershire, England, Edward Woodcock, bailiff to his Grace the Duke, set out pens and paper and began to write.

'To Silas Woodcock,

To my esteemed kinsman, greetings.

Please be advised that William Brown, also known as Peppermint Billy, is to be shipped from Deptford to Van Diemans Land on 16 April.

Please ensure that he does not arrive in Van Diemans Land alive.

His family have been ejected from the Vale of Belvoir; two more of the sons are in trouble and will face transportation, if I have any connection with the cases. I wish to rid the earth of their miserable existence.

I shall be obliged for the efficient working out of this duty.

I am, sir,

Your Uncle Edward'.

He pushed his chair back from the desk and lolled in it briefly, hands clasped together at the back of the neck. Edward stared out of the window, noticing the small yellow flowers of the winter jasmine still clinging to the corner made by porch and house wall. His wife, Sarah brought in a tray of fresh tea and the few remaining slices of a cherry cake.

"Here you are, love, fresh tea".

"Oh! Just right! Well timed, my love".

"Now, you be careful in that chair! It may not take much more of your lolling".

Edward brought the legs of his chair to the floor smartly. He relaxed over his tea, and gathered the crumbs of a slice of cherry cake with a damp finger. He savoured every sweet bite.

These reveries were interrupted by the arrival of a carriage and pair – the Duke and his Lady were visiting! The Bailiff and his wife were used to these visits, so swung into action. Edward went to the front door, Sarah to the kitchen to put on a fresh kettle.

"Good morning, your Grace and your Ladyship".

"Hello, Bailiff. We hope this timing is convenient?"

"Of course. My wife is just putting on a fresh kettle. You'll have tea with us?"

"That'll be lovely", said her Ladyship, "Actually, I wish to speak with Sarah. So why don't I follow her into the kitchen, whilst you two talk business?"

"That will be admirable, your Ladyship. Sarah", he called, "her Ladyship is joining you in the kitchen".

The two men waited until the ladies were comfortable in the kitchen, and then they sat down in the lounge.

"Now, Bailiff, you've dealt with the Brown brothers at the Assizes, but we are still plagued by these damned gangs rustling our cattle! Last night, two dozen head were taken at Muston, right under our noses!"

"I'm sorry to hear that, sir. I suppose they were shipped by train from Grantham the same evening?"

"Certainly. They do seem extraordinarily well organised".

"We did deal with the Brown brothers, sir, but this gang is well led by a brigand with no name – we don't know who he is".

"You don't know who he is?" echoed her Ladyship as she and Sarah entered the room with a tray of tea, and some buttered slices of Barn Brack Loaf.

"Yes, dear", replied the Duke, "We were discussing the raids on our cattle. We don't know who their leader is".

"Please have some tea, sir, it might help your thinking", chuckled Sarah.

"Thank you for saying that Sarah", added her Ladyship, "Worry will kill him you know".

Sarah served the tea and offered the buttered slices of cake. Her husband accepted the tea, but declined the cake. He felt replete with the earlier cherry cake! The Duke and his Lady accepted both and enjoyed the Barn Brack Loaf slices with relish.

"Now, Sarah", said her Ladyship smiling, "Please say you can help me with the next Hunt Ball and the refreshments thereof".

Sarah laughed and nodded, actually pleased and proud to have been asked to help.

"That's all fine and dandy", said the Duke, "But we are still no nearer identifying the leader of this gang".

The Bailiff was at a loss to suggest the next strategy, knowing better than most that the Duke was a powerful man in the district. If he didn't know what to do next, then Edward certainly did not. Just as the Duke was throwing his energies into the route proposals of the new railway through the Wye Valley in Derbyshire, he appeared to want to throw his energies afresh into the problem with the cattle thieving gangs.

"What we need is an *agent provocateur*".

"I beg your pardon, sir, a what?"

"A spy, dammit! Someone to get close to this leader, gain his trust and then betray him".

Billy was moved almost immediately thereafter down to the London river, where ancient hulks were pressed into service as floating prisons. Moonrise at Deptford found him in his temporary sojourn in a Napoleonic relic – a floating gaol for transportees; white water in the big river softly plashing at the moorings. It was the calmest, quietest white water he would ever see, though he did not know this in that moment of deep despair. Billy recriminated himself for his stupid folly, he started to wonder about Dick and what may have happened that dreadful night. The matter would only be resolved much later in another place. Indeed, he was in for a few surprises as his life took a dangerous path between hostility and brigandage. He was not alone, however; he found strong support amongst his fellow transportees.

Each day was the same, chained and walked to the wharf on the creek for a day's hard work that took them as far as the bridge; then returned to the hulk in the evening, and to the gnawing, scavenging rats in its rolling holds. Each day he was chained to a likeable fellow,

"I'm Billy from Leicester, Billy Brown, and you?" Billy enquired tentatively.

"Bob," came the reply, "Bob Thackray from Leominster." The reply was quick, calm and encouraging,

"What you here for?" he added.

"Stealing silver spoons, and you?"

"Horse rustling and what some men called 'knavish trickery' ".

Over the next few days, the two discussed the vicissitudes of their comparatively short lives, Billy's feud with the Woodcocks, and their knavish trickery that had already cost his family dear. Billy told Bob,

"My older brother, Jim, is already on his way to Van Diemans Land for cattle rustling".

Bob was speaking of his own older brother,

"Paul was shot dead in a brawl outside a Leominster hostelry, at the time of the New Year". Bob drew in a deep breath, "His death affected the whole family deeply; a blight on the New Year, and now myself transported for horse and cattle rustling".

Billy liked Bob - they had a common background. They were both from the Midlands, though Bob was from the west, and Billy from the east. Billy was encouraged by Bob's equable temperament to think they could be good mates. This friendship bound them together more firmly in the future than their chains.

*

Silas Woodcock read the letter from his uncle again on the creek shore at Deptford. He was not surprised at the contents. He knew his uncle very well, and his mood swings. It would not be the first time he had wanted someone eliminated – nor the first time Silas had done the eliminating! He noted the chain of convicts working as far as the bridge, and wondered if Peppermint Billy was one of them. It was an idle thought and idly dismissed, as he determined on a course of action. He made his way first to the shipping office and then found the tavern. In the tavern Jem Potter, his crony, joined him.

"I bought four berths for the trip to Van Dieman's Land. We have to be on board by one o'clock".

They ordered beers. Potter took a huge draught when the beer arrived.

"God, I was dry!" he gasped, "It's the thought of sailing. I hate it!"

"Stop whingeing, man!"

"Why are you sailing?"

"It's my uncle's bidding. There's one job I have to do. I must kill one of these convicts – or at least, make sure he'll not return to England".

"Really! Do you mean the two of us?"

"I expect two more, Knight and Churchill. We should be able to manage it with four!"

As if at a signal, the two extra of this cabal entered the tavern. Knight and Churchill asked for Woodcock, and the waiter brought them over to join Silas and Jem.

The four of them seated themselves and more beers were ordered. Knight took out a pipe, tapped the bowl on the end of the table, filled it with tobacco from a pouch, and lit it. He puffed at it contentedly. Silas felt he had to lay the ground rules,

"I've asked you here to sail as passengers with me, because I have instructions to eliminate one of the transportees. I want you to help me".

"Do you know which convict?" asked Knight, through a haze of smoke.

"Yes, I do. It's William Brown, also known as 'Peppermint Billy'. You'll recognize him because he has a gammy leg and a permanent squint in his eyes. This hasn't stopped him from making life difficult for my uncle".

"Poor uncle!" said Jem, "Is it he that wants Peppermint Billy dead?"

"Yes, it is. You know he'll make it worth your while".

The waiter reappeared,

"You asked me, sir, to remind you of the time. It is twelve thirty. I believe you have to board very soon".

"Thank you", Silas handed him a sovereign.

Knight tapped his pipe on the edge of the table, and all of them rose to make a move to leave. Silas settled the drinks bill, and then led the others out of the tavern and towards the gangplank. Silas observed a gang of convict labour at work, and some others already finished and returning to the ship. He led his group up the gangplank and reported to the Purser's office to collect details of their berths.

"You are on the portside. I've given you adjoining cabins. Your washing facilities are the heads aft".

A steward who looked very young led the four of them to their cabins. Jem might have thought 'young and tasty!' Jem made a fuss about getting his cabin door open, so the steward lent a hand. Jem struggled with his luggage, so the steward took it into his cabin and placed it on the bunk. As he turned round, Jem was very close – blocking the steward's way out. Jem's carnal feelings got the better of him, and he groped the lad as he embraced him. The surprised steward grunted loudly and began to struggle. As Jem placed his hand over the steward's mouth, the door opened sharply and strong hands grabbed Potter and hauled him away, thus releasing the very relieved young steward. A much older man, another steward, had noticed the disappearance of his colleague and was immediately suspicious. So he had come to investigate. He told off this passenger, raising his voice,

"How dare you! Keep your filthy hands to yourself!"

Potter turned away. Woodcock appeared in the cabin doorway with such a distasteful look on his face,

"You be careful, Potter, that your feelings do not get you into trouble again!"

Billy was among the chains of convicts working in the creek. They were relieved to find their labours terminated by noon and they returned to the ship. As the convicts trudged back to the gangplank, they were surprised to see a body of women, of all ages, at the quayside, and the Captain remonstrating with some official,

"This is a damned mistake. You can't put these women on a boat full of men!"

"But those is my orders, Cap'n. These are the remnants of the *Olivia* who have to be transported, so they are to take up the slack places on your ship".

"But look at them, man. Four are with child, fifteen are so old and wheezy, and I doubt they'll survive the journey".

"That's as maybe, Cap'n, but they is my orders".

The Captain finally acceded to this order and sent for the First Mate. The women were taken on board, and the chained gangs of men followed on bemused. They did not see the two men standing at the balcony of the inn. Peppermint Billy saw the men on the balcony but there was nothing to suggest they were a threat to him. Indeed, this picture meant very little to him at that time. But the conference between Silas Woodcock, Jem Potter and two or three others was highly significant. It was a private conversation. It did not reach the ears of Billy and Bob, or indeed any of the Leicester lads. Importantly, the results of the conference were felt almost immediately on board. The convicts were not told why their work had finished early, and did not see the passengers coming on board. They knew the river was busy, all kinds of craft moved argently up and down; others crossed from side to side in a seemingly random way. In reality, the waiting ship moored in the middle of the river by this time, was being provisioned and primed for that fateful journey to Van Diemans Land. The convicts saw little of the London River as the ship made sail and slipped its moorings. The raising of her anchor reverberated throughout the ship. Then the convicts understood. The calm was broken and swept aside as the open mouth of the Thames delivered them to the sea. The ship turned southwards then westward through the English Channel and headed for the Atlantic. Clearly, their route was mapped to the Cape of Good Hope and thence through the southern oceans to Van Diemans Land.

What sort of name was 'Good Hope'? Most of them on the ship had none of it! *Hast thou entered into the springs of the sea?* Men in leg irons fared badly as the ship rolled and reeled about the sea during several storms. There were now many women on board, wives of convicts, girlfriends, women of all ages from young girls to old hags. Four of the wives were with child, two of them very advanced in their pregnancy. At the height of a storm, one woman's waters broke and the birth process began. That young girl was Esther Carver, wife of John Carver, a coal higgler from Hereford, transported for playing fast and free with weights and measures. A couple of older women were deputed to assist, whilst the most vocal of the lot alerted the crew,

"Water! 'Ot water! 'ere you blackguards! You was all born, and there's a little one on its way now, so move will yer".

The crewman who had lingered the longest was drawn in to do errands. He was asked to report to the Captain with the most urgent need – for hot water. This was done, and the Captain as busy as he clearly was, issued an order to the galley crew to provide a bucket of hot water. He also sent a note to the laundry for a sheet to be ripped up and sent for the new infant's comfort. But comfort was not the order of the day. The mother to be was finding her circumstances difficult. Esther's screams, as the pains throbbed through, were arresting; they ripped to ribbons the torpid consciences of the convicts. John Carver heard his wife in agony and sobbed. The mother to be writhed on the wooden floor; first feeling cold and then stifling hot, in turn. The crewman returned to his Captain,

"The ladies say it will take hours, sir".

"Keep me informed, lad".

"Aye, aye, sir!"

As the storm abated in the ocean, the crewman rejoined the women to find the mother to be quieter for awhile, but then the pains of stretching began again in earnest. Esther screamed piteously, as the older hags encouraged and cajoled,

"That's it, gel! Push!"

This procedure was repeated throughout the hour. Then, the infant emerged all of a rush, caked in fat and flecks of streaky blood. One of the hags hoisted the infant into the air by its ankles,

"Ah, it's a little boy!" she cackled.

She administered a smart slap across the tiny buttocks and shook the bundle. It was as if the whole company, at least those in that wooden hold, were holding their breath, expecting the infant to cry. Another smart slap shocked the company into looking at the sorry bundle. It made no sound at all. The old hag wiped the child's face with a rag; she clasped it to her whiskered lips to breathe into its tiny mouth. It was no use; the infant was stillborn. She turned to the baby's mother and shook her head; then wrapped the sorry bundle in the rag and lay it down beside its mother on the blood-soaked timbers. All the women were agitated and pointing. Some began to cry. As the hag bent down, she noticed that the mother was also still and white, turning a subtle blue around the mouth. Both mother and child lay there, *the way of life and the way of death*. The crewman reported to the Captain in a choking voice,

"Sorry sir, we have lost them both, mother and child".

Any death is a time of terror. The Captain ordered the Ship's Log to be completed with the details. He seemed to be about to say something else, something tender or sad. But the sounding of an alarm interrupted him.

For the convicts below, the crossing was proving to be eventful, especially through that part of the ocean called the 'Roaring Forties'; where waves were so high above them Billy imagined the scarp at Belvoir that it might have come crashing down in a thousand red and silvery pieces. Chained as they were meant certain death if the ship foundered. Then, one of their number, John Carver of Hereford was receiving the most awful news of his wife and newborn child. He was told that they had both died soon after the childbirth. The man was distraught, inconsolable. A number of his friends found the moment so sad and shed their own tears. The affairs of the ship paid no heed to this moment of despair. An alarm was sounded – they heard the crew rushing about above their heads. A main spar had crashed down in the lashing rain and needed to be hauled up or replaced. The Captain saw the need for extra hands and gave the order, "Bring up a 'chain' of prisoners!"

The crewmen acknowledged the order and dived below to find the required number.

The chosen 'chain' of eight men included John Carver, Bob and Billy. It was the Captain's order that the men were unchained, and the iron hasp was knocked open and the trailing chain rattled through the ankle hoops. The men rubbed their ankles briskly to get the blood flowing through them and jumped into action. The sailors had roped the spar and it needed brute strength to haul it up to its rightful position. The chosen eight grabbed the ropes – a real mix of men and a mix of ropes, until the midshipman sorted out the main one that needed the pull. This they took up and began to heave. Inch by inch the spar was raised. Other sailors, like dots, clambered aloft to guide the timber. It was slippery work – a misjudgement at that height – a scream, and a lifeless body thumped the deck. The Captain shouted his orders afresh. He was not a heartless man – he knew the cost. It was essential to get that timber in place and roped to do its job. With help, even from prisoners it was achieved. They even felt a little pride in the job well done. Back to reality, the prisoners were chained again and then shown to their places in the hold. The chain was one short, however,

"Oh no! Not John Carver!" said Bob in horror.

"What?" replied Billy, "Surely a family can't be wiped out in an afternoon?"

"I reckon that's possible in this hell-hole".

After one more week of sail, the inquest on the Carver family was held. It was a very sad affair. The formality underlined the enormous wave of pity that seeped through the company – most of the company. John Carver, coal higgler and convict of Hereford was judged to be 'accidental', though some muttered that, in grief at the loss of his wife and newborn child, he took his fall deliberately. Esther Carver was judged 'in child birth'; a dangerous time for all mothers, and the infant child was judged 'stillborn'. The next morning, the ship hove to for the funeral ceremonies. Drum rolls signified the beginning of the shipboard funeral, so that everyone might attend the committal. Unusually, the Captain allowed three of the older women to attend representing the rest of their company. It was usual to keep all women separated and out of sight, but this was special, and their presence was deemed appropriate. The teams of men lined up in their chains to watch as the bodies in their shrouds were brought to the deck. It was a poignant moment that still shocked the company. It was clear that the infant in his tiny shroud was sewn into the mother's shroud. They were to leave this world in each other's arms. John, Esther and infant lay athwart the trestles set up on deck.

The captain stepped forward to officiate, and read the committals for all of them, and then asked that the boards deliver their burdens to the sea simultaneously. As they slid into oblivion, he intoned the words,

"We commit these bodies to the deep, in the sure and certain hope that they shall be raised at the final trump triumphant".

Bob and Billy were moved by the judgements and the funeral following in quick succession.

"It's a bit too quick for my liking", said Billy.

"Perhaps it's for the best, as most people are upset and the ship has to get back to normal working as soon as possible".

"Oh, alright, Captain Bob!"

There were those that did not feel their distress; did not share their pride, even resented their hard work. Angry voices were raised as the men were walked back to their berths; sharp replies were given. It developed into quite a spat with oppressive glares that heralded trouble further down the line. Bob shrugged this off, but he was clearly shaken,

"We are fortunate to be chained," he said, "since there may have been blows exchanged."

"I noticed a sullen clique, and one or two notables among them," Billy observed.

They kept their voices low, not knowing how many were trying to listen.

EIGHT

In Frisby, Leicestershire in England, Billy's younger brother was eighteen years old. He was familiar with the work both Billy and Jim did for Mr Heathlighter, so was quite prepared for the approach by one Harry Bainbridge who said he wished to join the gang and could Dick help him. The pair of them met up by the railway bridge below Scalford that was the appointed gathering place on a dark, windy evening.

"This'll get the draught up their arses!" Heathlighter was cheerful as he arrived.

Dick spurred his horse forward,

"This is Harry, Mr Heathlighter, he wants to join in".

"Does he? Well, Harry, we'll be glad to have your help. That's a fine looking animal you're on".

"Thank you. The horse was my father's".

The group of about fifteen or sixteen were now in place, so the ruddy-faced Heathlighter gave the orders,

"Right. We have a herd of twenty waiting for us at Waltham so we'll take the road from the centre of Scalford and go out past the Manor. Keep up!"

The first group of riders were moving out as Heathlighter spoke to Tommy Beattie, one of his generals,

"Keep an eye on the newcomer, riding with young Dick. Let me know what you think".

The whole gang was now moving at some speed through Scalford village and out into the countryside that sloped down to Waltham. The whole gang? Not Harry Bainbridge and not Tommy Beattie. Harry had stopped at the Manor and was speaking to the resident,

"It's Waltham in the next hour. Please get this message to his Grace as quickly as possible".

It took only moments before he remounted and was trotting on. Tommy was the last to come through the village in a sweeping up manoeuvre. He saw Harry pause, speak, and then move on. He made a mental note of this, and spurred on his horse to try to catch up with the rest. He even passed Harry as he cantered down the lane, but did not pause or speak himself. Tommy reached the main body of riders and signalled Heathlighter to rein in,

"Wait on, this new man has some explaining to do".

Heathlighter trusted Tommy implicitly. He seized Dick's reins and pulled the young rider to his side,

"Tell me about Harry Bainbridge".

"I don't know anything about him. He seemed to appear from out of nowhere. He wanted to join the gang, so I introduced him".

"You introduced him, not knowing anything about him?"

"I suppose I did, yes".

Heathlighter raised his voice to the assembled riders as Harry joined them and was immediately reined in by Tommy and two others,

"Our new man stopped in the village and spoke to someone. I want to know why!"

Tommy looked at Harry and nodded, so Harry spoke,

"My horse caught a stone in its foreleg shoe, so I stopped and a fellow in his garden poked it out for me. It only took moments. I'm sorry to have held everyone up".

Heathlighter nodded to Tommy, who ordered Harry to dismount. Tommy picked up the horse's foreleg and examined the shoe. There were marks where Harry had indicated. There was no way of knowing how old the marks were, but Tommy made a mental note that they were dull rather than bright. Tommy reported,

"It's as he says. There are signs of a stone being picked".

Heathlighter appeared convinced,

"Alright, let's move on. It's the sort of thing that can happen to anyone".

He swung his mount around and the gang moved off. Tommy caught up with Dick,

"It's not your fault, Dick, don't worry about it".

"Thanks, Tommy. What will happen now?"

"I'll keep an eye on Bainbridge. You're not to worry about him anymore".

The herd of two dozen were waiting for them in a field opposite the elementary school on the Melton Road, but such was the skill of these men that the beasts were walked out and away towards Branston before anyone realised. The quiet drover lanes in Branston had already been checked thoroughly by Tommy, who even now was bringing up the rear at some breakneck speed because he had seen riders in the village! Tommy was sure that they were Estate men working for his Grace, and that they could only be there because the alarm had been raised. He raced ahead to speak to Heathlighter, and then asked two others to help him. They found a wagon piled high with hay bales parked in a gateway, and they rolled it out once the herd were past, so as to block the lane. These three were armed, so they mounted a guard against the wagon. The afternoon sun was sinking fast, and the men kept their rifles at the ready. The entry to the lane remained quiet, so Tommy believed the danger may have passed. He remounted and entered the field to the left and worked a big circle back towards the village; as the hounds drew cover for miles around, so Tommy assessed that the riders he saw were now miles away. He returned to collect the other two, and then the three of them cantered down the lane, and then galloped on towards Hungarton as the beasts were well on. By then, Heathlighter was judging that this small number of cows could be entrained at Grantham without much fuss. It would also be a surprise, if any riders were watching Radcliffe or the routes to Radcliffe across the Vale. He let his generals know,

"It's Grantham rail yard, lads. Let's press on. Tommy, ride ahead and make the arrangements, usual prices".

"Alright, I'm on my way", he shouted, spurring on his horse.

"Come on, you lot, move your arses!"

The raggle taggle group quickened the pace, with Dick and Harry in the rear. Once they had cleared Harlaxton, they entered Grantham and were soon at the railhead. Tommy greeted them,

"Over here, the wagons are ready".

The beasts were first penned and counted. Tommy spoke to Heathlighter and the leader then settled the account with the yard manager. By four in the afternoon, Heathlighter was following his usual procedure and paying off his men and the group were dispersing their several ways. Dick was wondering if he was going to be shadowed by Harry Bainbridge, but he needn't have worried,

"I'll be seeing you, Dick", called Harry as he urged his horse on.

Tommy was watching as Harry departed in the direction of Barrowby. This could be an easy route into the northern part of the Vale of Belvoir, so Tommy followed at a distance to check which route Harry chose. Meanwhile, Dick headed south towards Skillington, then he intended to swing down to Wymondham, and from there he would travel through Burton Lazars to Frisby. Tommy canters through Grantham and follows the lane towards Barrowby Village. It was as he thought, Harry took the road to Woolsthorpe.

"My God!" thought Tommy, "That's in the shadow of Belvoir Castle!"

Would Harry turn to the Castle? Tommy urged his horse on to see more clearly. Harry swung right at the crossroads, so he was intending to go by the Castle entrance at the very least. Tommy followed in turn. Did Harry turn into the Castle entrance? In fact, he turned right again, in the general direction of Redmile, away from the Castle! Just at the next crossroads, Harry turned his mount into the farm on the right hand side of the road. Tommy was puzzled. Was Harry the farmer? Who was he working for?

*

In the Vale of Belvoir, the Duke's bailiff Edward Woodcock was riding towards Long Clawson Village. He had rents to collect, people to see. It was a bright November morning and his nag enjoyed the nip in the air. Edward Woodcock enjoyed a nip or two in the bar of the pub, *The Crown and Plough,* where he sometimes held 'court' and expected the rents to be delivered to him. He was known to hold 'court' also at Scalford in *The Plough*. Tenant farmer Bainbridge handed over five pounds and ten shillings for October, and further three pounds arrears for September. Edward Woodcock entered the amounts in his register,

"I'd be obliged, Bainbridge, if there are no further arrears built up".

Bainbridge stepped closer and leant forward to speak quietly but firmly,

"I've been working with the gang. I'm accepted".

The Bailiff's eyes widened and then half closed, as he studied the farmer's face. So this was the Duke's man! The tenant farmer was part of the thieving gang of riders, but working for his Grace! Clearly, he expected the Duke to show his gratitude in a practical manner – perhaps some rent relief. Edward Woodcock recalled the conversation a month ago with the Duke when this idea was first proposed. He did not think his Grace would find anyone suitable, but then Edward was talking with the double agent.

The Bailiff stood and asked the landlord for a private room where the two of them might talk over a pint. The landlord cooperated and showed them into his parlour while his girl went to collect two pints.

"You should be comfy in here, gents". She returned to the bar to serve a fellow she had not seen before, but who was keen-eyed and alert.

It was Tommy, who was sitting apart, out of the gaze of Bainbridge or the Bailiff.

"I'm obliged, landlord", said the Bailiff, and both of them sat down at the small table. The girl returned with the beer and set it down on the table. She retired to let them have some privacy. Tommy called her over,

"Is that the Bailiff in there?"

"Yes sir, it is".

"So, who is that with him?"

"Why that's Mr Bainbridge of the farm down the lane, Cherry Tree Farm I believe".

"I'm obliged, young lady".

In the side room, the Bailiff spoke first,

"Well, Bainbridge – er, Harry, isn't it?"

Harry Bainbridge was taken aback by this sudden display of camaraderie,

"Yes, Bailiff".

"Alright, Harry", continued the Bailiff, "What can you tell me of your activities?"

"Well, Bailiff, very little. You see - I have to report directly to his Grace on a regular basis. His Grace understands the need for secrecy in this matter".

Edward Woodcock was astonished by this answer. He, the Bailiff, should not be privy to the activities of the double agent?

"What do you mean, Harry? You are not allowed to talk about it to his Grace's Bailiff?"

"That's about the measure of it, Bailiff".

"Well I never!"

The Bailiff was clearly deflated. His beer was left unsupped, whereas Harry downed his in two swallows. There was an awkward silence, broken only by the chimes of the mantelpiece clock. Edward Woodcock was not used to receiving a negative answer. He was much more used to getting his own way in things. The Bailiff stood to leave.

"We'll have to go through the motions in there", he said, pointing to the meeting room.

Harry did not answer him, but followed him out.

"I'd be obliged, Bainbridge, if there are no further arrears built up", he repeated loudly for the benefit of others in the room.

"I do my best, sir", was the respectful reply, "but market prices collapsed and I could do nowt about it".

Edward Woodcock took a sip of brandy and water that had been placed on his table,

"You'll have to do something about it in the future, whatever the state of the market!"

The Bailiff was in a mood. It affected the rest of his meeting with tenants. Actually, there was only one more to see, even though he noticed two people in the bar. Tenant blacksmith Hewerfield was cap in hand and looking downcast. He had no rent and eight pounds, ten shillings and six pence was owing. Edward Woodcock struck the table with his riding crop,

"This is appalling! Rent is due, rent must be paid!"

Hewerfield flinched visibly and fiddled with his cap.

"I'll report this matter to the Duke. You should expect me by the end of the week".

Hewerfield withdrew a broken man. He walked through the village, past the vacant lot that used to be the cottage of the Brown family. The lesson it conveyed was not lost on him. He walked home to his family. Back at the bar, Tommy made notes that he felt sure would interest Heathlighter.

Heathlighter did indeed read this report with great interest as it concerned the activities of Harry Bainbridge, tenant farmer and spy! He determined that action would have to be taken at the earliest opportunity. He and Tommy tried a bit of subterfuge themselves. Heathlighter received information through the network that a prime herd of cattle was at Nether Broughton, in a field at the top of Chapel Lane. He had a word with Tommy who undertook to deliver the date and the timing to the gang, but also to vary the target when speaking to Dick. So it happened that on the fourteenth of the month, Dick believed the gang to be heading for Scalford Dairy Farm, and on the fifteenth of the month he gave this information to Harry Bainbridge who had called at his home in Frisby. The raid was planned for one week later, and the rendezvous point was fixed as the stocks at Grimston, an easy ride for Dick. On the appointed day, he rode to Grimston with Harry Bainbridge, who had again appeared out of nowhere. The riders who gathered at Grimston numbered fifteen plus Heathlighter. Heathlighter addressed the team,

"We need to be alert today. We need to be efficient and speedy. There is a change of plan that may not altogether be a surprise, but we are heading for Nether Broughton today".

Tommy was watching Harry Bainbridge; watching for any reaction to this news. There was no reaction. Heathlighter's news was accepted without murmur; the men were keen to get on with it. The signal was given for them to move out. Tommy purposefully placed his horse next to Harry's and rode with him. It was a very short distance to Nether Broughton, a village so familiar to Tommy that he turned down Heckadeck Lane by mistake, so had to swing back and take Chapel Lane instead. They all met at the right field successfully, with Tommy shadowing Harry all the time. Within half an hour, the village was quiet. The cows were walking steadily northwards towards the Cropwells and from there it was but a short hop to Radcliffe on Trent.

The usual terms were given at the railhead at Radcliffe and the cows were penned, counted and paid for. Heathlighter as usual, paid off his men from the proceeds as the cows were entrained. He had other business to attend to,

"Tommy please finish up here for me. Dick and Jack come with me. William and Harry come with me, there's something I wish to show you".

The file of horses and riders threaded their way through the wide streets of Radcliffe until they reached the river. Heathlighter led them down to a slipway, and gesticulated towards the mighty Trent. As the riders moved forward, Heathlighter motioned Dick, Jack and William to hold back. Harry moved forward, but seeing nothing remarkable, he swung his mount round. He found himself facing a rifle pointed at him by Heathlighter, which he cocked noisily. The other riders had formed a half circle around him, so blocking any thought of escape. Heathlighter was scathing,

"Traitor! In the pay of the Duke; carrying messages to his Bailiff!"

Harry said nothing; his horse stamped the damp incline.

"You have two choices. A quick bullet, or a swim for it", Heathlighter said pointing to the river throbbing past the slipway.

Harry patted his mount's neck, and stood in the stirrups as the horse peed. Perhaps his mount sensed the tension of the moment. Harry turned its head round. With his knees he encouraged the horse to enter the water, and then he spurred it on to lunge forward and started to swim. Those that watched, saw the horse and rider make good headway at first, but next struggled to make progress against the strong currents.

Within a few moments, the rider was unseated. Harry flailed about, but his heavy clothing and boots inevitably dragged him under. The horse bucked without the weight on his back, and valiantly tried again to make headway in the surging torrent. The horse was tiring; the dead rider's foot was still caught in the stirrups! The watchers saw the horse's head with crazed nostrils and staring eyes, suddenly turn over and dip under the water. Neither horse nor rider was seen again. Retribution had been visited on a spy. It was over. The watchers turned away; Dick was in tears. Heathlighter was at once tender and comforting,

"Difficult to watch, I know, lad. Don't worry about it now. Get off home".

Dick spurred his horse into action and took the road to Cropwell Bishop and then down to the Broughtons. From there it was an easy ride back to Frisby.

NINE

1843

"Lock down!" the cry of the late orders rang through the lower decks, and the chains were fastened securely. The prisoners settled quickly, especially if they were close enough to friends to be able to speak. There was activity in the women's quarters. They could only assume that another pregnancy had reached full term. In the men's berths, Billy and Bob were on the same eight, so had opportunity to discuss their circumstances; but conditions were cramped. Billy was the natural worrier; Bob was made of sterner stuff. Both had had difficult lives up to that point, but fate had thrown them together – and dealt a good hand too! Despite the awkwardness, the council of wit and wisdom in the chained confines of the hold was beneficial. Billy's wit convinced him that the troubles were directed at him, and that the source of them all was somehow connected with the Woodcock family. Billy could clearly see the hand of old man Woodcock reaching out for him,

"He's got 'is claws in my family alright! He wants to reach out to destroy us".

"Billy, if he really is out to destroy you, then you have to stay alert. The more careful we are, the safer this journey will be," Bob's wisdom advised Billy to stay calm. Bob was the rock, steady and trustworthy. It was he who provided leadership at this critical point; explained how he would enlist the help of the Officers,

"We need the support of the First Mate. I've spoken to him and explained the two factions that seem to inhabit this ship. I want a watch maintained round the clock".

He set a cycle of watchful eyes amongst the Leicester men, like young Richard Pratt, a nineteen year old ostler and groom, and a native of Rutland, then of Derbyshire; like Thomas Dunslow and Joseph Barlow, both lifers, and John Garner who got ten years the same as Billy and came over on the '*London*'. Bob had already struck up a nodding acquaintance with the First Mate, Stevens, who had obviously been impressed with this steady and powerful figure. Stevens himself was sharp, his dark eyes took in all he surveyed, every detail; they raked the decks and rigging.

The crewman who helped the Carver family was again deputed to help the latest emergency – Harriett Farley, the young wife of Jacob Farley of Gloucestershire. The crewman was Chambers, and he then collected a bucket of hot water from the galley and two torn up sheets from the laundry. Chambers was determined to make Harriett comfortable; he didn't want another disaster! He considered first keeping her warm, so drew in tables on their side to form a barrier against the draughts. Two of the older women ministered and fussed around her, making sure her clothing was loose. They felt able to inform Chambers,

"All is going well".

Chambers dutifully relayed this message to the Captain, who timed the information at midnight. The Captain decided to retire to his cabin, but left word,

"I want to be called when the baby is born – whatever the outcome".

Harriett meanwhile, was serene, not at all flustered. No one would believe it was her first child, but all was made clear when she explained,

"My mother remarried and I assisted at the births of three of my stepbrothers".

So she understood the processes; all was progressing well. The older women pressed Chambers for a bucket of fresh hot water. Harriett was comfortable. By three in the early hours, the baby was well on the way; the women were busy. At three-thirty, the listening women heard the first lusty cries of a newborn girl. A beaming Chambers was seen nursing the infant in his broad arms. The women encouraged Harriett to stand up, in order to release the detritus of the afterbirth, and the cord still connecting her to her baby was cut with Chamber's knife. A proud Chambers handed the little girl to her mother and left to inform the Captain. The Captain stirred reluctantly, but as soon as he realised the import of the message, he was alert and awake,

"Wonderful news, wonderful!"

Chambers returned to his duties with the mother and baby. He told Harriett that the Captain was delighted and she beamed broadly and laughed. Her laugh signalled to the whole company that all was well, and as if with one voice they laughed too, and clapped, such was their happiness. Very few were asleep, even at that early hour. The two old women finished tidying – very little to do and made sure Harriett was comfortable and baby was put to the breast. It was a moment made in heaven. The baby suckled naturally, instinctively.

"Have you thought of names?" asked the first older woman.

"What are your names, ladies?" replied Harriett.
"Our names? But surely you want family names?"
"Please tell me your names".
"Well, I'm Mary, and she's Sarah".
"Oh my mother is Mary. Then I've decided – my daughter shall be Mary Sarah Farley".
"Oh, that's lovely", said Mary.

Sarah was full of emotion and cried a little with happiness. Harriett felt suddenly tired and sleepy,

"It's her, sucking, and she's tired too".

Within a few minutes, mother and baby were sleeping peacefully in the first bunk, well protected by a couple of tables on their side. Chambers had worked hard. He left, but would return in the morning.

So it was that, one month after sailing, trouble flared below decks. The stables where young Richard worked were set amidships, lower deck. They were surprisingly roomy, but dark because kerosene lamps were only lit in an emergency. Richard worked with three others, and they all bedded down with the horses, using hay filled bolsters. The grooms got included in the ship's teams by rotation, so they got at least the exercise and the light! Richard knew horses well. He grew up on a farm with stables, at Hose in the Vale of Belvoir. He had few opportunities to talk with the other Leicester men, just when he happened to join their teams. In that way, once or twice, he had been paired up with the team containing Billy and Bob. Billy liked Richard,

"He has an easy, confident way of talking".

"He certainly knows a lot about horses", replied Bob.

"I was surprised, Bob; he's not a prisoner! He works with the horses, that's his job".

"Of course, the horses are valuable and need looking after. I expect they are used in farming and in transport just like they are back home".

It was on storm-filled nights that Richard and the other grooms had their work cut out. They did their best to calm the horses. With every crack of lightening, nostrils flared and eyes rolled wildly. The horses stamped and kicked back. Their stabling prevented them from rearing up, but the sharp hooves were an ever-present danger. Nevertheless, these lads did wonderful work in maintaining order and restoring calm. Conditions sometimes conspired against the best intentions. A storm had been raging for about five hours, and the lads were tired. Suddenly, a kerosene lamp, already alight, arced through the darkness and smashed in the furthest stall. Flames leapt up immediately and the startled horses crashed against their oaken walls.

"Fire! Fire!" the agonised cry went up.

Richard and the other lads grabbed at the water buckets and raced towards the fire. They seemed woefully inadequate, but were quickly replenished with seawater as other men were organised by the ever-vigilant First Mate, Stevens. With his help the fire was contained and finally extinguished. One groom was treated for burns to arms and legs. One horse was so badly maimed and burnt, that it had to be put down. Stevens organised the block and tackle, and the dead horse was dragged to the side and hoisted overboard.

The enquiry that followed praised the work of the grooms and of Stevens. It assumed that person or persons unknown threw the lamp maliciously.

Two days later, another incident challenged the good order of the ship. The moment that chains were loosed before morning work, a heavy man lunged forward and gripped a hapless convict by the throat, and started to throttle him. Leicester man, Lowesby, or as he was called Ponk, remained vigilant – just as well. That fracas was a blind. Whilst guards raced to separate the two locked in a deadly stranglehold, two other shadowy figures quietly slipped aft towards the chain line that held Billy and Bob. With chains loose, it was possible to launch an attack.

But Ponk shouted,

"Watch out, Bob!"

At that alarm, Tom Dunslow put out a foot and brought the first thug to the deck. Bob rose to meet the second who was already aiming a belaying pin towards Billy that could knock him senseless. His throw left his raised hand moments before Bob whacked his manacles into the man's ribs. Shouting to Billy to 'get down', Bob thumped his assailant across the head and he crumpled to the deck floor. Meanwhile, the stranglehold had been broken, and guards restored some sort of order, rounded up the two 'out of place' – one decidedly groggier than the other. As when the fox communicates with his mate with a bark or a cough, signals passed man to man among the Leicester men. Bob looked at Billy and wondered. What was this developing threat to Billy? What had Billy done? Who were his enemies? These were very big questions for Billy. His wit convinced him. He explained to Bob,

"Woodcock has been an enemy from the old days, as far back as Scalford when he organised the village to throw out my family," and added, " It was Woodcock himself who chaired the jury that condemned me to be transported over the seas".

Bob's wisdom conceded that this explanation rang true, but he remained puzzled.

"If Woodcock has successfully ejected your family, and effectively rid the country of you, Billy the thief and rustler, why is he still trying to reach out, to damage you or even to kill you?"

Billy blinked. He had no answers. His head was ringing as they were all led to their work. The salt air hit him and jolted him to breathe deeply. He braced himself and he and his best friend joined the team already swabbing the deck. Some Leicester lads joined them, whilst others of the group were to be seen aloft in the rigging. Bob assumed that the morning melee was a test, a jab perhaps? If so, then more and perhaps stronger forays were to be expected. His assessment of the state of things and of the warring factions was accurate. After the first test came the trial of strength.

In the *Capulet's* camp, Silas was in charge, having broken his word to the Captain and somehow secreted himself below decks. Indeed, there were two or three sailors keeping guard and obviously on Woodcock's payroll. He repeated the refrain,

"Get Brown," and with added venom, "or else!"

His lieutenants, including Jem Potter, took orders meekly, but were as iron with their own teams. Blades glistened in the half-light; cudgels were burnished good enough to reflect the images around them. Silas had more to say,

"The Leicester men are a careful bunch, or will be especially after we knock one of 'em overboard. We may use the speed of this ship to our advantage".

There was some laughter, but Silas cut this short,

"So surprise is important. A knife thrown has to find its mark! Do not get separated yourselves. Keep together in twos or threes, for your own safety."

The conspirators nodded in agreement and quickly arranged themselves in the indicated grouping.

"This may well be the last chance before landfall, so make it as strong as a rock smashing an apple!"

Silas did not share with them his own agenda. He was a man of ambition, prepared to trample over others to reach his goal. He was in his element, directing the rough crowd in front of him. They would help him to achieve his higher purpose, albeit unwittingly. He wanted no less than full control of the ship itself. With this in mind, he ordered his men into action.

The first attack was to the wheelhouse in an effort to wrest control from the Captain. Cudgels swung and fists flew as sailors and thugs got to grips with each other. The First Mate assessed the situation at a glance and brought up armed seamen and threw them into the fray. Silas took particular pleasure in stunning a fresh-faced seaman who dared to threaten him with his rifle.

The First Mate ordered his men to fire if they had to. At once, gun reports were heard and two of the thugs collapsed, one of them obviously dead. This was confirmed later. The battle swung to and fro. At the height of the disturbance, Potter slipped away with two others. They found that the young groom, Richard Pratt of the *Montagues* was alone – somehow separated from his fellows and his horses, perhaps temporarily. This was an opportunity that presented itself, disported itself, loins bestirred themselves, enough frissons for those three *Capulets* to grab him and drag him below by a back stair, out of sight of guards. They took him to a heads aft and on the windward side. Young Pratt was pretty handsome and nineteen, prime meat for Potter and his lusts. The other two tore off his shirt, then dragged down his pants and spread-eagled him across the floor. His post-pubescent manhood was exposed, no longer flaccid after rough handling – so the thickening cock was half-erect. Potter was in a frenzy. As young Richard was held fast, Potter threw himself at the boy's privates, took them into his slavering mouth and groaned with ecstasy. One of his captors, overcome by the sexual heat of the whole thing, fumbled for his own member and began to masturbate. Hard himself, Potter gave his orders,

"Turn this chicken over!"

The boy was raped long and repeatedly. He was soon covered in blood, but Potter was oblivious of this and continued to his own climax. The two then dragged Richard to the showerhead and turned on the water. Potter disappeared. His two minions, still feeling the ecstasy of the incident, pawing the boy all the time, pulled Richard to his feet and dressed him with his torn shirt and stained pants. Reluctantly but unsympathetically, they released him into the melee on the work deck where he was a dazed and wandering figure, lately at the mercy of the gathered hounds, almost torn to shreds by their naked aggression.

TEN

Young Richard was wandering around the f'c'stle deck, his trousers stained with blood and semen. He seemed not to understand where he was. Sailors rushed by and paid no heed; one collided with him and sent him sprawling on the deck floor. The sailor helped him up but then just as abruptly, moved on. It was around midday, as the bells rang twice, then paused, repeating this phrasing twice more, then a single bell. Young Richard was oblivious to the activity around him. He found the support of a stanchion portside comfortable and was beginning to slide down it to the deck, when a sailor walked purposefully towards him and was just able to say,

"You alright, son?"

Young Richard made no reply, but the imminent conversation had no chance to blossom, as two heavy, burly men descended from the rigging one each side of Richard. The first immediately stunned the benevolent sailor who slumped to the deck. With that one turned aside, the two grabbed the dazed boy and hauled him up as one would a sack of potatoes. Up he soared into the rigging; an observer might even have noticed that the boy was tossed to another pair of ruffians. Richard certainly didn't know what was happening, so he probably did not see the signal that passed between them, the nod of the head. In a trice, they threw him overboard like *Jonah* to the whale.

The *Capulets* had chosen their moment well. The ship was approaching the Cape of Good Hope, and all hands, including teams of prisoners with their leaders, were concentrating on the task of sailing with the following wind at speeds approaching twelve to fourteen knots. It was a rough ride to be sure, but these square riggers were built for this kind of work. So the almost silent disturbance in the lea of the companion way to the f'c'stle deck attracted no-ones' attention. One minute Richard was there, the next he was gone. The two villains, or was it four, removed themselves from the scene as quickly as possible, but not without Tom and Joseph noticing both their departure and the disappearance of young Richard. There was nothing to be done, of course. The speed of the ship meant that the doomed man was left far behind – a speck of frail dust in the mighty ocean; bleeding was also a signal for marine predators.

It was enough notice. It signalled that serious and deadly enemies were at work. It was f'c'stle business anyway, nothing whatever to do with the officers. However, the keen eyes of the First Mate had noticed how put out the two Leicester men had been, though unsure as to the cause. Not for long unsure, as he strode along the deck silently, imperiously. A quiet word with Tom and Joseph reminded him of the growing bitterness between two groups,

"Seems quiet, now. I'm sorry for the loss of young Pratt. Are you sure that your friends are safe?" asked Stevens.

"For the moment, thanks. But the gang intent on trouble is just biding its time. The first chance it gets and there'll be a disturbance," replied Bob.

"We'll watch out for that. I'm obliged".

The two men parted company and melted into the night.

That bitterness grew apace. Even though the Mate ensured that both groups were chained apart – one windward and the other leeward – such separation could not be maintained in the rigging! So, a few days later, the teams were working on the topsails, setting them after rounding the Cape to speed their crossing of the Southern Ocean. A sailor was put in charge of each team; Bob, Joseph, Ponk and Billy were with Johnson, a fit, wiry Northerner with steely blue eyes and a shock of fair hair. His warm smile lifted the lads' spirits and encouraged them so much they would follow Johnson to Hell and back. Johnson showed them how to cast off the gaskets,

"You must get this collar off before hoisting the sail". He demonstrated the action once only, he was so strict. The lads were very attentive and drank in all he said.

Little by little, the heavy yards were lifted by muscle power pulling on the lanyards. The mighty topsail filled out in the wind, and the lads felt the kick as the ship responded and picked up speed. It was a noticeable speed, as drifting birds flashed past them, or rubbish thrown overboard disappeared behind them very quickly indeed. The movement of the ocean threw dappled reflections across the billowing tarpaulins. Figures moving above eye level were but imaginary and fleeting phantoms. The speed of the ship through its watery forest was intoxicating. The lads relaxed as their task was completed, but in the same instance, three figures took solid shape, appearing from behind the spreading canvas. It was the *Capulets* falling upon the *Montagues* and preparing to do them harm! The first assault was against Joseph and Ponk, who immediately grappled with their attackers in a furious melee. Johnson took action, with two of his sailors, and dived into the cluster of fists and punches. These three assisted Joseph and Ponk to withhold the brutes. One of the villains seemed to stagger and fall. Johnson and Joseph pummelled '*Mercutio*', as Ponk seemed to have got the better of his assailant.

There was a swishing sound in the wind, a keening, a lament; it was a harbinger of tragedy. A nimble-footed, furious '*Tybalt*' came sweeping in on a rope and toppled Ponk and his adversary, still entwined in a struggle, from the rigging. They dropped like stones, in a deadly embrace, and lay still. Johnson deftly leapt to the spot on that spar holding the flying figure and stunned him with a sharp blow to the side of his head. He pinned the sagging figure to a rail with the very rope he had just used. A third wave of terror descended from the rigging, but Johnson by this time had his men on full alert and the three villains making a last ditch effort were soon nursing sore heads or broken bones. Joseph had quelled his foe. Some sort of order then prevailed, but had the ship become a powder keg?

The First Mate and the well-respected Johnson preached vigilance, both then in the cursory enquiry, but also during the daily working of the ship. Three deaths, and one man missing was a rare situation to be in on board. There were clearly two warring factions on the ship, which must be faced head-on. Everyone had to be in a state of alert. Thereafter, men moved warily, carefully. As when the fox skirts the chicken run looking for opportunity to dive in, teeth and claws flashing; so, the *Capulets* looked for opportunities to cause trouble. Murder and mayhem were a heady diet. The response to trouble was not always to throw the villains into the brig, to kick their heels. Their incarceration, however, was limited to ten days, or at the Captain's wish for any other reason.

Their time was up then because the drum rolls signified the beginning of the shipboard funeral, so the brig was emptied so that everyone might attend the committal. Two men died locked together as they fell from the rigging. Here they were locked together in death's rituals, sewn up in their own winding sheets. Both factions bid their own man adieu, as the two boards were tipped and each deposited its load to the briny deep. Some of the Leicester lads were thinking that Richard had no such send off. Tipped overboard from a speeding vessel was his unmarked nemesis. The Captain and First Mate thought that the funeral might offer a breathing space to both sides.

That plainly seemed unacceptable to the *Capulets*. Their Tybalt stood amongst his cronies, laughing even though this was a solemn occasion, shouting oaths even though the majority felt the ceremony deserved silence. Tybalt was emboldened by the last fracas. He was openly hostile as the men dispersed after the funeral, spitting, calling, and laughing derisively,

"Chicken meat, eh? Brown – you're dead!"

Tybalt was no dullard. His language was colourful and offensive, enough to make any man bristle and possibly reply with violence. Bob remained steely quiet. His hands and indeed his whole body said 'keep calm', 'do nothing'. Billy and the Leicester lads did as they were asked; no chuntering, just quietly walking on.

Tybalt launched into another spat, sometimes delivered with clenched teeth and wild, deep-set eyes,

"You'll feel my knife! Christ, you'll suffer."

His eyebrows met in the middle; promised a rising temper, particularly after his recent unceremonious bundling in his own rope, and the subsequent throwing into the brig. His behaviour was a reminder that difficult times lay ahead.

*

In Asfordby, Leicestershire, England, Mary Turner was talking to her Mam,

"I'm not going to see Jim again, am I?"

"My dear, he's been sent off to God knows where for fifteen years. Do they ever come back?"

"I don't know. I just feel that my happiness has been shattered", Mary cried.

"There, there, don't take on so", putting a motherly arm around her shoulders, "Life has to go on, you know".

"What do you mean? My life can't go on", Mary sobbed.

Mother and daughter rocked in the chair in each other's arms for a while.

"This won't do", said her Mam, "I'll put the kettle on".

She raked the fire into life, and placed a filled kettle on the black leaded hob. It was soon singing merrily, in stark contrast to the mournful mood of her daughter. She made the tea in a china pot, and clattered about preparing two cups and saucers from the matching set. Is that what she meant by 'life must go on!? Mary was not convinced,

"But, I love him so!"

"Look here, girl. You'll have to forget him!"

This injunction set off yet more sobbing and rocking. Mary's Mam gave her a cup of tea, in the belief that it could work wonders. Mary recovered sufficiently to manage the cup to her lips. She sipped at it quietly.

They both heard the knocking at the door, and Mary's Mam encouraged her daughter to see who it was. Mary opened the door to the baker's rounds man, Tony. Mary's breathing quickened as she noticed his lovely eyes, brown and smouldering. He's tall, she thought. Lovely,

"Hello", she said.

"Mornin'. Usual order, is it?"

Mary turned to Mam to confirm.

"Yes, usual order please, Tony!" called her Mam.

"That's two farmhouse loaves and a dozen crusty rolls".

"Can you put them on the table, please", enquired Mary.

"Of course. Here you are. Will that be all, then", he said with a winning smile.

"Yes, thank you, Tony", said Mam, "How's your Mother?"

"Oh, much better, thank you Mrs Turner. She's on the mend".

"Oh, that's good. Give her my best, won't you?"

"I will, Mrs Turner. Bye then! Bye Miss!"

"I'm Mary", she said, suddenly embarrassed.

"Oh!" Tony hesitated no more than a second, "Bye, Mary".

The rounds man left the house and by the time he was checking his next delivery, he was whistling. Mary closed the front door and leant against it with her back,

"Ooh! This Tony is lovely".

Her Mam smiled,

"That's what I mean, life must go on".

The pair collapsed laughing in each other's arms.

*

In Nottinghamshire, England; there was an inquest on one Harry Bainbridge, tenant farmer of Belvoir, whose body was found on the banks of the Trent. The body was clothed in riding gear and boots, which would certainly account for his drowning. The body showed rubbed ankles, so it was assumed that he probably got his foot caught in the stirrup. Considering his weight, it was also assumed, nay feared, that his horse was also drowned and lost without trace. A verdict of accidental death was made; despite evidence that there were no hunt meetings that went anywhere near the Trent!

ELEVEN

1844

Billy and Bob were in the orderly line of convicts being returned to their stations, presenting a dull pencil of humanity. At first, the line was orderly. As it progressed along the deck, the line began to waver, encouraged by Tybalt's lieutenant and a few others, tottering and stuttering as guards futilely tried to keep control. A bird's eye view would have revealed balletic movements. The *Capulets*' chorus pushed hard in one direction and the line broke up. Sweeping stragglers before them, the *Capulets* moved towards Bob and Billy and the rest. The sailor Johnson could see what was happening and alerted Stevens the First Mate.

Immediately and decisively, Stevens ordered six of his men to load their muskets and to follow him. They drove straight into the heart of the melee, using their muskets as battering rams, pushing men aside or before them. Thus, Tybalt's lieutenant was thwarted by being cornered at the end of a musket and the 'mailed fist' of the First Mate. One of the *Capulets* had drawn a wicked looking knife, but it found an unwitting victim as the crowd pushed by. As the man fell, a sailor emptied his musket at the knife-bearer. The sound of the shot struck the ears of everyone there, and the crazed dance came to a stop. Stevens and his team ensured that the men were returned to their stations forthwith.

Tybalt's lieutenant and two others of the *Capulets* were thrown back into the brig. Two fresh bodies, the latest casualties in a mounting toll, were hauled away to be fitted for their shrouds.

The fact that three of the villains were locked up did not seem to make much difference to the tempo of deck life for the Leicester lads. The usual teams worked aloft in the rigging where adjustments were necessary in the long haul across the Southern Oceans. Others worked on deck; cleaning, polishing and generally making everything ship-shape and tidy. If there was a period of calm, when the wind died, the paint pots were brought out, new ropes were fitted. Bob, Billy and the rest did not relax however, as the brig was emptied after ten days – the maximum stretch. With Tybalt and his henchmen free, the watchword was vigilance.

Billy was nonplussed to see that Tybalt often had conversations with one of the strangers. Up to that point, he had no idea why, and he certainly had no idea who this stranger was. Bob found it prudent not to say anything of his own suspicions, yet. But events moved on apace, and Bob found himself reviewing this decision.

The gruel that passed for food was unbearable. Desperate hunger might drive one to eat it; but on the other hand, there might be something else to do with it! Thus it was, that feeding time on the Sunday following descended into an uproarious skirmish with missiles of food flying about everywhere. What passed for stew was tipped over an unlucky convict, whilst another received a dish of grey vegetables in his lap - all seemingly innocent and good fun. This was the scene that greeted Billy as he arrived in the mess, after first checking with the First Mate and sorting out young Richard's chest. He had found a few papers but little else. A letter from his mother gave her new address because apparently she was moving back to Derbyshire after losing her husband. Billy wrapped the papers in an oilskin for protection. He would keep those safe.

So he entered the dining area known as the mess and made his way over to where Bob was sitting. As he sat down, Billy shouted as a knife pinned his shirt to the bench back; whilst a fellow prisoner in the next bay screamed as a dagger pierced his ribs. Bob looked quickly towards Thomas and Joseph further down the feeding hall. Thomas was already pointing to the source of the knives. Bob could see the leering face of a man who did not belong there. Somehow, this man had found his way to the lower deck and been the immediate cause of the trouble. Joseph meanwhile had reached Stevens who sent in a squad of six sailors to quell the disturbance. Stevens had the man brought to him and gave him a stern warning not to again go into the prisoners' quarters, not even to the lower deck. No proof could be established that this man threw the knife, so he sent him packing to the upper decks.

Serious work was undertaken the next morning. Thomas and Joseph found themselves high above the decking, in an attempt to repair the t'gallants' winding gear. Eight men in all, including Tybalt and one of his lieutenants, made up the team. Two sailors, one of them Johnson, were overseeing the operation. Under their direction, the men were ranged around the main mast and began to pull on the cables that lifted the sails into position. One cable clearly did not complete its task; it was sticking some six feet above their heads. Johnson gave the order to clear the obstruction to Joseph, but Tybalt, the personification of Mischief, pushed forward roughly – so that Joseph had to be careful not to fall.

"I'll mend it", he shouted, nimbly taking the stepped mast and rising to the seat of the problem. Johnson shouted to him to cut the rope that linked with the cable, but was now snagging. Tybalt wielded the knife he had been given, with a glint of mischief in his eyes, leering at Joseph. As he cut the rope, he looked to his footing in an attempt to launch himself at Joseph, but there was a resounding thwack as the rope, now freed of tension, whipped inwards and wrapped itself round Tybalt's neck. The weight of the rope could not be held, so the burly frame of Tybalt then flashed past them and landed in a tangled heap on the deck some sixty feet below. The sailors immediately brought the team down and Johnson reported to the First Mate.

Quickly assessing the situation, Stevens had Johnson sent to his cabin 'on report'. The reason given was 'lack of control' – a convict loose with a knife!? The First Mate ordered the clearing of the fallen tackle, and with it the removal of the corpse entangled in it. Tybalt's neck was broken, snapped in the fall. He was dead before he hit the deck. Inevitably, Johnson was punished; the rules applied to all, heroes included. At dawn the next day, a drumbeat was sounded as he was lashed to a capstan and given twenty strokes of the cat o' nine tails. The ship's surgeon threw a bucket of salt seawater over his bleeding back as the assembled company dispersed.

Over the next few days, Stevens made counsel with Bob. The *Capulets* were well organised and these two men wanted to find out why and how, and most importantly by whom? These discussions did not include Billy, or the rest of the Leicester lads. So Billy was unaware that the First Mate had made an astonishing discovery – that the ship had passengers! This was incredible, but apparently not unknown if the right influence and the right cash could be employed. This explained the 'stranger', the man below decks – he was a passenger! Stevens made further enquiries as diplomatically as possible. He returned to Bob a few days later with a list of three names, Jeb Knight, George Churchill and Silas Woodcock. Bob almost tore the paper from Stevens' hands. He spat out the name with an unusual vehemence, 'Silas Woodcock!' This explained everything that had happened on board, prison ship or no. The man's name was enough. No need to know more of the sod's family tree. So Billy was right after all – the long hand of old man Woodcock was stretched out by means of this relative, or at least kinsman. For the moment, Bob said nothing of this to Billy. Instead, he instituted a roll call, mentally counting up the members past and present of the Leicestershire Lads. Joseph and Thomas supported Bob and Billy. They had lost Richard and Ponk. The *Capulets* had lost four, one by Tybalt's hand toppled from the rigging; then Tybalt himself when his neck was broken in the bungled repair job; and another knife man by a sailor's musket fire. A fourth fell to his death in that first struggle in the rigging. Both sides had others in tow, sympathisers, and men of principle or none.

The star-filled seas were smooth that night. They had sunk down the globe for about one hundred and ninety days, and were just a few hours from their destination. Bob decided Billy should be told before landfall. He should be made to understand that even though his instinct was true; that it was Woodcock reaching out to crush him; he had to realise that life was very much more dangerous from now on. Of course, in Van Dieman's Land, he was still a convict and still under supervision.

"But, Billy, does this make any difference to Woodcock?" asked Bob. The band of brothers made preparations for the disembarkation. And so they came to Hobart, lately named a city, and stood off a while to allow a pilot aboard. Van Diemans Land then had them in its iron grip that matched their chains. Bob and Billy and the Leicester lads had a chance to pause on the gangplank, Billy in a prophetic mood,

"When the old mapmakers reached the end of the world, they wrote, '*Beyond here there be dragons*'". The lads laughed, but laughter was perhaps a little premature, as the prophecy was to ring true before 'ere long.

TWELVE

Horses neighed, a Dixie band played, men shouted - Billy heard the familiar hubbub of a thriving work place as he stepped onto the welcoming quayside of Hobart in Van Diemans Land. It was a noisy place. All was bustle and business as hundreds of people flocked to the newly created city. He hardly had time to notice that the women were being moved further along the quay to another vessel, but almost at once there was shouting and wailing. Young Harriett Farley with her infant child, Mary, was aghast that she was being separated from her husband.

"Oh my God! You cannot do this?"

Jacob Farley was distraught,

"Harriett, my love, I don't want to lose you!"

Billy was upset; he turned to Bob – equally shocked. Bob turned to see Stevens, the First Mate at the top of the gangway,

"Stevens – what on earth is happening here?"

Stevens walked down the gangway and reached Bob,

"Now then, what you see is orders".

"Orders!" shouted Bob, "Bloody orders! You cannot separate this man from his wife and newborn baby. What sort of bloody regime do you represent?"

It was a comment that found its mark. Stevens wrestled with his conscience; he was mortified,

"God! I didn't think it would come to this".

He gave orders for Harriett Farley and the infant Mary to be brought back and put aboard a carriage that would take them and some rough convicts to Launceston,

"I cannot release the convict husband, but at least this way he sees his wife and child – who knows, they may be able to start a new life in this land".

Jacob Farley from Gloucester and his wife and infant daughter were put aboard the carriage in double quick time. Stevens indicated to Bob and Billy to join them, and they in turn asked Tom, Joseph and John to follow. Three more and their carriage was full. Stevens turned back to the ship. He had to tell the Captain what he had done. Billy got down again to speak to Stevens, as the rest of the women disappeared on to their new vessel, bound for the mainland. Bob estimated that up to one hundred, maybe one hundred and fifty convicts were being disembarked. The quayside was all jostling and pushing. Their guards had real difficulty in beating a path to the waiting wagons, through the flotsam and jetsam of the human zoo. There were drunkards arguing and fighting, thrashing about hither and thither that made their route hazardous. There were mothers slumped on the pavement, rather worse for the evils of drink. Some even had their toddlers running bare-arsed around them as they slept. Other women, painted faces and sunken eyes, lurked in doorways hoping for the attention of passers by – especially men! Convicts were a familiar exhibit, and thus a focus for laughter and ribald joking by these onlookers. They made a lot of noise and clamour for the notice of all and sundry. Some shouted for their children,

"Come 'ere where I can see yer!"

Others plied their trade,

"Want a good time, darlin'?"

"You feelin' lucky, sir?"

Billy mused over how best to respond to these entreaties, but realised at once how impractical that could be – what with his chains and everything! He had thanked Stevens and stood there listening. Suddenly, a cry went up,

"Stop thief! Stop thief!"

On hearing this shout for the thief to stop, Billy looked round to see where this familiar cry was from. So, he was surprised that the young man fleeing collided with the chain of prisoners on the quay and stumbled towards him. Billy did no more than stick out a foot and the lad tumbled to the ground. In an instant, hands grabbed him and hauled him away. An official thanked Billy, for his prompt action!

Bob was wreathed in smiles; he saw it all from the wagon,

"Takes a thief to catch a thief!"

Billy saw the funny side of the matter and laughed out loud, only to be prodded by an over zealous guard,

"Quiet there! Keep in line!"

Billy climbed up again to sit with Bob.

Wagons and horses conveyed the men, including the *Capulets* and the *Montagues*, from that teeming quayside, and climbed into the quiet hills that led them north. There was no knowing what had happened to the passengers, because they had not seen them leave. Where had Woodcock gone? Billy kept his thoughts to himself for the time being, and wondered at the reddened sky. It clothed the mountains to the south of them in scarlet finery, including Mount Nelson, but the scene was soon blotted out as they moved onto a broad plateau. The rolling scenery was rutted with signs of human traffic. The track was wide to allow for passing, so it was a matter of concern when one of the trundling wagons lost a wheel. The shout went up from those in the following wagon. Men chained together were flung to the ground in a heap as the drunken vehicle lurched to one side. No one was injured, but the scene was suddenly mayhem as one of the young convicts let out an awful scream; leapt up holding his arm. The nearest guard raised his rifle with the butt end downwards and struck the ground two or three times. He turned to announce,

"Tiger snake. Strikes out when trapped. The lad is unlucky!"

He kicked the dead specimen away further, because even the fangs retained their venom for years in crystalline form. The stricken lad was pale, and was suffering a massive headache. He went limp and the guards lifted him gently on to the nearest wagon. A guard moved forward to speak to their superior and to explain what had happened. The order to camp was eventually passed along, and the wagons were circled to keep better order. The superior ordered four of his men to beat the ground within the circle, to guard against any more somnolent snakes. A fire was lit, and billy cans put by to boil. A crew of six moved off to repair the broken wagon. By that time, most of the day had passed, so a camp and the preparation of supper was the most beneficial thing to do for all concerned. It could have meant an early start for the next morning. For the stricken lad, however, there was no more to be done. His skin had turned a greenish yellow, and a knowledgeable guard shook his head,

"Liver failure!"

An hour later, the lad's life was extinct. It was a shocking introduction to Van Diemans Land. Everyone was aghast at the ferocity of the attack and the speed of its deadly effects – nature in the raw!

At early morning, the sound of a single drum was heard, accompanying the coffin to its final resting place. The watching men mused how unreal this event was – not in this damned country a day and already burying one of their number! An hour later, a burial party had returned from its sad duty. Camp was drawn and preparations for moving off were completed. It was a quiet, contemplative party aboard the wagons as the file of guards took their positions and the order was shouted,

"Move on! Move on!"

The horses took the strain and the wagons rolled and pitched across the terrain. Within the next hour, they entered a deep forest. Billy could hear the chatter of what sounded like crazed wood pigeons, that he later learned to call kookaburras. Their singing echoed round the dry forest and somehow lightened the burden of their enforced trek. They continued along the prominent north road that was dotted at intervals with military outposts – among them Oatlands, and its sandstone buildings. They spent time at that place, more for their guards to take refreshments, as it was a warm day. Grudgingly, they were also allowed some weak beer and a crusty biscuit. Jacob and Harriett were released from their chains so that they could go with their baby to find a quiet spot where the infant may be fed.

Chained and shuffling forward, Billy stumbled. He noticed a wagon keeping up with them but on a parallel road to their right. He thought he caught sight of Silas Woodcock sitting next to the driver, but rather than say anything, he made out he was struggling with the stiffness gained in the wagons. Bob was close and quickly caught him in his strong arms. The guards hesitated, at first it looked as though they would dive in, but seeing the Christian act of one prisoner helping another, they relaxed, just as other rough elements leered at them. The cool beer and crusts were very welcome. Afterwards, groups of the prisoners with a guard were unchained to allow them to walk round the square, and to notice the sand coloured buildings stretching in every direction. Billy had a chance to mention to Bob what he thought he had seen, so the two of them could be seen heads down, in deep conversation.

"I tell you, I saw Woodcock!"

"You see that man everywhere," replied Bob, "and nowhere. He's probably a hundred miles away by now".

"Bob, I know what I saw!"

As they walked around they come across Jacob and Harriett enjoying the sunshine. The infant Mary was asleep after her feed.

"You've picked a nice spot here", said Billy.

"I can think of better places in England", replied Jacob.

In reality this was a brief moment before resuming the wandering with the guard. Billy was to learn much more about sandstone and its preparation for building, and just how close his enemy was as they walked. Their meanderings were interrupted by the uncouth and menacing voices of a group that caused the guards to rush towards the hubbub. They did not notice two figures alight from a wagon parked near by, and come racing towards Bob and Billy, with obvious evil intent. Bob noticed and was equal to the task, first flipping the leader onto the floor and delivering a well-aimed kick at the second. The latter collapsed holding his private parts and groaning. The leader, he with the broken nose gained presumably in bare-knuckle fighting, struggled to his feet, glowering at both of them. Bob stepped forward in a threatening manner. The two retreated. This gave him the chance to look at the parked wagon and to see Silas Woodcock in the driving seat, calling them back. So young Woodcock was not a hundred miles away, but tagging their movements as the fox keeps his prey in sight. It would be a long time before they could put a name to each of these miscreants, but the one Bob had felled, he with a broken nose, turned out to be called Pitts. Their wagon was driven off and disappeared up the road ahead of them. It was still a great puzzle to them to imagine the reasons behind this venom, even if they thought they knew the source of that evil.

Meanwhile, again in chains, they watched the sorry procession of wagons winding ahead of them towards Launceston. The prison camp was two to three miles out of Launceston set at the front of a sandstone outcrop. The Leicester lads and Jacob and Harriett Farley were moved on to another wagon, but had time to say cheerio to Billy and to Bob. They were off to the rope works. Billy and his friend waved them off as the second wagon moved on and finally disappeared round a bend. Billy and Bob were moved thereafter to their bunk bed accommodation and told they started at dawn the next morning. The planning was cunning. Billy quickly found out in the morning, that his work consisted of scraping at the sandstone with a chisel. It was hard labour alright! They were expected to fashion building blocks, five hours chained and five unchained. What's the saying…'idle hands'? Needless to say, one's chisel became very precious indeed.

Not yet a 'model' prisoner, Billy was full of fun; he saw opportunities to cause such uproar without blame of any kind. Bob was enthusiastic, not that he thought it all out; he took the idea into his being as he did breath into his lungs. Bob worked in the next gulley, working on what appeared to be coping stones such as you'd fix on top of a big wall. The intricacy of the carving merited frequent inspection, so the men downed tools and paid careful attention. In the lull, it was a simple job to tip a chisel over the blocks one to another. They had such fun seeing the panic as the men turned back to their tools, the shouting, and the blows as one blamed another. Bob said nothing, but quietly dwelt for a moment on the sheer fun they were having, against a backcloth of unmerited violences. The two of them allowed themselves a smile. All manner of men were incarcerated here, for bad pledges, deep debt on the one hand, and for stealing, horse rustling on the other. Even his own two brothers were transported for horse rustling. Jim only lately arrived, before Billy, and he made what enquiries he could to find him. Within a year, his brother Dick was brought over on the *Blundell*. This was a surprise, unwelcome, but nevertheless news that shook Billy rigid. What was his Mam feeling then, with three sons on the other side of the world?

*

In Asfordby, Leicestershire in the East Midlands of England, Mary Turner married Tony Hickman, the baker's rounds man. Elizabeth Brown, sister to both Jim and Billy, was one of her bridesmaids. Mr and Mrs Jack Brown were guests that day. Ann Brown reflected on what might have been,

"If only Mary was marrying Jim", she said.

"Don't be silly, Ma!"

"Well, I know it was not meant to be. I'm very happy for Mary and Tony".

"So you should be".

"Mary is level headed and sensible", said Ann, "I wish my own children had such qualities".

Jack and Ann had a lovely day, and laughed and joked as good as the rest in the wedding breakfast. Ann was suddenly quite pale and wont to faint. Jack caught her in his arms and she leaned back in her chair,

"Take me home, Jack".

Jack complied, with a word of regret to the Turner family and the bride and groom. Another guest loaned a carriage, so they were soon well on the way to Frisby, and to the home of Ann's sister Evelyn, and her brother in law Richard, Evelyn's husband. Jack Brown helped his wife into the sitting room and laid her on a large settle. He was concerned for her health. Ann had never really got over the enforced move from Scalford, and now three sons were overseas! That was a great disappointment. Yet they were both well supported by Evelyn and Richard. Their children had grown up together. The fact that Ann had to suffer the transportation of three of her lads was all too much for her.

Now Ann was coughing and getting weaker. She took to her bed. Her daughter Elizabeth made a warm broth and helped her mother to sip it from a proffered shaking spoon. Ann smiled her 'thank you's, too weak to speak. Evelyn tore up soft linen squares, into which Ann might cough. These could easily be scolded and washed. It was evening and Ann had eaten a little stew and potatoes. She settled comfortably. A sudden racking cough began and Evelyn held her back for support, and offered a linen handkerchief. Ann was shaken by the attack that at last subsided. Evelyn took the linen piece to Richard and Jack – it was stained red with bloody sputum. Jack turned away, his shoulders heaving silently. Richard put his hand on Jack's shoulder as though to steady him. Evelyn discarded the linen square to the back of the fire.

On the fifth day, Ann died in Jack's arms. Elizabeth was with Evelyn and Richard and they heard the moans from the bedroom, and gathered what had just happened. Ann's fight was over. She was at peace. Billy and his brothers in Van Diemans Land did not know this had happened. Billy did not know for a long time; not until his return to England, when he reached Bedford Street in Leicester after travelling from the ship.

*

In Van Dieman's Land, Bob saw that Billy was troubled and offered a twist of tobacco. The two of them settled with a pipe-full and fell silent. Billy remembered the old adage, *'The earth is made round that we might not see too far down the road'*. He learned more about their situation,

"Isn't Launceston a very big place?"

"It is a developing port with its river connections to the sea".

Chained gangs made up of convicts with brute strength, or with the necessary skills brought from home, were known to work in the shipyards, or to build roads and bridges.

"I wonder if we will get to join such gangs".

Bob thought he knew someone to talk to,

"Perhaps someone in the supervisor's office can tell me".

"Quite possibly", said Billy thinking what a likeable chap he was, and evidently their guards thought so too.

Billy came to realise that not everyone appreciated Bob's easy way with the guards. It was involved with privileges, both real and perceived, and brought him enemies, and thus enemies of their group. Within a month, Bob and Billy were transferred to a bridge building gang with half a dozen guards and headed out for a place on the South Esk River called Perth. There they were directed by architects and other planners and began to build wooden caissons to keep back the river so they could build the first piers of the new bridge. From the first moment, they realised what a difference in the guards, snappy, supercilious and one or two downright evil. The working area was damp, muddy and dangerous. Men chained to other men were clearly in peril. Their pleas fell on deaf ears. Hour after hour they dug out the footings of wet clay, replacing it with heavy stone blocks. These had to be mortared together and the first pier slowly rose piece by piece.

On the third afternoon, the work suddenly hit a problem. In short, tragedy struck. The heavy stone block being hoisted into position began to sway violently – possibly a rope snapped, or someone had interfered with it – and dropped with sickening force on three men below, each chained to each. They had no chance. Their bodies were pressed into the mud and disappeared. A fourth man also chained to them, screamed in desperation.

Give him his due, a guard leaped into action and swiftly uncoupled this man from his deadly load. It all happened very quickly indeed. Men everywhere, Billy included, were reeling from shock. The poor unfortunate who had been rescued was incoherent with the trauma. One of the sadistic guards ordered them back to work, firing his gun in the air to reinforce his message. Slowly, the work resumed and brought some sort of order to the scene. The errant block was lifted, as were three bodies chained together for their journey to God. Was this a warning? If so, from whom? They wept over them, noticing the blueness of their innocent mouths.

The blueness of a wound, Billy said, *cleanseth away all evil.* They quickly forgot the symmetrical beauty of the bridge now spanning the river. Their days were swifter than a weaver's shuttle. They lost all hope. With the bridge completed, Bob and Billy were moved to the rope works – evidently with good reports of their working habits. What they did not realise was the growing antagonism and jealousy of a small clique, but principally Woodcock's cronies, including the man they thought was called Pitts, he with the broken nose. Bob, however, spoke to Billy,

"Woodcock is no longer with his helpers. Where is he?"

THIRTEEN

The riverside in Van Diemans Land was a melee of wharves, piers, boat building sheds, and rope and sailcloth workshops. One big workshop that – Billy thought of it often – but then his life was idle in the prison cell, and he cried bitter tears. But it was no use. The time for pleading had gone. His own mouth condemned him. Anyhow, that despair came and went. They were put to work, he remembered, straightway hauling twine and hemp bundles in the rope workshops.

"You see these hooks and the flywheel?" grubby-fingered and bewhiskered, the foreman showed Billy and the others how to fix the strands of hemp to the hooks.

"There are five hooks, but, mind, use only three of them", he said, fingering the hooks required to explain better. One got the feeling he'd been doing this for years, so that he could string up the hooks in the dark.

"Any questions, then? he asked. He did not expect questions, nor did he get any. The convicts began to move away, following their team leaders, but Billy lingered,

"What is the rope made from?" he queried.

"Hemp", replied the foreman, relieved to find a serious student, "but it needs tarring to make it seaworthy".

Billy's lesson may well have continued, but he was called away to join his team. Billy thanked Chapman, the foreman, and raced off. It was in the rope works that Bob and Billy fell in again with other Leicester men, Thomas Dunslow, Joseph Barlow and John Garner. Bob and Billy also saw Jacob at work and wanted to know how they had settled in.

"How's that precious baby? asked Billy.

"We are doing well, thanks. We have a hut to live in just within the camp perimeter, and everyone makes a fuss of little Mary".

Billy and Tom were in number one workshop, and Bob and Joe were in number two. They did not learn which team John joined until much later. The workshops were so vast they could accommodate ropes up to a hundred feet long; and vats of tar stood at the far end. The distinct smells were pungent in their nostrils. Thus, there remained many dangers in rope making, as Billy and the Leicester men soon realised.

Towards the end of the second day, Bob and Tom noticed the First Mate, Stevens, with two men, soberly dressed, heading for the Office.

They also noticed the darkened clouds as if a storm was brewing. Within the hour, they had rain and Tom had two names – by devious means – or his liaison with a lad from the Office. The names were ominously familiar, George Churchill and Jeb Knight, representatives apparently of a rope making establishment in Bridport, Dorset, England. Bob recognised the names immediately,

"They were passengers on board ship, alongside the scoundrel Silas Woodcock! They're here for no good reason", he exclaimed.

"Representatives of what?" mused Tom.

"I'd be surprised if it was only for rope!"

"Do you think they are in league with Woodcock?"

"Dead right! That's it!"

Bob sought out Billy and Joe as soon as their evening started in the mess tent. The wind and the continuing rain were picking up, as he quickly outlined to Billy what, and who, they had observed that day. Billy was puzzled,

"What are businessmen doing, mixed up with Woodcock?"

"That's just it, we don't know, yet", replied Bob, "but if the First Mate introduced them, perhaps he can tell us more".

The strong smell of hemp surrounded their discussion; a cloak of mysticism at least as potent as the connections they had found, or the tobacco-filled atmosphere of the mess tent, where Bob was talking to the First Mate, Stevens, an hour later. There was a tuneless piano tinkling with soul-less ditties in the background. Bob greeted Stevens,

"You well, Mate?"

"As well as can be expected".

"Are you in port for long?"

"We sail in five days time, after provisioning and some keel re-fitting".

Bob posed the important question,

"Can you tell me what you know of your passengers, Churchill and Knight?"

"Why do you ask? What's up?"

"You recall the trouble on board between two factions of prisoners, and the interference by one of your passengers, namely Woodcock?"

"Aye, I do that".

"Well, we believe that feud is to be carried on within the Rope Works, indeed throughout this Penal Colony".

"Are there enough of 'em to do that?"

"They are bullies. Woodcock has his lieutenants, but they recruit others to their cause by frightening 'em".

The Mate considered for a while, then,

"George Churchill asked too many questions about you men, especially you and Billy. We began to feel that his purpose in Van Diemans Land was more than looking after business interests. But having said that, I do not remember seeing him with Woodcock anywhere on board".

"Woodcock is clever enough to control these men from behind the scenes. He must have some sort of hold over Churchill and Knight, or he simply threatens harder".

*

The albino was in a hostel in Launceston reading the postal packet he had received. It was postmarked Hobart and dated just three days before, and the quadroon, Mordecai, grandson of a French medical man and an Aboriginal maiden, was interested because he was expecting a communication. It was from Silas Woodcock and spoke of a task and a target. The albino associated with white folk, and like them would give no comfort to any dark-skinned aborigine. He was a self-taught reader, a man of strength and determination who enjoyed these games; perhaps this stemmed from his French ancestry, but whatever, the games were profitable.

"A convict to be trapped and killed", read Mordecai, "He is William Brown, also known as Peppermint Billy. Not to leave Van Dieman's Land alive".

Albino read the figure at the foot of the page and whistled,

"Well worth it!" he thought.

The albino stepped outside, wet a finger in his mouth and held it up. There was a slight breeze, but Mordecai sensed that was gaining in strength. He went to the stables in the rear, and began to saddle up his chestnut gelding, *Beau Brocade*. He walked the gelding out into the early evening and *Beau Brocade* pricked up his ears in anticipation, and struck his front hoof on the cobbles. Mordecai stroked his neck and whiffled - here was another human who could communicate with horses - and mounted. The albino controlled the impatient gelding with a tight grip on the reins. At last, he used his knees to spur the horse on, and they were away into the dark.

Mordecai knew where the camp was that was mentioned in the letter. He was born here and lived here still. He remembered the place, about two miles west of Launceston. It was recognisable by the cluster of huts. Near the gate, he encountered a figure emerging from a hut and immediately enquired,

"Peppermint Billy?"

"Not 'ere, mate! Try the Rope Works", he said, pointing east.

The albino was surprised that his question was answered. After all, what sort of a name was 'Peppermint Billy'? He had also been there long enough to know where the Rope Works were. He turned the gelding on to a well-defined track - he knew a short cut across country to the Works. This was the part the horse loved; a stile and a low hedge of juniper to jump. *Beau Brocade* was in his element and covered the ground at speed. At half a mile distance, Mordecai could hear the revelry in the beer tent, actually the mess tent. The large tent was all lit up. He encouraged *Beau Brocade* to walking pace, and moved into the shadows of a hut near the perimeter fence. He dismounted and tied the reins to a bar on a small verandah. He stood and listened; he sensed that the hut was occupied. He could smell a baby!

Jacob turned over and opened his eyes. In the dark, and hearing her steady breathing, he realised Harriett was asleep. Did he hear something? Why did he wake up? He felt the need to relieve himself, so he got up carefully and moved to the back door of the hut. A bucket stood inside the door, intended for just such a purpose. However, he was sure that his peeing into a bucket would be too noisy, so he opened the door and stepped out onto the verandah. He closed the door and placed the bucket strategically. As he began to pee, he looked around idly; he could hear the noise from the mess tent. He finished, turned back towards the door, then realised that there was a horse tethered to the rail,

"What the ...!", he uttered a strong oath, but could not finish it.

Mordecai in that instant, struck Jacob with a piece of wood much like a cudgel. He caught Jacob about the head, and Jacob crumpled to the wooden floor, out cold.

FOURTEEN

Mordecai moved to open the back door of the hut. Jacob's body was in the way, so the albino dragged it further over. He opened the door, and listened. All was quiet. He carefully stepped inside and closed the door behind him. The smell of the baby, like warm milk, was stronger now as he crept into the bedroom. It was dark, but Mordecai sensed that a young, fertile woman was lying there asleep, perhaps half asleep and waiting for her man to return.

Those very thoughts and the inner warmth brought tightness to his loins, and he was aware that he was already stiff and erect in anticipation. Mordecai removed his coat, a jerkin. He loosened the belt of his trousers, let them fall and stepped out of them, kicking off his shoes. He stood there in his shirt, and quickly stripped that off, so that naked he slipped under the single knitted cover. Keeping her face under close scrutiny, he snuggled down. Harriett was pleased that her Jacob had returned. She moaned softly and turned, rolled towards him, and felt his manhood hardened and alert, brushing against her leg. Harriett took a deep breath, and was suddenly aware that something was different, not right. This smell was wrong! She opened her eyes in urgent panic, and opened her mouth to scream, but was stopped by a very strong hand clapped about her face. She was looking into very strange eyes, as he felt for the soft, pliant centre and entered her immediately. Harriett struggled and arched her back, but the albino was heavy and insistent. He began a rhythmic thrusting that got stronger and deeper. She tried to kick; she tried to claw, but Mordecai was oblivious. His strength controlled the girl, he shrugged off her protests; he came to his climax and gripped her tightly as he dipped his head to the pillow, and began to extricate himself from that warm nest. He looked again at the girl's face full of terror. He indicated with a finger to his lips that she should be quiet. He pointed threateningly to the crib, and Harriett's eyes widened as she understood.

Mordecai got dressed. He moved to the back door and stepped out on to the verandah. The man was still out cold, so Mordecai left on foot; he left his horse tied to that rail. He moved in the direction of the mess tent and soon found cans of kerosene stacked at its rear.

"The fools!" he thought.

He took a can, and found an open flap. He moved inside and began to sprinkle kerosene liberally on the canvas and on some folding, wooden chairs stacked at the back. He removed one of the burning lamps and smashed it among the chairs at a point of great noise from the partygoers. This breaking glass was not noticed in the general merriment, and the chairs quickly began to burn and crackle. As he left, through the flap, he saw three figures moving towards the tent.

"It's Brown", he seethed. He raced straight for him, hoping for a quick kill, but only managed to bowl him over in the darkness.

"Here, what are you playin' at, you blackguard!" shouted Billy.

Tom and Joe tried to grapple with him. Billy tried to grab him, while Tom and Joe threw their weight against the albino, but Mordecai proved very strong and threw them off easily before hastening away.

The figure had gone, disappeared. Tom and Billy had noticed the man's strange eyes. Mordecai reached the hut; noticed that the man had now gone inside the hut. He could hear raised voices. He took the reins, led *Beau Brocade* quietly a little further away, and then mounted. He heard shouts at the mess tent and smiled. What a good evening he'd had, so far. He spurred on the gelding and rode back to Launceston, leaving mayhem and mischief in his wake.

*

The lamps stuttered as the tent flap moved. It was Chapman, the works foreman, who stepped inside, and preening his whiskers, looked round and recognised Bob and Stevens, and made straight for them.

"Evening, gents, the wind's freshening".

Stevens nodded and ordered him a pint. One of the workmen went to the piano and immediately enlivened the proceedings with a quick time tune. Bob fished,

"You had visitors today from England".

"Yes, I did. So?"

Stevens made his point,

"They don't seem much like businessmen".

"Well, funny you should say that, 'cos I feel that right now".

The noise of a sing along interrupted their talking, and they could see up to a dozen of the workforce enjoying the piano accompaniment.

"Tell us what you mean".

"The two of 'em were more interested in the list of employees and convicts. They asked very few questions about the quality of rope making".

The smell of hemp grew noticeably, until Chapman recognised the odour of something burning. In that same moment, there was a flash of light at the end of the mess tent and a mighty roar as flames leaped up the canvas. Voices were raised, and agitated figures began to dash about.

"Fire! Fire!" and others, "Bloody hell!"

A disciplined team rushed for the pumps – a wheeled carriage that brings twenty or so gallons to the base of the fire within two minutes. It seemed to have little influence. Chapman wrinkled his nose again and gave his opinion,

"I smell kerosene. Something big is afoot tonight!"

As he spoke, there was a general move of men towards the tent entrances. As Bob and the First Mate reached the open air, Billy arrived at their side, breathless and bothered,

"I've had a run in with one of Woodcock's villains, a very pale, red-eyed sod!"

"You alright, Billy?" asked Bob, concerned.

"Yeh! Tom and Joe sorted him out", he laughed and pulled the two Leicester lads into the light. Tom was shy and looked at his feet. He described Billy's would-be assailant,

"An albino, I reckon. Quite the strangest fellow I've clapped eyes on".

Joe, whose name could be blunt, agreed,

"Yes, he made a show of threatening Billy, but realised he was not alone and moved off into the crowd".

Bob looked enquiringly at Stevens, who shrugged his shoulders and said he knew nothing of the albino. Bob assumed,

"In that case, he was already here when we arrived. Somehow, he has been recruited to Woodcock's cause, so we have to be on our guard".

The evening lamps were lit as usual. They spluttered, dripped and flared in the breezy night. The friends smiled as if to agree that all was under control even if the elements indicated to the contrary. *They are confident of their own righteousness.* Indeed, the fire was now well and truly out with the mess tent in tatters at one end, but still standing proudly at the other. Chapman took his leave and was joined by Stevens as they walked in the general direction of the quay.

*

Jacob and Harriett's life together was in tatters. Jacob had moved inside after finding himself lying on the verandah. He remembered a blow on the head after relieving himself in the bucket. He and Harriett had gone to bed very early – they were both very tired and after young Mary herself was asleep, they had soon dropped off. Jacob returned to the bedroom to find Harriett in a state of collapse. She was unable to speak – yet. He swept her up into his arms, but she was unresponsive; she flopped and fell back onto the bed. Jacob was nonplussed; Harriett could do nothing but cry. What was wrong? Harriett the merry girl, the proud mother – now her personality was in shreds. What happened that this should be so? Jacob began to wonder about that blow to the head that knocked him out. What or who hit him? That was it, whoever it was attacked them! Did the assailant get inside the hut? Oh, my God! Jacob fell to his knees and sobbed. His wife had been attacked -attacked and maybe worse? Jacob buried his face in his hands. He needed help. He checked the infant, undisturbed. He reassured Harriett that he was going for help and left by the back door.

Jacob headed for the mess tent, to find as luck would have it, that he was walking towards Bob, Billy, Tom and Joe, and a couple of others that he did not recognise.

"Bob, Billy!" he shouted and began to run towards them, "Help me, help me!"

Bob ran towards Jacob and they met with a hug,

"Jacob, whatever's the matter? What happened?"

Billy arrived, anxious and disturbed,

"Are Harriett and the baby alright?"

Jacob tried to explain, gulping in air and holding his chest,

"We were attacked. Harriett is in a bad way, but young Mary is alright and sleeping. She slept through it all!"

Bob looked at Billy; they were both alarmed,

"Attacked? What do you mean?" asked Bob.

Stevens held back Chapman; Joe and Tom hovered close by, all the time looking round to ensure their safety.

"I was stunned, and I'm sure Harriett was attacked inside the bedroom. I can't explain it; all she does is cry".

"Do you mean you were knocked out?"

"Yes. I got up and went out the back to pee – oh! Yes. I went out the back and found a horse tethered to the verandah rail, then it all went black".

Bob and Billy began to walk quickly and Jacob followed. Stevens and Chapman decided to return to the main tent to alert the managers and crewmen still there. Tom and Joe walked slowly along their intended path. Jacob led the way into the hut by the back door, pointing out where he had seen the horse tethered to the verandah rail. A lamp was lit in the bedroom, and Harriett was sitting up with her knees tucked up to her chest. She recognised Bob and Billy. Jacob sat beside her and put his arm protectively around her shoulders. Harriett was weeping silently.

"She's in pieces, look at her! Where's my bubbly, happy Harriett?" moaned Jacob.

Bob tried to talk to her,

"Harriett, I'm sure it's difficult, but try to tell us what happened here. We only wish to help".

"A man came into the bedroom. He got into my bed", she looked at Jacob with terrified eyes, "He forced me!"

Harriett buried her face in her hands.

"Do you remember anything about this man?" asked Billy.

Jacob hugged his wife,

"It's alright, gel. Try to think if you can".

Harriett looked up,

"There was something. This man had strange eyes".

Bob looked at Billy, and in unison, they said,

"Albino!"

Jacob looked bewildered, so Bob reassured him,

"It's a blackguard we've had trouble with at the mess tent. He set fire to it, causing mayhem. We think he's made his escape – probably on that horse you saw".

The infant Mary began to cry.

"It's all these visitors, talking", said Jacob.

"I'll feed her now", said Harriett.

Bob and Billy began to move out,

"You'll be alright now, Jacob. Just look after those two precious bundles".

"Thanks, lads!"

Bob and Billy walked back with Tom and Joe to meet Chapman and Stevens on the main path.

"Is everything alright?" enquired Stevens.

"The villain that fired the tent had already attacked Jacob and Harriett. The baby is fine, she slept through it all".

"Are the couple injured?" asked Chapman, "Were they hurt?"

Bob held his hands out in mock restraint,

"Hold on. The albino knocked out Jacob and then raped Harriett. He apparently came and went on horseback".

"Who is this albino?"

"He works for that bogger, Woodcock", replied Billy, "He was after me!"

"Woodcock you say", mused Chapman.

*

Bob and Billy were walking with Joe who seemed a little bereft because Tom was walking off with Alan - the boy from the Office. Stevens checked his walking and moved back a little to Bob and Billy. These two and Joe stopped in their tracks. Stevens said,

"You might be interested in something Chapman has just said to me".

"Oh", said Bob, " What can that be?"

"It seems he had reason to chat to the man from the shipping office – and they have an interesting passenger travelling back to England. His name is Silas Woodcock!"

FIFTEEN

Tom appeared the following morning, after spending the night with Alan – the boy from the Office, but he was dishevelled, soiled and heartbroken. His speech was slow and he choked out the words,

"Its ... Alan...dead", Tom sobbed and Billy looked questioningly at Bob. Tom tried to continue,

"We were asleep at Alan's house ...Alan lived there with his father...we were raided by four or five hooded men. I saw one very pale-faced! They killed his father in his bed with long knives – no sounds at all as they held a pillow over his face. They grabbed Alan and pulled him away from me – two held me fast and forced me to watch. First, they played with his privates and leered at me silently. The next was so awful!"

Bob gave him a glass of water, and Tom continued,

"Two, three, I'm not sure. Anyway, they forced Alan to bend over the bed towards me. Alan had the most fearful look on his face. Then, the pale face drew one of the long knives, inserted the point into Alan's arse, smiled at me and then rammed it to the hilt with all his power. Alan's face creased, he went limp and died in front of me. They threw me out of the window, and left as quietly as they'd arrived".

It was obvious that Tom had found it difficult to relate. He collapsed sobbing and Bob supported him to a chair. Bob's voice had urgency about it,

"You know this means we have to try to change our situation. We may not be able to shake them off, but we can try. I will see Chapman this morning".

Chapman was dismayed by the events that Bob described, sending two of his men to retrieve Alan's body and that of the boy's father; but he felt it impossible at the present time to arrange for the Leicester group, including Bob and Billy, to be transferred to the dock area. The changeover might not be possible for months.

*

Harriett Farley was complaining of stomach pains. She was five months into an enforced and unwanted pregnancy after being raped by the intruder with wild eyes. Harriett did not know the word 'albino', but she could describe this man's eyes as 'staring and bright pink'. She got upset as she remembered that night, and was appalled by the thought of the threats he made against young Mary. Jacob was concerned, because he found his wife inconsolable,

"Harriett, my love, how can I make you comfortable?"

"I'm not sure; I don't know where to put myself!"

"I've had an idea, but you may think it's silly".

"What? Go on, say what you're thinking".

"Harriett – you can't rest, you can't get comfortable, so let me take you to the river. You may feel a bit cleaner if you have a soak".

"Jacob, that's a good idea. I think that may be the answer - if I can just float".

Jacob hugged Harriett. He was relieved she liked the idea,

"I'll organise a wagon; let me go and talk to Bob and Billy. I'm sure one of them or both will look after Mary".

Harriett found the drive in the wagon irksome. She was pleased when they reached the riverbank of the South Esk, a little way downstream from the bridge at Perth. Jacob helped her down after steadying the wagon and putting a rock under its wheel. They clung together and tried to negotiate the bank at a small inlet. The water lapped her feet as she moved into the basin. She exclaimed with delight, as she was able to sit down, so that the water was up to her chest. She felt it important that here was a current refreshing the basin constantly.

"Jacob! It's already working. I feel pain".

She staggered a little as she rose to her feet, so Jacob jumped in and took a position behind her, holding her round the waist.

"I'll hold you, you'll be alright".

"Jacob, I'm sorry", she cried and trembled.

There was the telltale staining of the water, as Harriett lost some blood. It was diluted in the running water very quickly, so Jacob felt comfortable to stay with his wife. Harriett grabbed Jacob's arms, as a spasmodic movement began to terrorise her loins. She bore down as she had been taught.

"Oh! Oh!" she groaned, "It's coming!"

Harriett made a mighty push down; something she could do in water, but not on land. The detritus of that fateful evening was ejected under water; a small image of a human being was seen beneath the surface. Harriett looked at it fondly, firm in her own mind that she was getting rid of something unclean, but still going through the motions of a good mother.

"No! No!!" she screamed, "Those eyes!"

The small face had opened its eyes, its pink eyes, and she imagined the baby looking at her. Harriett collapsed in a paroxysm of shock. Jacob struggled; he staggered back, but managed to keep hold of her. At the same time, he was able to kick away the bloody bundle.

"I've got you! It's alright, gel!"

"Oh, Jacob, that was horrible!"

Jacob said nothing to Harriett as he heard an animal commotion further down the stream,

"It's gone now, love – no need to worry anymore".

Jacob helped her towards the bank, a gentle slope of a bank that was comfortable for his wife. He wrapped Harriett in a blanket taken from the wagon and encouraged her to climb to the seat. He supported her carefully. Jacob made a fuss of the horses, kicked away the rock from the wagon's wheel and climbed up to sit beside Harriett. Jacob pulled the reins to the right and the horses turned away from the river and back to the track.

"Let's go home, love", said Jacob.

Harriett held fast to his arm and put her head on his shoulder. She made no reply; she was a bit sleepy.

*

Chapman indicated to Bob that a transfer to the dock area might be possible within the next two weeks,

"It seems there are vacancies after half a dozen terminations – men serving out their allotted time".

"Thanks", said Bob, "I'll let the others know".

Bob's concern was for the Farleys, especially for the young Mary. He sought out Jacob and gave him the news of the transfer,

"So you see, we shall not be able to keep an eye on you after we move".

"Well, surely the danger has passed. We haven't heard of the albino since".

"Don't be complacent. This warfare will rumble on when you least expect it".

On the eighth day after this conversation, Chapman asked the Leicester men, including Bob and Billy to bring their gear to the office, where transport was waiting for them. There was not a great deal to pack. Bob had time to see Harriett and Mary and to wish them well,

"Take care, I'm sure we shall meet up with you again".

The wagons pulled away at two o'clock in the afternoon, and the men began to look forward to their work at the docks.

*

It was varied work in the dock area; they sewed sailcloth sections, or carried timber planks along the quayside to a dry dock, where the framework of a new ship was rising by the hour.In the dock area, Bob and Billy, Joe and Tom, and John Garner and two or three others, regularly found it possible to brew up and rest a while by a disused shed. The guards plainly maintained their high regard for Bob, and thus with his friends. Billy was pleased to count himself among them. He wished it were still so with all his heart. Anyhow, the bays to the side of the shed were mostly empty, save for a pile of spent or broken fruit punnets. The next spring, they found a stump robin nesting in one of these. Before long, a clutch of three spotted eggs was to be seen, all pale green. It was delightful, watching the robin care for the young 'uns - in and out with titbits. The men were in and out to work, sometimes days on end. When they noticed the next time, the robin was nowhere to be seen. Surely not time enough for the fledglings to leave the nest? They could not understand it. John Garner was sent to investigate. He looked all round, moved a box or two, but in a very short time they saw him turn away and retch. After a while, he described as best he could,

"Black soldier ants have invaded the nest and eaten the young alive!"

That shook them, especially as they'd grown fond of the little blighters. John was the older of them, a matter-of-fact sort of fellow, rather thickset and shortish. One just wondered how such an independent, straight-ahead nature got him into this mess. Billy expected he fell in with a bad lot.

Thinking of a bad lot, there was an incident in the shipyard during the early summer, when Bob was shifting timber planks to the base of the dry dock where the cladding was being done. He took a plank from the neat stack at the side of the dock. Billy was working with Tom and Joe on the opposite wall with tar brushes and a hot tub, painting beams as thick as a man. Billy could see Bob moving about through the ghostly framework of the boat. There was all of a sudden like, a twittering – a murmuration of starlings? No, the timber on the dockside began to rock then fell – straight towards Bob some thirty feet below. Billy shouted to him,

"Bob – look out!"

Joe and Tom waved their arms frantically. Bob heard the shout in time and leaped to one side for his life, as the wood crashed down and splintered viciously. A spar slammed into Bob's left leg, and he lay bleeding. Instinctively, Billy looked back to where the pile of planks should have been – shock, disgust; he saw three figures, the albino, Potter who was Woodcock's closest ally and the leering face with a broken nose - Pitts! Billy understood that a jealous spat had developed into a dangerous feud. But what of Bob? He was carried to the dockside, an awful struggle up the stone steps. A fellow cleaned up the wound – he seemed to have some sort of medical training – and made sure every splinter was cleared. Bob bore all this impassively. He knew the timber pile had been pushed. They were chained back to camp and had a chance to tell him of Potter, the albino and Pitts, and in return, Bob was able to explain about Woodcock returning to England. Bob swore quietly – he not being the sort to cuss usually, perhaps because his leg was sore.

It was a sort of notice that these blackguards would have to be dealt with one day – probably one day soon. Bob was rested for two or three days – no use to man or beast until his leg had healed. When Billy could, he spent time with him. He well understood the difficult situation that was developing. Yet he advised caution – *the price of wisdom is above rubies* – though Billy was more temperamental and fool hardy. Within the week Billy crossed swords with the broken nosed Pitts. They were road building in the Esk valley, not far from the new bridge. John and Tom were with Billy, mostly carrying buckets of broken stones that had to be pounded into the ground. These were then doused in hot coal-coloured glue sort of; when it cooled it made a firm surface, especially after another pounding. Anyhow, Pitts must have thought it a good opportunity to make mischief. A bucket of hot stuff landed at Billy's feet. He scarce had chance to jump aside. With a shout, Billy threw it back – the guards rushed him and held him down. That little fracas earned Billy a whipping! At least the taste of the whip made him think more clearly. 'Woodcock' – the name seared his brain. He remembered the times that his family had been plagued by this man, or by his family. It was a Woodcock who was chief man in the jury that sent Billy here. Was this man a relative? Was Billy to be mocked and taunted by this family? This was the first time he resolved on revenge.

About this time, the work gangs became more systematic. At least the men got as much time inside, say in the rope workshops, as they did outside, in the boatyard or on the roads. New arrivals got only the quarries! Bob was recovered, and Billy's back had healed when they rejoined the rope works. The year was getting on, and the shelter from the rising, warmer winds was very welcome.

"Do you realise, back home, we would be sheltering from cold rain, even snow at this time", said Bob.

"The world's topsy-turvy!" replied Billy, "Life is pretty settled, and has been for a month or two. Is it a fool's paradise?"

Billy was within two years of finishing his sentence, of earning his certificate. The feud with Potter and broken nosed Pitts was simmering away, and would soon come to the boil. They worked in the rope-making industry through the winters; but come the spring and they returned to the boatyards. They also came by old friends, the Leicester lot – Tom, Joseph and John, also recently transferred. They had news of their old friends, Jacob and Harriett. Young Mary was five already and another brother or sister was due. Bob took Joe on one side and asked,

"What became of Harriett after her encounter with the albino rapist?"

"Oh, she recovered after a short illness, and nothing resulted".

"Well, that was a blessing, and now a new little one expected. That's wonderful news".

Bob got to wondering what the short illness was, though he was worldly and sensible with a strong family background that enabled him to make an educated guess. He said nothing to Billy or to the others.

SIXTEEN

Together with Bob and Billy, the Leicester men made a formidable team, and they were recognised for their efficient work. But *'death was at work in us'*. Being placed on another half finished hulk was their just reward. The carpenters sped up as they deftly produced the planking. Their hammering noise created a tattoo of rhythmic beating, sustained by the delivery of yet more planking. The good works of this team quickly spread abroad. It was to be expected that others would be jealous of their success, or more precisely jealous of their good relations with the guards and the carpenters. The jealousy of Woodcock's cronies was as *'unyielding as the grave'*. Within fourteen weeks the hull and decking of the ship were in place. Masts, lofty things, were installed together with their cross beams and crows' nests. Tar and caulking became the focus. It was about this time that Billy started work in the smithy – hot, sweating labour shovelling fuel for the furnaces. It was not all brutish. One or two true artists worked there. Billy met a silver smith, Edward, who had his termination certificate and was a hired man for his skills with silver. He was working on a tea service silver pot, for the Captain's table.

This was when Billy saw the fining pot, the bubbling of the silver pieces as they dissolved. He imagined they were pieces of the Manning silver. Edward was pleased to be his teacher; showed him the way to raise the heat sufficient to receive the silver pieces. Meanwhile, back on the ship, Bob and the others had to contend with the feuding still going on, getting bitter and dangerous. A wayward chisel dropping menacingly from the decking, a mallet wrapped in a cloth and swung by a rope along a walkway; such were the mean and deadly tricks they encountered. They gave as good as they got. Pitts with the broken nose was too close, his foot in a loop, a pull on the knot at the side of the mast and Pitts was hoisted involuntarily aloft. His shouting saved him as one of the crewmen quickly lowered him back down to the deck. He was ashen faced, *'a pale horse'*. At least he looked ashen from a distance, John said. Again, where decking was still not secured, the unwary were likely to tread into thin air. So when their friends cornered Pitts with his broken nose and had him backing away, he could not see the danger. He spat and cursed, looking wildly about for support, but Potter was nowhere to be seen. Joseph lunged at him, Pitts staggered back and as the decking gave way, he threw up his arms and uttered a whining yell. He disappeared. *It became strangely calm.* Then a shout went up as his body was discovered. His neck, as well as his nose, was broken, the swinging ends of deck above him the only evidence. One thing was obvious; the feud had stepped up a gear. They were at loggerheads with Woodcock himself, but fighting his shadow – fighting his cronies in his absence!

Working with Edward, Billy became engrossed in the silver work. Truth to tell, he neglected his pals. He was off his guard. So it was that Billy did not notice the spat Bob had with Potter. By all accounts, Potter had taunted him with a hot caulking iron. This Bob had ignored until it got too close for comfort. With the speed of a striking snake, Bob dropped down, grabbed the twine cable that slithered across the wooden decking and yanked on it – hard! Potter was upended, lost his hold on the caulking iron that circled above him *like the sword of Damocles* and in falling whacked him smartly across his chest. Bob stood with arms akimbo, shaking with mirth. It was not appropriate. The five of them held a council of war.

"He's too strong", said Tom, looking at his feet.

Joe disagreed, and put forward a plan to attack Woodcock's trusty lieutenant, this man called Potter. Jem Potter was a waspish man, with darting looks and a restless tongue. Snakelike. Bob believed they should attack when he was distracted. Tom laughed and drew on his own experience,

"That's easy, a pretty boy and he's well distracted".

Billy was surprised; he had not noticed this trait in Potter. He had no idea what happened to young Richard on the ship. Nonetheless, it seemed a germ of a good idea. Tom agreed to find a decoy. They agreed the poop deck – an area that was finished, but with an occasional carpenter around. They would need to get secreted away in there, so a carpenter's crate and aprons were obtained, and the rear cabin was prepared. Tom had no difficulty finding a willing stool pigeon. The plan was explained to this lad as soon as Tom knew he could be trusted. It seemed the lad had some experience of certain men wanting to paw him or being a mite too 'friendly'. The lad took obvious pride in being able to 'distract' others, even though he was not of that persuasion. He knew the man to be a brute, and disliked Potter's nature and his darting eyes. He concurred with their overall plan. They agreed it had to be done quickly, not even a week should pass.

Accordingly, three evenings later, the decoy – Billy called him 'Mark' – made sure that waspish Potter had noticed him as work finished and blokes were milling along the dockside. Four of the lads were hidden by this time, Bob, John, Joe and Billy. Tom was outside, keeping watch on the unfolding drama, as Mark turned back to the catwalk and climbed aft. Potter followed at a distance, having swallowed the bait, and with his eyes darting about from side to side. Discreetly, Tom was some way behind him. Woodcock's usual cronies had seen it all, and left their main man to his foibles. So Potter, snakelike, entered the rear cabin alone.

Mark approached the large table and turned, smiling and fingering his groin. Potter lurched forward with undisguised lust. It was the signal they had waited for. Billy launched himself at the back of his neck; his right arm he threw around the neck and his left knee was jammed in the small of Potter's back. John clung to his left, and Joe to his right. Bob brought his full weight to the task and manhandled the writhing mob. Mark withdrew to a corner. Then Tom walked in and found them piled on the cabin floor with Potter virtually stunned. In this state, he was bound hands and feet and was dragged to a window opening to stern. The only lamp in the cabin, that had illuminated that soft moment when both characters had betrayed their venal intentions, was now extinguished. Waspish Potter was pushed out of the window on a noose that tightened with his weight. In that way, Potter was extinguished. They congratulated Mark for a job well done. It was agreed that they leave the cabin singly at intervals. Mark left first. An hour later the cabin was empty. It was evening, everywhere quiet. The bluish water in the dock lapped almost noiselessly. Billy reflected on the immense burden that had fallen on them with the death of Woodcock's lieutenant, and the war that killing announced. What a story to take back to England!

*

In Leicestershire, England, on the other side of the world, it was the day of the funeral. Ann Brown had died a week ago. She was the wife of Peppermint Jack, and mother of four sons, including Peppermint Billy, and a daughter. There was light dusting of snow that showed the black horses in sharp relief. The horses waited, occasionally striking the hard ground with their hooves. As their heads dipped, the black plumes on their bridles bobbed up and down. The silver trim on their tracery, contrasted brightly with the dark hearse. The two carriages behind were filled, in the first by Jack the widower and Jack's daughter, Elizabeth, and in the second with Sam and Tom and their parents, Evelyn and Richard. The Funeral Director nodded to the three coachmen, and then took his place ahead of the horses. All was in place and ready, so he began to walk slowly, with his top hat tucked under his right arm. When the sad procession reached the bridge over the Wreake, the Director leaped aboard the hearse and the three vehicles picked up speed as the horses broke into a trot. It was a short distance to the church, where the Director and his men carried the coffin inside. There were trestles before the altar that received this burden. The small congregation took their seats as the Vicar welcomed them and began the service. Mary and her mother were there to pay their respects.

A short while later, the pitiful group gathered at the graveside, waiting for the interment of the body. The surround of the open grave was lined with carpets of grass; the traces of the strapping for lifting or lowering the coffin were stretched out each side. Elizabeth supported her father by linking arms. Jack gratefully acknowledged this move by clasping his hand in hers. Otherwise, they were both numb with cold, with apprehension and the enforced pause before the Vicar was ready for the committal.

"... ashes to ashes, dust to dust", he intoned.

The mourners turned away at the finish, and the two gravediggers began to fill the gaping hole. Jack and Elizabeth, still clinging together, stepped back to the pathway and thence to the path and road leading to the churchyard gate. Suddenly, they hugged each other as the empty hearse and carriages rattled past them, pulled by eager horses heading for a feed. Evelyn and Richard and their two boys caught up with Elizabeth and Jack.

"It was a nice service", offered Richard.

"Yes, a good send-off", added Evelyn.

Their replies were no more than weak smiles as Elizabeth and Jack turned and followed Evelyn, Richard and the children towards home.

*

SEVENTEEN

1853

The celebratory occasion in Van Dieman's Land was the completion of Billy's term. Ten years served, and then freedom beckoned. The happiest coincidence was that Bob his staunch companion and friend, had also gained his ticket of termination. There was merriment and a few drinks as the friends organised the departure of two of their number.

"Good luck!" said Tom, close to tears.

"Take care!" advised John, Mr Matter-of-fact.

Joe turned away, overcome by the moment.

Even foreman Chapman arrived to bid them adieu, and he brought a surprise guest to see Billy – old Edward the master smithy who had taught him to melt down silver. The two greeted each other with a warm hug and a handshake. They moved to one side and began to gossip,

"It's lovely to see you again, Edward".

"Likewise, but you don't know, do you?"

"Know what?"

"Chapman brought me because my sight is failing with all this close work".

"Oh, Edward, cannot spectacles help you?"

"I'm expecting some from England soon, but how soon that will be, God only knows!"

They moved back into the merry fray. His mates all wanted to know what Billy would be doing.

"I'd like to try to learn something of my brothers", he said.

His friends knew that two of his brothers were in Australia, somewhere, under a sentence of transportation, and that any search of this kind was hopeless from the start, as none of the postal services were available to convicts. Billy was awkward as he hugged his friends, blinking furiously because it was an emotional moment. Bob, on the other hand, shook hands crisply and firmly, before the two of them finally offered 'goodbyes' and then moved off towards the carriage that would take them to Launceston. They had not taken more than a dozen steps when they saw two figures with a child approaching them. It was Jacob and Harriett with young Mary – come to see them off, and with a surprise bundle! Cradled in Harriett's arms lay the infant Robert William. He was a year old and one month. Bob and Billy were overjoyed to see their friends and their children. Jacob spoke,

"We hope you don't mind us naming the young 'un after you?"

Bob gasped,

"Oh! I didn't realise. Robert – that's me, and William – that's Billy"

Both were overcome. They hugged Jacob and kissed Harriett's hand to show their pleasure.

Harriett told them,

"That's settled then. We can go ahead with the christening. We are just sorry that you will be unable to attend next month, because you will be away. Do you know where you will be?"

"Eventually, around Hobart, we expect", replied Bob.

Both made a fuss of young Mary before getting up on the carriage. They waved their goodbyes as the carriage pulled away. Billy turned aside, already upset by the leaving.

*

Their first sojourn was in Launceston itself, at Ma Whittle's place. Flo Whittle ran a hostel for the many tradesmen and craftsmen that found work in the growing port. Twenty years or so, she'd been a widow woman. Yet every day, always dressed in her pinafore she complained,

"My man left me short-handed", or,

"My man was useless!" all the time rubbing her voluminous chest, "useless!"

Bob and Billy were not the sort to quarrel with Flo Whittle's version of her difficult life. They nodded vigorously in agreement – indeed, as vigorously as Flo rubbed her chest!

They made themselves very useful – making beds, washing pots and pans; Bob, the practical man, even fixed the squeaky door. They drank with these men, saw them slobber and fall into their cups and carried them to their beds. Ma Whittle paid them for this work – and they had free board and lodgings. There were a number of ways they increased their 'wage'. Ma Whittle was so pleased with them, she recommended their services to her neighbours – so Bob mended a roof, or the two of them put right a drunken fence. Men a little worse for drink do not notice the odd shilling or two that disappeared. But one night, a heavy drinking orgy, they had to carry each of four mates to their room. They shared the four beds in that room. As Billy delivered the last burden, quite a stocky fellow, to his pit, he noticed a handsome watch and chain dangling from the bedpost. He suddenly wanted it. As Billy removed the man's boots, he checked that the rest of them were already asleep and one snoring enough to wake the dead. He placed the boots under the bed, at the same time lifting the watch and chain carefully from its stowage.

The next morning was an entertainment for Bob and Billy alike.

"You've 'ad my watch, you bugger!"

"Who you accusing?"

"Give it back, or by Christ you'll be sorry!"

These two were cursing and swearing something shocking even for a hardened criminal like Billy the thief. Of course, the watch had been missed. But each blamed the other; and they crashed into the other two in their anger,

"Look out, you oaf!"

"Who are you pushing?"

and the four of them tumbled in the narrow confines between the beds. With an almighty crash and a few oaths, they emerged into the living room,

"Thief! thief!"

"You fool, you've lost it – I haven't got it!"

Ma began to fret,

"Oh Billy, they'll do damage", and added,

"Throw them out, won't you?" furiously rubbing her chest.

Billy chose the watch's owner first and helped him through the door with a hefty push. The other three quickly followed, helped along by Bob's boot. Their noisy quarrel could be heard clearly for a full five minutes more as they wandered off. That watch did not work except for that ancient servant called the devil, and eventually became one of the causes of Billy's own date with death.

They stayed with Ma Whittle a full year – summer to summer. In that time, Billy practised semblance as an itinerant preacher. The role struck him as a suitable and expected one. Bob agreed if somewhat rily. Billy took to the road comfortably as a preacher – he was always quoting the scriptures,

"*All scripture is God-breathed and is useful*".

Verses of scripture came so easily to mind – even to his evil mind! – through a habit he had acquired when young and attending chapel with his Mam. *Like God knowing good and evil.* The guise suited Billy well as they began to move generally south, with Hobart and Port Arthur their destination. Crossing Van Diemans land was achieved in easy stages along the military road. This also helped them to keep close to sources of information.

"Keep your eyes and ears open", said Bob as they trudged along, "There's traffic of souls on this highway".

"I see soldiers and hangers-on", replied Billy, "But no Woodcock – not for years past".

"I reckon he's back in England, working some mean tricks. We'll only see his hangers on – if at all".

The military road winded its way back to Gonara, and on to Campbell Town, where they again sought out a hostel, such a hostel – full of night noises and spent energies. Of all kinds, so you could say they were *'enslaved by all kinds of passion'*.

Billy slept soundly as was his wont. In the morning, he and Bob took a passable breakfast of tea and bacon – shared with an old traveller who spoke little, but puffed on a long, tapering clay pipe. Billy admired the way he damped it down in the bowl, with a fashioned tobacco-stopper. After a wonderful supper on the verandah, Billy considered,

"Would have done Ma Whittle a treat!"

Bob caught his eye; they both creased up with laughter, both furiously rubbing their chests. The old traveller was bemused by their antics, but intervened,

"I make these, you know", holding the stopper forward.

Billy recovered quickly and leaned over, very interested,

"It's beautiful".

"It's whittling wood, that's all".

Billy's keenness pleased the old man, George by name. Just George – no other name he owned to. It became a common sight, the two of them at eventide, nattering away.

George was full of stories,

"Have I told you about my time in Africa?" he said, continuing without waiting for a reply, "I was in a clearing, deep in the jungle, when a fierce lion came charging at me from the undergrowth!" There was a half smile around his mouth,

"What do you think I did?

"What did you do, George?"

"I pushed my fist down its throat, grabbed it by the tail, pulled it inside out, and off it bounded back into the jungle".

They laughed heartily together, he for a good yarn, and Billy because he had not heard it before. He was a good soul, George. He paid no heed to Billy's infernal blinking, but he watched his ambling with the gammy leg. He recognised the help that Bob's strong arm afforded him, but felt he could suggest an improvement.

"Swing your leg at the knee", he opined, "Take a step, swing the foot forward".

Billy was so comfortable with him, he took his idea and he tried it. It slowed him down at first, but as he got the knack of it, so he got quicker. He trained Billy round that yard like a chicken! Several days later, he had a better gait – felt easier too.

George wondered about their way of life now Billy was free to move around,

"You realise, some ex-convicts live the life of bushrangers".

The very idea amused them,

"An unprepossessing hero, I'd make!" Billy laughed.

Both Bob and George saw the funny side of it and also laughed. But the germ of an idea was sown. The war with Woodcock was far from over. He had no wish to change his appearance as an itinerant preacher, but he could make use of a bushranger's pistol,

"For my own protection, you understand".

George made a show of thinking hard, then,

"It's not impossible, but it may take some time to acquire one".

There is a time for everything!

*

In Leicester, England, Billy's brother John and his wife were worried about Jack, Peppermint Jack, since he had lost his wife about two years before. Jack had lived on at Frisby with his sister in law Evelyn and her husband Richard. He was the usual handyman about the farm; he was good with the horses and the cattle. Lately, Jack had been moping, so that John and Ann were wondering if he would agree to join them in Leicester at their home in Bedford Street. They accepted that Jack had been a great help on the farm, but now agreed with Evelyn and Richard that he was "getting on" and deserved to retire. It was not as though the farm could not spare him, with both Sam and Tom, sons of Richard and Evelyn, now working effectively as their father directed. Jack was their uncle.

Nevertheless, Jack was at first resistant to the move,

"I'm not ready for the scrap heap yet!"

"We're not suggesting the scrap heap", replied Evelyn patiently.

"Now that Mam's gone", added John, trembling a little, as he did under any kind of tension, "you should take things easier".

Sam and Tom and their sister Evelyn were listening intently, part of the family group now seated round the breakfast table – the largest, most comfortable area in the farmhouse. Evelyn handed round mugs of steaming tea. For the moment, Jack ignored his tea,

"I know you all mean well. I've enjoyed working with Sam and Tom", he smiled and playfully ruffled Sam's hair, "Am I not still useful?"

"You're not as sharp, Jack", Richard was quick to respond, as Evelyn put her hand on his arm as though to caution him. Richard was gently spoken now,

"You've been worrying over poor Ann, and we hope you won't have to worry any more".

Jack's eyes glistened as he turned towards John and Ann,

"I do miss her, me' ducks". He took up his tea and drank, "She was my wife and my best friend". Jack caught his breath and sobbed.

The issue was decided. Jack would move to Leicester with John and Ann. Sam snuggled into his Uncle Jack's arm, and the two of them clung together warmly for a while.

*

Six months later, in Van Diemans Land, George, Bob and Billy talked on the verandah in Campbell Town at evening. Instead of parting for their beds, George beckoned Billy to his room where he took a package from under his bed and unwrapped the green cloth. The pistol was of a large bore, nearly a foot long and with a bullet fully two ounces in weight. Those who knew about those things said it was next in size to the bulldog pistol, with a bore quite as large as the horse pistol. Billy noticed a mark on it.

"Is that the mark for Birmingham?"

"Well done! That's well spotted".

They shook hands on the price - £6 of Ma Whittle's funds – no problem! George threw in a whittled tobacco stopper as well. This pleased Billy a lot, because it was a kind gesture from a good friend.

Within a week, they were on route to Hobart, and yet another boarding house – but Flo Whittle's sister, Edna Courage, ran this. Unlike her sister Edna wore the apron only for domestic chores. At other times, she was in a dress that was prettily printed with flowers, and a matching choker at her neck. She liked to look presentable for her man, Charles Edward Courage. They were received well by this couple, especially as they had recently been helping Flo. Edna clearly appreciated having a preacher as a houseguest,

"Now, sir, you're room is ready and I hope comfortable".

"Thank you, Mrs Courage".

"I've put Bob your friend right next door, and there is a connecting door should you need".

"That sounds most suitable", said Bob, picking up the bags and moving towards the stairs.

"Billy, I'll call you early – tomorrow being Sunday, and you'll want to be in church, I'm sure".

"Shall we say eight in the morning, then?"

The two travellers retired, both tuckered out. They slept well, through an uneventful night.

*

Albino was uncomfortable. Silas Woodcock wrote that he was unhappy. He was uncertain as to the whereabouts of Peppermint Billy and his crony. He had a report almost a year old, more probably, since Billy's ticket of completion had been issued.

"This is not good enough!" he wrote.

It was a year since Jem Potter was killed, so the year had been spent quietly regrouping and licking their wounds. He was not so brave as to say this to Woodcock.

"Where are the sods?" raged Woodcock in his letter, "They have to be dealt with! It's probable that they have both done their time and are out on licence, but what are they doing?"

Albino wrote in explanation that they had lookouts up and down Van Diemans Land,

"Sooner or later, we shall have news of them", he tried to reassure Woodcock all those thousands of miles away in London.

*

Sunday morning in church was amenable to Billy and Bob. They were comfortable within the songs and prayers. An invitation to Billy to preach was accepted with aplomb. His sermon, though brief, was directly relevant to souls seeking paradise and the redemption of sins. A dose of fire and brimstone was added with relish. There was warm fellowship at the end of the service, but Billy and his friend declined the offer of tea and made their excuses to leave.

"People will think we are trying to hide", said Billy.

"Let them", replied Bob.

The next Sunday they were in Huonville, and the one after that in Richmond. So welcome were they, the churches sent a pony and trap with driver to ferry them to and from Mrs Courage's Boarding House and the meeting place. Billy was always spick and span, well turned out, so that people noticed him on the streets of Hobart,

"Mornin' preacher", said one, remembering Billy from the previous Sunday. Who else amongst the watchers might remember him?

The hamlets at Cygnet in the southwest, and Sorell in the northeast were also on Billy's itinerary for preaching. The two friends were well received wherever they went. These different communities were very appreciative of a visiting preacher and his assistant. Bob had become an efficient assistant – he took the collection, read the lesson, made himself generally useful. This pattern of visits on Sundays lasted for another year. Bob and Billy were quite settled to this way of life. Were they relaxing too soon?

EIGHTEEN

Billy first met Susie-May on a Sunday jaunt to the hamlet of Sorell. She was not a raving beauty, but well built and buxom. She cut a flattering figure in the hay, where she was stacking the bales into the barn. Hay got everywhere. It littered the floor all around the barn entrance. It was in her hair and in her blouse. Billy was impressed! Bob began to use uncomplimentary language; he called her a 'slattern', but he suddenly noticed the disturbance of the hay – indeed, a shower of hay in the doorway, and through it tumbled Josie Trivet. Bob was instantly charmed by the appearance of yet another beauty, and she noticed him with a winning smile. If Bob had even thought of the Sunday lunch waiting for them at Mrs Courage's Boarding House, if he had even thought to say,

"C'mon Billy, our grub's getting cold!", he thought better of it, and grinned at Billy instead.

Josie and Susie stood there laughing, and sorting the hay from their tousled hair. Their stance was inviting, and Billy and Bob needed no second bidding. They entered the open gateway leading to the barn and walked slowly towards the laughing pair. Billy stood as best he could with his gammy leg; he blinked more rapidly than usual. Susie approached him and placed her fingers on his afflicted eye. She took his hand and pulled him gently towards the barn door. Josie had already wrapped her arms around Bob's waist, so now they turned and walked into the barn. Whatever their purposes, Billy and Bob maintained a polite distance between themselves – indeed, Bob and Josie climbed a ladder to the hay loft, whilst Billie and Susie-May found a quiet area in the far corner.

It was hot in the barn. Susie's nubile strength was enough to unwrap the prize parcel, layer by layer. She stepped out of her skirt – the only layer! Billy laughed and pulled her down to lie across him. He stroked her firm breasts and flat stomach. Susie was ready. She turned to sit astride him and guided his manhood, now erect, into a warm, moist nest. Susie lay down and smothered Billy with kisses. At the same time, she began to work her hips up and down, increasing the excitement for them both.

Bob found Josie submissive. He took charge and the two were soon locked together in a highly charged embrace. Josie's skirt on the rail signalled surrender and the rutting began, stronger and stronger. Josie lay back; her fingers gripped the hay bale and found the twine binding to hold on to. She was unaware that the twine was cutting her fingers; she was ecstatic as the surge began. She felt Bob stretching as though trying to stem a tide but failing in a glorious liquid culmination. Susie let out an animal cry as her own climax began to rip. She hugged Billy as his body shook with emotion. They clung together in a warm, sticky embrace, and lay still, listening to the steady beat of each other's heart. However, their reverie was interrupted by a rifle shot. The bullet sang past and ripped into the stack of hay bales. The marksman was the farmer, Josiah Trivet, Josie's father. He was in a rage,

"Where is she? Where's my Josie?"

He fired off another shot into the hay. His threats were obvious. Susie hurriedly dressed, and Billy fumbled with his trousers.

"I don't know where she is!" shouted Susie defiantly.

The fracas had startled the listeners in the loft. Josie and Bob got dressed silently. Bob saw that Josiah Trivet was standing below him. Quietly, Bob realised that a bale had only to be nudged – which he did. The bale crashed down and struck the furious father on the shoulder, throwing him to the ground. Thankfully, the rifle was thrown into the hay harmlessly. Josiah was stunned, giving Bob and Billy sufficient time to make good their escape. The girls raced for the farmhouse and Mrs Trivet, to explain no harm had been done.

Bob and Billy resumed their ramble through Sorell. They headed for the chapel on the hillside, its red roof glistening in the afternoon sun. Appearing from nowhere, the Sexton welcomed them to the Chapel for the evening service.

"Where's your driver. How did you get here?"

Billy and Bob laughed and explained they had walked, but would welcome a ride back to the Boarding House. The Sexton's house was next door, so he invited them in for a drink and a bite to eat. Both men could not believe how hungry they were, so were a little embarrassed as the plate of food was cleared in record time. The Sexton was not at all put out; he went to put the kettle on,

"Have you sorted your text, Preacher?"

Billy turned not a hair. He surprised himself with the ease of his reply,

"Of course. I shall use the passage in *Luke* 3 that speaks of producing fruit in keeping with repentance".

Bob sat open mouthed in astonishment, then both collapsed in peals of laughter. The Sexton returned with the tea,

"It is good to hear laughter in this house again!"

The evening service in the Chapel was smoothly run. Bob helped as sidesman and by taking the collection at the appropriate time. Billy's sermon was listened to with great care, and was well received in the brief discussions that followed. Billy was thanked for his efforts. Bob was intrigued to notice a member of the congregation, now moving out of the Chapel at the end of the service. This member was albino. This member lingered a while, watching them both. Bob encouraged Billy to finish talking to the Sexton, and they walked down the steps to the waiting carriage. Mordecai, the albino quadroon, stood at the foot of the steps with a leering smile about his lips, watching after the disappearing carriage.

Sunday jaunts could not be the same. Bob at least realised that their present location was suddenly unsafe. Around the Boarding House and everywhere in the area, the two were extra vigilant. Even so, it took a while for both of them to realise that they were being followed. They recognised the same faces at different points in the street. This was something they were definitely not used to. They had been lulled into a false sense of security. The spies posted in all major venues had tracked them down. They did not realise how murderous it could turn out.

Three of Woodcock's sidekicks kept them in sight, taking turns to accompany them into any building, and making a pig's ear of the business. Bob even waited inside a doorway and greeted his follower with a loud,

"Hallo!".

The blackguard's reply was a threatening growl that Bob stifled with a rapid blow across his mouth with the back of his right hand. The follower staggered back, bleeding from a cut lip. The enmity between these two was as tangible and terrible as the fox, cornered by the hounds. Just as the fox found an opening in the hedge, the encounter only delayed this man - it did not stop him.

Back at the Boarding House, Bob advised they move on,

"There's an afternoon coach that travels north".

This would retrace their course towards Launceston, and Billy argued,

"Isn't this exactly opposite to Woodcock's expectations".

Bob grinned at him in agreement. He alerted their landlady to the fact that they had to move on. Edna Courage was upset that this must be so, but she provided a pack of food for them to travel with,

"You'll need to keep your strength up, if you're travelling". She began to weep a little, and Bob – ever the gentleman- hugged her and calmed her down.

"Many thanks for your hospitality. We've been very comfortable".

With the farewells completed, Billy and Bob made their way to the carriages at the docks.

But Woodcock's watchers had established themselves in the docks at Hobart, so their boarding of the coach was witnessed and soon they were aware of a couple of outriders flanking them on their route north. Before the familiar sandstone buildings of Oatlands came into view, Bob climbed to the driving seat and chatted to the coachman, clearly reaching an understanding and a handshake. The break at Oatlands was taken at a tavern, an old way station. Bob warned Billy,

"Be watchful, lad".

Within half an hour of their arrival, the two outriders strode into the tavern and lost no time in picking an argument. The first rider was short, but stocky and thick set, the second taller and thinner, a beanpole. 'Stocky' dominated a card game; he seemed to know enough of the rules of whist, both finessing and revoking so that he earned the opprobrium of the other players. Matters came quickly to a head with 'Stocky' accusing the card players of cheating, the dealer of underhand methods. Stocky berated the dealer to the point that pistols were raised. All eyes were fixed on this fracas, but not Billy's. He noticed 'Beanpole' moving just out of vision, then reappearing behind a column, getting closer and closer to Bob. Billy was surprisingly calm as he took his pistol from his belt, aimed and fired. Beanpole dropped lifelessly to the floor; in the same instance Stocky swung his pistol round to fire, not at the hapless card player, but straight at Bob. However, Bob had been forewarned by Billy's own shot and leaped to one side firing as he did so. Stocky was only winged. In what seemed an age, both men reloaded. Bob was aiming as Stocky attempted to raise his own pistol. The shot knocked his pistol from his hands and tore into Stocky's neck, ripping the major blood vessel apart. Stocky collapsed quite dead. There was a stunned silence, broken by Bob's urgent call to Billy

"Get moving, get out of here!"

No one made a move to stop the two fugitives.

"It was clearly self-defence, Bob" Billy panted.

"At least this cannot be denied" was the quick reply.

Because of this situation, they changed their course. Within the hour they were again on the move, on the coach to Hobart! They reached the city in the evening and took rooms near the docks. Bob and Billy talked together earnestly about the incident,

"You OK, Billy?" enquired Bob.

"I think so".

"We're both alright, aren't we?" encouraged Bob, putting an arm round Billy's shoulders.

"Of course. I just feel apprehensive about the voyage".

"It will be fine. Just think – home to England!"

"What do you mean – fine?"

"We shall find friends, I'm sure. We'll not be alone".

They reviewed the attempts to learn something of Billy's brothers. Bob was pretty sure that Dick and Jim were not in Van Diemans Land, but in the penal colonies on the mainland of Australia. This meant they learned nothing of the boys' fate before embarking for England.

*

In the Vale of Belvoir, Leicestershire, England, Edward Woodcock the Duke's bailiff was riding to the castle. He had said nothing to his wife, Sarah, but he was summoned to explain the mounting total of unpaid rents.

"There's upwards of a hundred guineas still owing!" thundered the Duke, "What's your explanation, sir?"

"I need time, yer' grace, having been laid up this last winter".

"Laid up, sir! That's no use to me!"

"But I can quickly put matters right, your grace", he was thinking of laying more heavily on the likes of the blacksmith, Hewerfield.

"I shall put matters right now, man. You are dismissed my service with immediate effect".

Woodcock was non-plussed. His instructions could not have been clearer. He acknowledged his Grace stiffly but courteously, and retired from the room.

He rode home to Scalford to his wife, after arranging for his horse to be collected the next day. It was a life-changing move. Within days, he received a message from his Grace, offering him the sinecure of collector of tolls at the Gate on Thorpe Road, Melton Mowbray. This was just the ticket, he thought, for his retirement days – with a cottage attached and a small garden where they may keep a few chickens. This was something they could both manage. The appointment was from Lady Day. He shared his planning with his wife, but was unprepared for what happened next.

Sarah, his wife of the past quarter of a century, the mother of his two sons, was unwell and became seriously ill. She took to her bed and her temperature was clearly rising, as she perspired profusely. Edward was worried and sent for the Doctor, who arrived during the evening. Their two sons, Sam and Phil were pacing up and down. Samuel was married and within the next half hour his wife, Helen arrived. No long examination was needed; the Doctor stood up, shaking his head and advised Edward,

"I'm afraid you must prepare yourself for the worst", he adjusted his spectacles, "She's worn out. And please boil your water before use. It's very similar to cholera – rife in big cities, but surprising here in the East Midlands".

"My wife has lately returned from Birmingham where she has been nursing her sister".

"That'll be it", said the Doctor emphatically, "I'll be calling back tomorrow".

Sarah had little sleep, too warm, too thirsty. Edward ministered to her as best he could, and Helen was a great help. As dawn slanted in at the windows, and the baying, throaty call of the dog fox faded into the distance, so Sarah faded. By the time the Doctor arrived, it was all over. The Doctor confirmed that her life was extinct and, with an impressive copperplate hand, wrote out the certificate.

Edward moved to the cottage on the Thorpe Road, alone. He worked hard as the collector of tolls, and enjoyed visits from his grandchildren. James in particular, now nine years old and one of the children of Sam and Helen, began to stay over, keeping his grandfather company.

*

In Hobart, Van Dieman's Land, all was a hive of activity as the ship was readied for its return to London. Billy and Bob, now passengers, were newly arrived on board. When they joined the ship, they were well aware that they had company – undesirable, threatening. They also had a surprise companion travelling with them!

NINETEEN

Hobart had changed since Bob and Billy first saw the fledgling city. The place was bustling with people, visitors and merchants. The port was well stocked with ships, laden with basic goods and provisions; lines of carts were waiting to be loaded to enable distribution throughout the island, of dry goods, even livestock! Their tickets of leave had secured a berth starboard side, so Bob immediately checked the entrances and exits of their stowage; checked the stairs and stairwells and the portholes. The cabin had a bunk bed, Billy took the top and Bob slept below. He made sure the door was locked and lay with feet towards it just in case.

Billy swore he was no sailor, but the ship seemed newly repaired. She had new yards and canvas, and spares to see her through a hurricane or two. Billy would like to say his thoughts turned to Ann, but he had no idea that she was waiting for him in Leicester. Billy was very busy with the troubles in hand, wondering what Bob was managing with the First Mate, Peter Anderson. Bob was hoping to forge an alliance with him. Very early on, Captain Parry called the ship's company to a general meeting at which he lay down the 'rules' of the impending voyage. Bob and Billy were delighted and amazed to be joined again with Tom and Joseph. These two explained that John, Mr Matter-of-fact, was also on board. They had been released and given their tickets of leave because of their good work in keeping order through the troubles with Woodcock's cronies. This did not ring quite true to Billy, more the machinations of evil to get rid of good men. Why, it could even have been the work of a Woodcock ally, influencing the authorities, gaining clear ground for their continued dominance. He had no idea how close to the truth he had come.

It did not take two shakes to realise that in that company there were half a dozen men that seemed associated – cliquish *Capulets* – a force to be reckoned with. One in particular, a man with pink eyes, caught Billy's eye. The response was cold, heartless, menacing. He could not say he had much colour, just those steely pink eyes and white hair long before his old age. Bob recognised this one of old; from that night at Jacob and Harriett's! He remembered calling him the 'albino'. He was very much to the fore on the morning they drew anchor. Before the ship moved an inch, there was a commotion on the quayside, and a small party of three or four with sparse luggage demanded the gangplank. Crew hurried to comply and the men started up the walkway. No! Second in line – not his usual place – came Silas Woodcock!

"How the hell has he got here?" said Billy, as Woodcock came on board ostentatiously, "Lord Muck!"

Woodcock felt safe in the company of his friends and hangers-on. He was generous with his smiles and pawed the arm and shoulder of the pink eyes. Albino greeted him as a long lost brother, a sight that filled Billy with utter revulsion. The show was quickly over, as Woodcock and his cronies disappeared below – no doubt to discuss their evil purposes.

The ship's crew resumed their usual tasks after this unheralded interruption. Men shouted, chains clanked as the raised anchor was lashed to the side; weights and counterweights crashed about. Ropes snaked across the deck; canvas rippled as it was stretched. Slowly, the sails rose up, momentarily blotting out the sun, but then billowing as they caught the breeze at the harbour mouth. The very frame of the ship picked itself up on its haunches and strode off into the watery fields. Bob's face was a picture. He plainly shared Billy's feelings, but sensibly pulled him away to meet the others and to declare an immediate state of war, and this on the high seas, because the ship was already a fair distance from port. With Woodcock now returned from England to lead his minions on this return passage, and the effect this had on his gang; the threat from his cronies was now more sinister and more deadly than at any time before. After all, they were going across a turbulent ocean, no easy escape! The fateful journey to England had begun.

Bob sought an urgent meeting with Peter Anderson, the First Mate. Peter was a man of decision; despite the typically quizzical expression his face mostly wore. He recognised the qualities of the Captain had passed their best. Now, he supported him as best he could, took decisions, kept order; trained his 2nd Mate, explained his duties to the man. Peter Anderson was a man of firm purpose. He had had to be, after losing both his parents to pirates operating in the Azores, some twenty years before. Peter was twelve years old when he was orphaned. His Uncle Ben Anderson took him in and raised him with his own two sons and a daughter, on the exposed Lincolnshire coast, near Grimsby. Growing up by the sea, Peter was a skilled sailor who earned his Mate's ticket in record time. Now he was First Mate to Captain Parry, watchful, professional and jealous of the good order that reigned on board. So he was very attentive as Bob and Billy explained the situation on board – the two opposing factions, the continuing feud between Billy and the villainous Woodcock. He was appreciative of being forewarned of possible trouble,

"I'm obliged, gentlemen, for this information. I shall of course share it with the Captain and will muster my men to alert them and stand guard".

Captain Parry was an experienced man, with twenty-five years of service, including the last twelve as a Captain. He had been in charge of ships in most of the world's waterways, except the Pacific. The run to and from Van Diemans Land, via the Cape was very familiar. Routines were familiar, but crews changed and had to be trained again. Officers were mostly the same, except this time, for the young 2nd Mate, inexperienced and a little headstrong, but he could be moulded after a passage or two. Captain Parry was tired. He leaned heavily on the stalwart First Mate, who could be trusted to make decisions and to see to the efficient running of the ship. In the past, the Captain had earned respect from his men, as when the ship's carpenter, Thomas Sarah – a gentle and friendly Cornishman, fashioned an elegant cabinet in rosewood with oak banding, and three drawers with a fold-down writing block covered in green felt. This he presented to the Captain on the tenth anniversary of his promotion. But now, the Captain's tiredness made him somewhat ineffective. He authorised the use of his able-bodied passengers in the crew's teams, so they had to learn to be nimble with buntlines and clewlines and braces. They quickly came to know the hard life of sail. Captain Parry did, however, intervene to recognise the limitations of Billy's awkward gait and squint,

"I think it would be best, Billy Brown, if we were to place you with Thomas Sarah, our carpenter. You'll like him, and the workshop will offer some protection if there is any disorder on board".

"I'm obliged, Captain", replied Billy.

Thomas had wide skills, from the cobbling together of beam and spar, or fashioning a new mast when required. His skills with the chisel and knife were used if the ship's surgeon was somehow incapacitated. Indeed, these skills were to come in useful on Billy's behalf later.

They were well out to sea on a rising swell, making their first leg to the Cape; it was the thirty-fifth or the thirty-sixth day of sailing and the routines were proceeding well. They were passengers and not chained convicts – a big difference to their movement around the rigging! The first inkling of trouble was the attack on John Garner, their Leicester mate, when in the rigging. The teams were checking the buntlines and braces, when a jab with a knife cut the rope that bore John's weight. Consequently, he fell down a braceline very quickly indeed. Fortunately, he had the presence of mind to check his fall with a secondary rope, so that he did not smash into the mast as the villain intended. Billy had to admire John's coolness in this crisis, because this incident was noiseless but for the wind in the sails. No shouting by John, but plenty by the knifeman as Bob caught up with him. In a trice the man was swinging by a single looped ankle, his head making a circle in the air. His knife dropped harmlessly to the deck, some thirty feet below. The would-be assassin was lowered on the rope. The Mate, the wind spattering his ruddy face, stepped up to the villain with fists already clenched and quietly felled him with a sharp punch to his temple. The Grim Reaper appeared momentarily for either man or both, but had been denied for now. What cannot be denied was that Woodcock orchestrated the affair. He was clearly seen directing his minions to the rescue of the knifeman. Thus, John reported to Billy,

"How could Woodcock do this within the jurisdiction of a Captain?"

Billy could not say these two colluded, but,

"The Captain is ineffective! He was unable, for example, to draw up lines of demarcation between the factions on board. It would have been enough", complained Billy, "for the Captain to lay down the law and keep the Leicester Lads to port and the others to starboard. This Captain spits in the wind!"

The inexperienced 2nd Mate, who was supposed to manage the sea lawyers, the malingerers and the hard men among the sailors, compounded the problem.

Bob observed,

"Hard men among the passengers are beyond his capabilities. Fortunately, Peter, the First Mate is decisive. He has no authority to discipline anyone on board without the Captain's express permission or approval; but the Captain's only response is to turn on his heel and walk aft to his cabin. Clearly, the Mate would have no truck with the likes of Woodcock and his gang!"

But this incident was the precursor of more violence. *'The Lord answered Job out of the storm'*.

The First Mate and a small company of the ship's crew – about ten or a dozen, backed up Bob, John, Joseph and Tom Dunslow. The Captain kept his head down – wisely perhaps, because within the first hour of the skirmish the 2nd Mate was foolhardy enough to rush the starboard side of the galley only to be struck down with a pistol ball through the heart. He sank to his knees, face ashen, and tipped forward quite dead. Billy was suddenly fearful that this might have given Woodcock an inflated idea of his power. Sure enough, four or five of his men, including the Albino, moved forward towards the f'c'stle, and another four aft towards the workshops and the poop deck. The Mate had wisely issued arms to his company, and now these were brought to bear on the approaching villains. It was enough to stem their advance. Bob and the others raced aft to see how things were progressing. The workshop was filled with smoke from small arms fire. The exchanges were deafening. Poor Tom raced up and was immediately cut down viciously by Woodcock himself, before the latter ordered his men to retreat in the face of the new support they had attracted. Bob and John went to Tom's side, but there was nothing they could do. Gray unlocked the workshop and they all gathered to assess the damage.

The Mate, Peter Anderson arrived and explained the loss of his deputy,
"With Woodcock now retreating, the attacks have become desultory. In fact, I think I may now say that some sort of order has been restored".

They all moved inside the workshop for added safety, but all gunfire had ceased. The smoke was clearing quickly and Peter continued,
"We have at most another forty days to the Cape, so I'm hopeful we can batten down the hatches".

Bob wondered,
"And what of Woodcock? Will he try anything again?"
"I'm keeping him at arm's length for the present; we'll try to ensure he is restricted to the port side at the stern".
"Will that work?" asked Bob.
"I have half a dozen soldiers in transit to England, that say it will work", Peter replied with a smile. With a following wind, they made good time to the Cape, reaching the harbour at Simons Bay on the thirty-fifth day after the workshop meeting.

TWENTY

Simons Bay near Cape Town was a pleasant spot, despite their recent difficulties. The ship could be provisioned and the men would be able to bring a number of packages and a few livestock on board to be stowed. The opportunity for repairs would be taken, especially some new rigging and a new mainsail after a close inspection revealed tears and shot holes. Captain Parry estimated that the need for refreshment and repairs might have kept them in port for three days, and recommended passengers disembark and explore Cape Town. Bob immediately went to seek out Peter Anderson, the First Mate,

"We may have trouble ashore, Peter".

"Do you really think that's likely?"

"Woodcock will take every opportunity to attack Billy – he's the real target".

"I'll see if I can persuade the soldiers to accompany you. Would that be suitable?"

"If they can, that would be splendid".

So, it happened that six soldiers who were in transit to England from their recent duties for the Governor in Van Diemans Land accompanied Bob, Billy, John and Joseph. Simon's Town was a naval base, so the atmosphere was very reminiscent of Portsmouth or Plymouth. The sergeant and corporal led the four privates and Bob and Billy tried to get into conversation with Sergeant Collier who hailed from Wiltshire,

"Thank you, Sergeant, for offering to escort us", said Bob, falling into step with him.

"That's alright, sir. My men appreciate the chance to stretch their legs".

On this bright morning, the nondescripts and the uniforms could be seen walking down Adderley Street in easy union. A kookaburra could recognise the laughter that passed between the men, relaxed and comfortable.

"What were duties like at Government House?" asked Billy.

"All starch and gaiters, sir", replied Private Knowles, grinning widely enough to show his gap teeth.

"We was well fed, though!" chimed in Private Adshead.

Bob was suddenly alert, as he saw the albino moving silently across to the left of his field of vision,

"Take care, Sergeant Collier!"

"Close order, now!"

The soldiers moved immediately to form a ring of firepower around Bob and Billy, but marching steadily down Adderley Street. The soldiers were well briefed. This incongruous group arrived at the site of St. George's Church, and stood around the engraved foundation stone dated 1830, inscribed with the name of Sir Lowry Cole. Bob read it studiously, whilst Billy blinked rapidly and stood awkwardly with his gammy leg. Although they saw the albino walking by on the other side of the square, there was no immediate threat, either real or supposed. Indeed, there was the unmistakable smell of bacon and eggs cooking. It wafted by the men's nostrils. Sergeant Collier had a quick word with Bob, and the group moved as one towards the pleasant odours of a bar.

"We'll call this lunch, eh?" asked Bob.

Sergeant Collier agreed. The men needed no second bidding and settled down. Orders were taken rapidly and fresh cooking arrived soon after. Billy, John and Joseph found a table apart, but the soldiers insisted it was dragged to form a longer table with their own. This done, the Leicester lads sat down. Bob stood guard a while longer, but the albino had disappeared – presumably back to the ship. Bob sat as the orders arrived, so the party was soon in full swing. Indeed, Private Adshead had a glorious tenor voice that he now exercised in a quick rendition of Stephen Foster's *Old Folks at Home*. There were few dry eyes as he finished that one. Straightaway, he launched into a strong new song, Benjamin Hanby's *Darling Nelly Gray*. A crowded room of the customers welcomed his singing that lunchtime. Private Adshead acknowledged the acclaim, but was not prepared for an encore; he would not give an encore. The meal was continued and enjoyed to its conclusion. This incongruous group took its leave, and the walk back to the ship began. Bob and Billy noticed the albino several yards ahead of them, also retracing his steps to the ship. They said nothing to the others. Albino had clearly observed them for most of the day. Where did he have his lunch? Albino went aboard and again disappeared below. Bob, Billy, John and Joe boarded quietly with their escort.

"Many thanks, Sergeant Collier", said Bob.

"That's alright, sir. Same again tomorrow, perhaps?"

"Yes please", chimed in Billy, laughing.

The lads retired to their cabins starboard side and soon settled and slept happily through to six bells – the end of the morning watch. Billy's timepiece was not working, so that could be of no help. The bells won the day!

The second day of the ship's inertia almost followed the same pattern. Sergeant Collier and his team met Billy and his mates. The nondescripts and the uniforms walked into the port and thence to Cape Town. Again, the albino, who walked behind at a 'respectable' distance, shadowed them. Sergeant Collier gave a command,

"Close order there, gentlemen!"

The corporal and privates walked smartly to cover the lads, whilst the sergeant fell back with Bob to put pressure on the albino. The ploy worked. Mordecai hesitated, and then walked to his left into the market area behind Adderley Street. The sergeant and Bob resumed their positions with the men. They walked on and the bar hove into view. The owner was already on the doorstop with a pleasant smile and a wave indicating they should enter and be comfortable,

"Sirs, you are very welcome", he said in good English. The uniforms and the nondescripts accepted the invitation and found the long table already reserved.

"For you, sirs, as before!" said the owner.

As they sat down, there was sustained clapping from the diners in an already crowded dining room – they remembered yesterday. Orders were taken, cool drinks arrived, and the men relaxed. Billy turned to Private Adshead on his left,

"Where did you learn to sing like you do?"

"I'm largely self taught, though I sang in choir at chapel for a couple of years before enlistment".

"Chapel, eh? That's splendid. I love to hear the choirs at chapel. They sing with such enthusiasm!"

"That's what I found, enthusiasm and a good conductor".

Their conversation was interrupted by the arrival of the food, and the men's appetites took control. They tucked into a delicious portion of lamb shank with onions and green vegetables. The meat positively dripped from the bone and the sweetness of a red sauce could be tasted.

"Is this red currant?" asked Bob.

The reply was lost in a sudden hubbub and panic mixed with desperate screams as a knot of perhaps half a dozen Cape cobras was thrown amongst the crowd from the darkened doorway. The writhing mass of snakes was angry; their hissing was enhanced by the enclosed space within the restaurant. Customers and waiters alike were keen to distance themselves from this threat; they left their food uneaten, their drinks were abandoned. Sergeant Collier ordered his men to load their rifles and to be on guard,

"Keep your eyes open. If one of the buggers even lifts its head, blast it!"

The cobras were equally desperate to escape, sensing the movement around them. They slithered across the floor, causing consternation. The bravest amongst the diners sat or stood quite still, knowing that the cobra reacted to movement. But the leading snake encountered a desperate man stumbling to get out of its way. With a gleaming eye and darting tongue, the cobra raised its upper body to assume a threatening posture – then fell back as gunshot blasted through its head. The shot, unfortunately, caught the stumbling man in the thigh, and he yelped in pain. Bob and Sergeant Collier hurried through the alarmed dining room to the rear of the building. They found a group of men sitting around a card table, laughing and joking. The albino was one of them!

"Hey, you!" said Bob, pointing an accusing finger at the albino, "Stand up!"

Mordecai, the albino was shaking with laughter as he stood,

"What do you want?"

"Do you get your fun by frightening folk with a bunch of snakes?"

"What!" he laughed again, "I've no idea what you are talking about".

Bob appeared about to strike him, but Sergeant Collier checked his arm,

"C'mon, lad, there's nowt to be done here".

Bob and the albino were aware of each other, exchanging fierce looks that bode ill for the future. Sergeant Collier and Bob returned to the dining room where folk were settling down, the owner was fussing and the immediate danger now receded. The sum total of loss was three large eggs from the kitchen as the cobras made their escape. The injured customer had a bandaged thigh, otherwise comfortable. The sergeant nodded to Private Adshead to lighten the proceedings.

TWENTY ONE

The third day of inertia dawned with news that their ship's idleness was at an end. All was made ready for sailing. Provisioning went on apace; fresh vegetables and fresh meat even live meat on the hoof for future needs. Indeed, the live meat was very lively. A line of beef steers was approaching the ship across the cobbled quay; it was a wavy line as the cows wandered left and right. The hands that accompanied them had a hard job steering them in the right direction. It was made doubly difficult when one of the cows refused to step on to the gangway that led to the holds midships. The cow dropped its head and lowed in a plaintive voice, as though it knew instinctively that its future was bleak if it joined this vessel. It backed away, inevitably colliding with the following beast. This blockage had instant repercussions across the quay, as cows sensed the distress of one of their number, and something amounting to panic set in. The trouble stemmed from the cobbled surface of the quay – not very reassuring for the cloven hoofed. One of the cows moved too close to the edge of the quay, and in the crush it was pushed over and fell into the water. Nothing could be done. The ship at its moorings would crush the poor beast, or it would drown. The hands redoubled their efforts to control the cows, in case there were more fatalities.

Bob and Billy pressed their faces to the small porthole in their cabin, which had a good view of the quayside. They found the dramas acting out before them, funny and there was rare laughter. Bob returned to his upper bunk to read the papers he had bought in Cape Town. The cows were rounded up and encouraged to mount the gangway; they followed their leader on board without more fuss.

The new rigging and yardarms were in place. Thomas Sarah, the carpenter was to be congratulated! Sailors swarmed over the buntlines and the crew-lines making all taut and ready. Sergeant Collier drilled his men for a couple of hours. They were sparkling in their pristine uniforms, polished and pressed. All passengers were temporarily sent to their cabins, so that the decks could be cleared for action.

"Cast off ends!" cried the Captain.

"Anchor's free, sir" reported the Bosun.

The ship inched forward; its sails began to billow and fill in the breeze. It delicately steered its way to the harbour mouth through a navigable channel already lined with ships from around the world. A salute of flags was hoisted, to offer respect to Cape Town and to the port of Simon's Bay.

As the ship strode into the strong currents of the bay, the flags were taken in and stowed. The next landfall was expected to be England. This was very much the expectation of Billy. He thought of England, not as a green and pleasant land, but rather as the haven and refuge of his archenemy – old man Woodcock! In the same breath, Billy thought of his homecoming, his Mam and Dad, his brother John and his sister-in-law, Ann. He thought of his true sister Elizabeth and her husband. The cold air against the porthole refreshed him, replenished his energies, and he fell back on to his bunk, avoiding Bob's waving legs because he sat on top, still reading. Their quiet time was not meant to last, as the Captain then needed passengers to join teams as usual to set full sail.

Men shouted, men answered, as teams were formed. Bob and Billy were together as their team raced topside to deal with the t'gallants. They caught sight of John and Joseph in a team far below them, but there was not even the chance to wave. The salt spray from the prow even reached skyward to hit Billy and Bob. This they found very invigorating, but would have preferred to work in the dry! It made no difference to the sailors in their team – they loved it! From their eyrie in the t'gallants, Billy and Bob imagined the surface of the ocean.

"It's like glass", said Billy.

"But too far to see your face in it!" laughed Bob.

With full sail, the ship picked up speed in a following wind. The Captain directed a northwestern course in the hope of picking up the Gulf Stream to carry them northwards; the ship was picking its path carefully through sometimes-mountainous seas. No longer a looking glass, the sea was boiling up. Was it coincidence, that as the teams were stood down, tempers began to boil up, especially in teams using Woodcock and his cronies. Some supposed slur led to a fistfight, with a small crowd quickly growing and jeering them on. The First Mate, Peter, ordered in the soldiers to restore order. Sergeant Collier and his men, under some pressure with the roll of the ship, soon separated the combatants and sent them packing. All passengers retired to their cabins, exhausted. Their rest was interrupted within half an hour, by the sounds of small arms fire. This began portside, where Woodcock had committed his cronies – possibly a dozen men, to sweeping the cabins, routing out any resistance with force. Peter alerted Sergeant Collier who despatched a couple of privates to see what the trouble was. The privates were inexperienced. They had never seen hand-to-hand combat, but now it was very real within the confines of the portside gangway, where one of them was cut down almost immediately. The other one bent over his colleague, but could see that the shot was fatal. As shocked as he was, he made his escape and returned to report the situation.

"Vandals with pistols have killed my colleague, and they are now trying to take control of portside aft, and the starboard side is already being evacuated!"

Indeed, Bob was already leading Billy and the Leicester lads forward to the f'c'stle.

"Wait here Joseph, and you Billy", said Bob, "whilst John and I take a quick look".

"Take care, Bob!" urged Billy. Bob picked up a belaying pin, weighed it in his hands and then moved off.

The crossing of the South Atlantic was a hard one, but the ship successfully settled into the Gulf Stream. It ran immediately into squalls, spouts and hurricanes in a pitiless storm that reflected the tempests on board. It was soon clear that Woodcock had committed his troops to an all-out assault, as though to try to take command of the ship. Sergeant Collier acted upon the information he had received, and moved his small force towards the stern to engage this very present threat. They met Bob with John, recently evacuated from their cabins.

"If twenty-two sailors had done this, it would have been mutiny", said Bob, "on the high seas!"

"What are they trying to do?" asked Sergeant Collier.

"Probably take over the ship, and then kill Billy", replied Bob, "He's their principal target".

Bob returned to the f'c'stle. He was anxious for the safety of Billy, who might have presented a target in that messy brouhaha. He thought to move him to a place of safety,

"C'mon lad, I'm taking you to your friend the carpenter".

Billy acquiesced without comment. He liked Thomas the carpenter. Billy shook Joseph's hand and turned to follow Bob as he made tracks for the carpenter's workshop. Once there, Billy realised that Thomas and Gray, the Captain's Steward together had barricaded the door of the workshop, so that it then acted as a refuge for all three of them. Bob then explained,

"I'm going back to Joseph and the others, so keep your heads down".

He gave Billy a hug and they parted. Bob was about to pick his path carefully back to the f'c'stle. He froze in the shadowy lee of the workshop when he saw a figure creeping forward. Bob wondered if he was a sniper, looking for an opportunity to kill. As this figure drew level with him, Bob swung his belaying pin and struck the man over the head. The creeping figure was surprised; it slumped to the decking. Bob raced back to the f'c'stle and told Sergeant Collier about the man he had knocked unconscious, so that a couple of the more experienced soldiers were sent to capture him.

TWENTY TWO

Elsewhere, the fight raged, as the ship raced northward. Bob was with Joseph and John and the soldiers, meeting the villains head on near the f'c'stle gangway. They had their hands full with raid after raid. Privates Smith and Noond checked their rifles and picked up some extra ammunition. They moved forward towards the maelstrom at midships. The ship was still moving at speed, but one could still hear the crack of gunfire and the clip, clip of the snipers. Private Smith believed he'd found a target and stepped slightly to his left to take aim. He squeezed the trigger, then stumbled and fell to the deck – a neat bullet hole in his forehead was glistening red. His squeeze of the trigger, however, sent a shot that clipped the neck of George Churchill – one of Silas Woodcock's cronies. George was surprised, and felt the blood on his collar by moving his right hand up to his left. Unwittingly, his collar then presented a red badge, and within a few moments more a well-aimed shot found Churchill's collar, and George collapsed quite dead. So even snipers enjoyed only a short life.

There was a general rush on the starboard side, where Sergeant Collier and the Leicester lads, Joseph and John, prepared to face an advancing group of men shouting and some small arms fire indiscriminately whizzing about. They dealt with it effectively by the use of a salvo of musket fire from the line of soldiers, and the charge was halted. Bob thought it opportune to send Sergeant Collier to make a report of the 'state of play' to Captain Parry.

Billy was safely barricaded in Brian Farah's workshop, together with Gray, the Captain's steward. They could only listen, and imagine what was happening. Sea spray anointed the dead and dying that littered the deck, including young Private Smith, and George Churchill. The loss of life was mounting in the face of this evil. *'Woe to those who call evil good'*. There was the occasional smell of spent cordite, as the wind willed. Mordecai, the albino and three minions tried to rush their positions on the port side, but the quick thinking Corporal Knowles was able to repulse them with his young marksmen, Privates Hall and Adshead. Woodcock for once was indecisive; he clearly signalled a withdrawal, but no one could guess how long this would last!

It was a time of regrouping. The Captain and his sailors had their hands full with sailing at speed, so he was quite happy for the First Mate to keep order with these unruly passengers. Peter made his own report of the fatalities and the injuries. He invited the Captain to the workshop, where the soldiers and the Leicester lads, Brian the carpenter, Gray the steward, Billy and Bob, were gathered for a conference. What next?

"Their leader is Woodcock", said Peter.

"My arch enemy", added Billy.

"You have said he bullies these men to do his bidding. So if he can be eliminated, won't they melt into the woodwork?" asked Peter.

"You're right", replied Bob, "He's a bully!"

No one in the company could have imagined that Bob was already thinking of a way to attack Woodcock, though he said nothing. The meeting broke up without a decision, other than to continue their defences as required.

"Same again, lads", said Sergeant Collier, "We have sufficient ammunition".

His words were suddenly drowned by the sound of small, repeated explosions. Captain Parry looked at his First Mate. Peter reacted immediately and asked Collier and his men to follow him. They dived out of the workshop and headed towards the stern and the weapons store. As they neared the end of the run from the cabins, they smelt burning – the weapons store was on fire! The men formed a chain of fire fighters, buckets of seawater – too little, too late! At least, the seawater prevented the fire from spreading further. The fire was still truculent, and the damage difficult to assess.

"We have the ammunition already issued, and no more!" said Peter to Sergeant Collier. Peter judged it was time to return to the workshop, where he spoke to Bob,

"The weapons store has been fired, Bob, so our ammunition is suddenly in short supply".

"OK, we shall have to play our ace", replied Bob.

No one thought to ask Bob what his ace was, because the bosun interrupted them,

"Message for the Captain!"

"Yes, Bosun?"

"Fire is out, and some boxes of ammunition have been saved".

"Well done, Bosun. I believe that's good news!"

"Very good, Bosun!" added Peter, who asked that the ammunition be brought to the f'c'stle as soon as was possible.

"Aye, aye, sir!" The bosun stayed to join in the conference.

The Captain thought aloud, repeating what he had heard and claiming it as his own original thought,

"It seems to me we have to deal with this man, Woodcock, who seems to be orchestrating this mutiny".

There were murmurs of agreement.

"That's right, sir", said Peter, "I know I have said this before, but if we could stop him, I feel the rest of his cronies would be ineffective without his leadership".

"The only other diehard is the albino", said the bosun, "He's been very troublesome".

Bob made a fist,

"Give me the albino!" he said, vehemently.

"Don't do anything foolhardy," replied Peter, placing a hand on his arm in mock restraint. Bob seemed to sulk; at the least he went very quiet.

The Captain thanked Peter and followed the bosun, whilst Sergeant Collier brought his men to attention and they marched off towards the f's'cle. Bob and Billy took their leave of Gray, the steward and Brian, the carpenter,

"An uneasy night, eh?" asked Gray.

"Could be", replied Billy.

Bob was still quiet and contemplative. The steward and the carpenter had made their billets within the workshop, so Bob and Billy left for their temporary quarters forward.

In the early hours, Bob was restless. He woke to find Billy sleeping soundly, with an occasional snore. He climbed down from the top bunk, and dressed. Billy turned over, but was soon quiet again. Bob checked his knife and again wrestled with his conscience,

"Am I right? Am I wrong to try this on my own?"

The argument ran on silently. He satisfied himself that his purpose was within his capabilities and the right thing to do. He stepped out of the cabin. During this first watch, there was very little movement. Certainly, none was expected amongst the passengers. The ship creaked, the sails were half full in a rising wind. Both soldiers and sailors were taking turns to keep watch. Bob began to slip down the gangway in the lee of the main mast. No one noticed this silent figure. He reached the orlop deck and moved aft and towards the port side cabins. Bob crept along the passageway – he was playing his ace card. If he could eliminate the albino, Woodcock would lose the advantage.

Bob was determined and fully awake. He climbed into the rope stowage, so that he could better observe the half-lit run of cabins. Bob observed a couple of figures moving about even at that hour. Knight walked along the passageway talking, but Bob could not make out what he was saying. Knight entered a cabin and his conversation ceased. Bob assumed this was idle chatter, rather than serious planning using midnight oil! He heard Pitts talking at the far end. He was smoking and relaxing, talking to someone within the cabin – possibly Woodcock. Bob stiffened as the speaker emerged into the gloom. He recognised the albino immediately, and at the same time wrinkled his nose due to the effects of the rising pipe smoke.

Bob had to make a sudden movement to stifle a sneeze. He must have made a noise! Albino must have heard it! Bob fell back behind a stanchion, and froze. Sure enough, the albino was walking towards him to investigate this noise. Bob was thinking he would never have such a good opportunity again. He was higher and astride the walkway, so the albino walked beneath. Bob gripped his knife tightly and as the man turned round, he launched himself onto the albino's shoulders, slashing downwards with the blade. As the blade slices into his shoulder, Mordecai let out a roar and tried to dislodge his assailant. The noise had already disturbed the occupants of the cabins, and a small audience gathered. Bob was able to stab the albino's other shoulder, perilously close to the brute's neck. The two were locked together and thrashed about. Mordecai found his own blade and managed to plunge it into Bob's thigh. Bob twisted his blade, thinking he could despatch the albino. Indeed, Mordecai cried out as though he was mortally wounded. With a great show of strength, the albino drove his blade into Bob's lower stomach.

Woodcock himself had arrived, and it was he that held back the other onlookers,

"Let them fight this one to the death!"

Bob rolled to his left as the albino momentarily choked. In an instant, Bob rolled back again, driving his blade into his opponent's throbbing neck. At the same time, almost exhausted, Bob grabbed the albino's head and pulled it back. His fingers found those pink eyes and Bob began to apply pressure, as though to gouge them out of their sockets. Mordecai let out a blood-curdling moan, and grabbed Bob's wrist to try to pull his hand away. There was very little strength in the albino's arm, and even Bob's was beginning to sag. Both combatants were now desperately wounded. Bob twisted his blade again, and the albino's carotid artery finally snapped. Mordecai's head reared up; his eyes glazed over as the fountain of blood began to sap away his life. Bob collapsed, himself mortally wounded. An onlooker made to move forward and was instantly reprimanded by Woodcock,

"Stop, leave them be! It's not quite finished yet!"

Bob turned his head towards the albino and could just see his sightless eyes – the brute was dead. The struggle had been a bloody battle of behemoths, with no outright winner. Bob, however, was satisfied that one of their greatest dangers had been eliminated. He was saddened that he could not take this news to Billy and the others. With a last gasp, he died.

*

Billy woke up to sense immediately that he was alone in the cabin. Bob's bed in the upper bunk was empty. Billy was not worried at that point, because he remembered Bob slipping out in the night. He decided to dress quickly and to seek out his friends. Indeed, as he finished dressing, there was a knock at the cabin door. It was Joseph with John, come to see how he was,

"Did you sleep well, Billy?" asked Joseph.

"I suppose I did, but I'm worried about Bob. Do you know where he is?"

"We've not seen him this morning, Billy", said John.

Joseph sought to calm Billy down, by suggesting,

"I'll go and speak to Peter, the First Mate, in case he knows anything".

Joseph left straight away, and found Peter by the mizzen gangway, where he was explaining their duties to a five-man sailor team. As he dismissed them, Joseph took the opportunity to ask,

"Excuse me, Peter, but have you seen Bob this morning?"

"No, I haven't. Is he missing?"

"Billy is worried because apparently Bob left the cabin in the early hours".

Peter stroked his chin, clearly thinking if he should say something. He decided,

"There is something you are probably not aware of".

"Oh!" said Joseph, immediately interested.

"My men have reported some sort of disturbance amongst Woodcock and his cronies. They are not sure what it is all about".

Joseph indicated that he should get back to his friends, and Peter promised to inform him of developments. In the meantime, Peter asked Sergeant Collier to ensure a constant vigil with his small detachment, and to be ready for any trouble.

TWENTY THREE

John was speaking as Joseph returned,
"They seem to be in a right temper".
"I've not seen Albino at all today," added Joseph.

Billy's anxiety was not helped by these comments, but it was not until two days later that Billy was roused at dawn by Joseph and wakened with a friendly tussle. Billy woke in the earnest hope that it was Bob rousing him – but it was Joseph, looking anxious. Joseph put a finger to his lips, urging Billy to come quietly. Billy's curiosity was aroused and he followed meekly, as Joseph led him to the ship's rail. Billy gripped the cold iron, and Joseph indicated that he should follow with his eyes and pointed upwards. Way up on the yardarm a figure was swinging, twirling in the light breeze. John joined them with a heavy, hang dog look.

"It's Bob", he said quietly.

Billy staggered and Joseph steadied him. Joseph and John exchanged glances, and mutually agreed to take Billy back to his bed. As they closed his door, they heard him sob and sob.

A couple of hours later, Billy woke up to his cruel loss. His mood had changed, hardened, his head was clear, his purpose was clear. Billy had to deal with Woodcock and soon. In those two hours, Joseph and John had gone to the bosun's office and arranged for a small party to bring the body down. An official enquiry was quickly opened, for four bodies, Bob's and Albino's found after a diligent search below the f'c'stle gangway; and also for poor Tom and the foolhardy 2nd Mate. The enquiry was as quickly closed. Four more fatalities were of no real consequence. Three of them were only passengers!

Billy went straight to Brian Farah, the carpenter and told him the whole story. For the first time, he guessed the relationship between this villain Woodcock and the Edward Woodcock in Melton who had sent him to Van Dieman's Land. Were they father and son? Were they uncle and nephew? Billy never knew, not even to the end of his days. Brian Farah understood his need for revenge. Billy told him more than once that he would do for Edward bloody Woodcock! In his anger, Billy stumbled around the workshop, first sobbing for his friend Bob, and then shouting against his sworn enemy. He swept tools and cans to the floor, filling the room with smells of resin and, possibly, cordite and oil.

The cans clattered around a framework of wood that was Brian's latest piece of work. Billy was shocked and put out his arm as if to protect it,

"Sorry, sorry Brian, I didn't mean to damage your work!"

"That's alright, Billy. No harm done!"

Brian found a sharpened chisel amongst the tools spilled on the floor. He bent to pick it up, and placed it in Billy's hands as he rose,

"Will this be useful, Billy?"

Billy grasped the chisel with determination,

"I'll go and speak to the Mate".

He stumbled in blind rage from the workshop and used the mizzen gangway to reach the Mate's quarters. Billy now had nerves of steel. Peter Anderson, the First Mate, was writing his notes for the logbook, but he noticed at once the determination on Billy's face. Peter welcomed him in and offered Billy a seat. He also noticed Billy's 'weapon'.

"Your not going to use that on me, are you?" he laughed.

"Not likely, Peter, it's for that sod, Silas Woodcock".

"Oh!" Peter was surprised and imagined that Billy might have problems what with his leg and his blinking, "And how might you manage that?"

Billy was in no mood to be deflected by mere considerations of leg or eye. First, he walked better then because of the tuition from George at Ma Whittle's in Van Dieman's Land; and second, his blinking eye did not hinder a well-aimed blow! Billy was shaken by Peter's amiable conversation. Did he not realise Billy had the heart of a lion? Well, at least a dog fox following a scent.

"I'll need your help, Peter", emphasised Billy.

"Precisely, how?"

"I need this villain in chains and helpless, so that I can despatch him".

"This man Woodcock has caused a great deal of trouble on board. For this reason, I suppose I could arrest him!"

Billy wondered aloud if this arrest would offer him the chance to act.

"He can be put in chains and locked up next to the weapon store".

"I know where that is Peter, shall we say in one hour's time?"

Peter smiled; again Billy's determination shone through,

"OK, I'll get on to this straight away", said the First mate emphatically, "I'll send you word when it's done".

Billy withdrew from Peter's cabin and made for the mizzen gangway. Peter left his writing, and went to the guardroom to get Sergeant Collier and Corporal Knowles. He explained their mission, and the three of them headed for the portside cabins. They were met by Knight, who blustered but was cast aside, as the trio moved on. They found Woodcock alone in his cabin. It was a simple job to bind his arms behind him and then march him aft to the weapons store. The First Mate chained him to the inside bars, and turned to the two soldiers,

"Thank you, gentlemen. Mission accomplished".

The two soldiers left. Peter addressed Woodcock,

"You are detained here for mutinous behaviour".

"Your superiors will hear of this nonsense when we dock in London", sneered Woodcock. The First Mate left the store and found a sailor to take a message,

"Find Billy Brown in his cabin starboard, and tell him to meet me here at 2 a.m."

"Aye, aye, sir!"

Peter watched the sailor disappear on his errand, and was shaken by the startling development of a stalker. The sailor was being followed by a shadowy figure that probably was now unaware of being followed itself by the First Mate! The sailor used the mizzen gangway and turned aft for the starboard cabins. It was Joseph who opened the cabin door, to find a young sailor collapsing into his arms with a blade in his back. In the same instance, Joe heard a shot ring out, and a shadowy figure fell about eight feet away from the lighted doorway.

"Close your door, now!" shouted the First Mate. Joe hauled in the sailor, and closed the door. The young matelot was reviving, with the blade missing vital organs, but he was still groggy. Billy made him comfortable with a coat under his head to act as a pillow. He and Joe exchanged puzzled glances for a few minutes, until there was urgent knocking at the door. It was Peter!

"I sent this poor man to give you a message. I might as well do it myself, now!"

He stepped inside the cabin, carefully stepping over the unfortunate sailor,

"I'll get him attended to, and the other one removed".

"What was your message, Peter?" enquired Joseph.

"I want Billy to meet me at the weapons store at 2 a.m."

"Thanks, Peter", replied a shaken Billy, "I'll be there. Can Joe come too?"

"Of course, pleased to meet you, Joe".

The First Mate left to find the sawbones and to organise the removal of a body.

Billy was gratified to receive this message – a clear commitment from the Mate. His own plan was now taking shape. He and Joe knew well the location of the weapon store – at the end of a run from their cabin. Joe bunked with Billy now that Bob was dead. John was alone in the next-door cabin. Joe and Billy stirred themselves in the early hours. Joe peeped in to see that John was alright,

"Sleeping like a baby", he smiled at Billy.

They met Peter close by the weapon store on the dot of 2 a.m.

"Hi Peter, all quiet?"

"Yes, Billy, now! You alright Joe?"

"Fine, thanks", replied Joe.

"Right, can we do this thing quickly?" asked Billy.

The Mate showed the two of them the store. Woodcock was in the corner against the wall of what could only be described as a cage. Billy, even at that critical juncture, reflected on the Mate being a most unlikely ally, but he supposed that Peter was angered by the way Woodcock and his cronies hijacked the ship's routines. He also had in mind, no doubt, the murder of the 2nd Mate. Mate skirted the wall of the cage, pulling the door open. Joe entered the cage and stuffed a kerchief into the villain's mouth. The Mate passed the chain holding Silas through the outer bars, and went round to pull it taut. This had the effect of pulling him tight up to the bars, presenting his neck to the uprights. Billy's instinct told him that this scene was biblical, *'thus was the lamb led to slaughter'*.

He thought of Bob, his dear friend, as he raised the sharpened chisel. He thought of his family back in Leicestershire, England, now separated from three sons by transportation – and at the hands of a Woodcock! Billy plunged the chisel into the jugular. It broke cleanly and there was a heavy surge of blood. It fountained across the cage, splashing Billy and Joe. Joe threw a blanket over the dying man's head and shoulders. It was quickly soddened with gore, but the spray was controlled. The First Mate, Peter, slipped in the sticky mess, slackened his grip on the chain; and Silas Woodcock's form sank down making a soft gurgling sound, then silence.

Peter passed the chain back through the uprights and Joe threw it to the opposite corner. He retrieved the kerchief from the dead man's mouth. Peter indicated with a wave of his hand that all was finished and they needed to leave. As they reached the rail of the ship, Billy threw the chisel into the sea. Again with a wave, Peter suggested a clean up for themselves in the heads aft. There they bucketed water over each other whilst fully clothed in an effort to wash away any traces of blood. The urgency of this job did not allow for the natural hilarity – it may have woken others. Piece by piece, they stripped their garments and made a sodden pile of them. The three naked conspirators finished their ablutions in silence, picked up their bundles, and dissolved into the night.

Billy went to sleep thinking of his dear Mam, and spoke silently to his best friend, Bob – told him the job was mostly done, only the old sod Woodcock to do for back in England. Joe saw that John was sleeping on undisturbed, and was soon himself snoring contentedly. In the morning, the First Mate informed the Captain that a prisoner was attacked in the night by person or persons unknown, and that the prisoner was dead. He added that the man was the same that caused mayhem on the first leg of the journey. The captain recorded the event in the log.

"Make the usual arrangements, Peter – say, 10 a.m. tomorrow".

With the removal of Woodcock and the Albino, the troubles on board dissipated in the wind. The brief committal service was held that morning with a bold display of red and gold provided by Sergeant Collier and his men. The bosun informed the Captain that the ship had just passed Trafalgar, and that England lay nor-east of here. Within two more days, the ship docked at Deptford on the Thames. Billy reflected that they had come from the other side of the world. His life had come full circle, because he had left Deptford some thirteen years earlier. John, Joe and Billy found the First Mate, Peter, and thanked him for his help.

"Well, Peter, we've arrived safely, thanks to you".

"Only doing my job, Billy – got to keep order on board!"

All four laughed at this idea, shook hands and the lads left him to get on with his 'duty'.

"Good luck, Peter, and best wishes for your own command – sooner rather than later!"

"That's very kind, Billy, Joe and John. Now you take care".

As Billy and the Leicester lads left the deck, the Captain and his First Mate, Peter, saluted them. Billy raised his arm in acknowledgement and felt warm and comforted for the first time in ages. If only Bob could have shared that moment! It was a brief moment, however, because as they descended to the quayside, they found themselves in a mighty bustle of bodies including passengers from other vessels along the quay, including a British man-o'-war, and now a company or two of the 30th Foot, lately arrived home from the Crimea. The noise on the quayside was clamorous and perhaps confusing, as passengers and military personnel tried to find their route across the quay to their rendezvous. There was even a regimental band marching in full dress uniforms!

"Over here, Henry!"

"Sarfend lot follow me!"

The army band broke into its version of 'Lillibulero'.

"You alright, Billy?"

"Thanks, Tom, I'm alright".

The Leicester friends made a supreme effort to keep together, but matters weren't helped when they were overtaken by a group of euphoric foot soldiers. Laughing and revelling at their homecoming, two of them picked up Billy between them and carried him on protesting for a further fifty feet. They dropped him at a tea stall where Missionaries were serving mugs of steaming beverage. They suppressed Billy's continuing protests by handing him a mug, and laughing, moved on. Within a few moments more, the Leicester lads caught up with him and straightway decided that a drink was a good idea at that time. The Missionaries fussed over them and found them seats and proffered hot mugs of tea. The lads settled down to watch the flotsam and jetsam of humanity pass them by.

"This is welcome after the slops on board!" said Joe.

"Make the most of it lad, we shall have to be off in a mo'" replied John.

"I can't wait to see Mam again!" said Billy, burying his face in the mug.

They thanked the Missionaries and began to make their way to the railway. This was an astonishing development since the lads went overseas, and they were full of wonder. The man in the ticket office explained they could buy a ticket to London where they must change stations and buy a ticket to Leicester. They followed his advice and had only a quarter of an hour to wait for the next train, during which they also took the opportunity to use the rest rooms and relieved themselves.

TWENTY FOUR

May 1856

Ann, 'my brother's wife' – these were words that burned into Billy like a red-hot poker. She and Billy were warm together for a brief while – her warm touch, her warm smell, and her warm smile. Fact was; Billy and his brother had a blazing row. Billy visited his family in Leicester at the end of May. He had travelled to the city with his friends, and on this marvellous new train system, so was in a buoyant mood in which to meet his Mam and Dad and after such a long absence. He took his leave of his friends at the station, hugging each one in turn and thanking them for their support. His friends said their goodbyes and moved off in their different directions.

Billy walked on towards his brother's home. As he turned into Bedford Street, his Dad was waiting for him at the door, obviously troubled. Billy looked for his Mam – she was not there! His Dad was tearful as he explained that Billy's Mam died while he was serving his time in Van Dieman's Land. Billy was stunned and soon beset by sharp feelings of guilt that racked through him. Why this guilt? If only he had not been so stupid; not been so venal and grasping as to steal silver spoons. He might have been able to see his darling Mam again; he might have been able to hold her warm face to his and enjoy her chuckles. It could not be. Billy needed comfort; his Dad had turned away – overcome himself. Billy and his sister in law began chatting. Ann knew that Billy needed to cry; she knew he was heaving silently. She folded him in her arms and his tears gushed forth; Billy was aware of her warmth through his anguish. Ann steered Billy to a chair, and sat beside him. Ann wiped Billy's tears with her own sweet-smelling handkerchief. Billy was appreciative of her ministrations; liked the closeness. His hand lightly brushed hers. He cheered up and smiled at last, albeit weakly. John, his brother, observed the exchanges between them and was distrustful; he was suspicious and began to shake, as he usually did under any kind of pressure.

The mutual feelings that affected Ann and Billy developed to the point that both realised the bond between them was strong, was good, was worthwhile. For Billy at least, here was a woman who cared, who accepted, and was prepared to ignore his faults and imperfections. For

Ann, here was a man who was young, vibrant and fit – all right, he squinted and had a limp, but these were nothing as she felt his strength and warmth against her body. She found no strength or warmth in her husband, John. The mutual understandings that overtook Ann and Billy developed apace. They came to the point where they decided to go away for a few days. Just to see if they could make a go of it like. John didn't think much of this idea, but he saw he could do little about it.

"Get away from her, Billy!" shouted John, "Get away from my wife!"

John was by now trembling almost uncontrollably.

"Ann, how can you do this to me?" John sobbed, "Please, Ann, think what you are doing".

A neighbour, Mary Ann, who had come in to 'borrow' a cup of sugar, tried to comfort him but he pushed her away vehemently.

"For pity's sake, Ann, don't leave me!" John collapsed into a large armchair.

Ann and Billy saw an opportunity to leave quietly from the house. Stepping carefully over John's outstretched legs, they headed for the door as Mary Ann leered.

"Ann, you can't be doing this! Think of your brother, lad!" his father intervened.

"It's no use, Dad. We want to be together. We'll send word when we're settled," said Billy.

Ann grasped Billy's arm tighter as they left the house and began the short walk to the railway station. They were oblivious of curtains twitching; of gossips at the street corner. They huddled together as though to blot out the rest of the world; to take this combat to the upper reaches of the Empire, wherever necessary. Ann was comfortable in Billy's arm, and he supported her capably in view of his limp. They snuggled together, speechless, shocked. Silently apart from a polite enquiry and a 'thank you', Billy bought the tickets. They travelled on the train in silence too – got to Quorndon and booked into the *'Royal Oak'* for the night. They got to the hotel room, and Ann straightway threw her arms about Billy's neck and kissed and cried over him ever so long. It does a woman good to have a good cry – then after feel as right as nine pence. Indeed, Ann cheered up, especially after some supper – bread, a piece of pork pie and beer.

"Oh Will! What have I done?" she cried, "What have I done to John?"

These were not questions that Billy was meant to answer. All he could do was to be strong and to hold her. Ann was clearly in torment, forever worrying if she'd done the right thing. They talked and talked.

"Will, I do love you!" avowed Ann in a determined voice. She always called him Will – not Billy.

"But what have I done to John?" she again broke down, "I've hurt him something dreadful!"

"Shush, Ann. It's me that has hurt John," replied Billy, "I've wronged my own brother and I regret it".

"Darling Will! Hold me tight, I feel suddenly cold," appealed Ann.

Billy thought of himself as more than a rough and ready cove,

"Ann, my darling, I want to be your great Captain. I want to out-Marlborough Marlborough".

That only served to increase Ann's anguish; and this, in turn made him as gentle as if he was nursing a newborn baby. They retired for the night and both slept exhausted, in each other's arms.

*

John, Billy's eldest brother, reached Nottingham from Leicester on the regular coach and four, sitting on top to allow the breezes to wash around him. He preferred the coach to the trains. It took longer, but time was not important in this circumstance; his wife was now with Billy, leaving him bereft. John trembled, as was his usual reaction to stress. He left his father fretting at home in Leicester; he was in Nottingham to see his sister Elizabeth, and her husband Joseph. He walked into Ferguson Street and found their house by the old brick works. John knocked and waited. The door opened – it was Elizabeth.

"John! What are you doing here?"

"Hello, sis! I need to talk to you".

"Come in, come in".

They hugged and John's emotional state burst forth in floods of shaking tears.

"John! What is it me' duck?"

"She's left me," he sobbed.

"Do you mean Ann has left you?"

John nodded in agreement, still sobbing, still shaking.

"My God! What is she playing at?" asked Elizabeth rhetorically; then, "I'll put the kettle on".

Elizabeth was a business like homemaker, kept everything in order and tidy; meals were prepared for the moment. She explained,

"Joseph will be home for his tea around six, so we've another two hours to talk. Come and sit down, lad".

John followed her into a sitting room and the two of them chose the settle by the window. Elizabeth remembered the tea and went to collect a tray. She returned and set the tray down on a convenient table. She had added a plate with slices of barn-brack loaf, well buttered. For the first time that afternoon, John smiled. The way to his heart might well have been via his stomach.

They enjoyed the tea and cake, and then nestled down to talk.

"Come on, John, talk to me".

"Well, you know Billy came home and found Dad and me at Leicester".

"Yes, I knew he was expected".

"He was upset at the news about Mam".

"Oh, of course, he could not have known".

"That's right. He was so upset and Ann was able to comfort him".

"What do you mean, 'comfort him'?"

"Well, that's it! She put her arms around him and", John was trembling now; this was a difficult story for him to relate, "She … held him tightly… She…pressed herself against him".

"Oh, I can see the scene. How awful for you, John".

John took his cup of tea in both hands and held it to his lips,

"Even we do not hold each other tightly".

Elizabeth put down her cup, slightly embarrassed by this revelation, and looked at the clock,

"I'll have to be getting Joseph's tea on. Would you like another cup?

"Yes, please, don't let me hold you up. There's a stage at half past the hour".

"Oh, John, you'll stay for tea with us, surely?"

"If that's alright, I'd be pleased to".

"That's settled then, I'll prepare enough for three".

Elizabeth busied herself in the kitchen while John read a local broadsheet full of farming and market news. By now it was just after six, and Joseph entered the yard, and then came into the kitchen by the back door. He greeted Elizabeth warmly,

"Hello, love! Everything alright?"

"John's here, me' duck. He'll have his tea with us before going back to Dad".

Joseph looked at Elizabeth quizzically, but she added no other comment. He moved through into the sitting room to find John. They shook hands.

"Hello, John, it's nice to see you again. Is not Ann with you, this time?"

John stared at him blankly and began to tremble.

"She's left me", he blurted out.

Elizabeth walked into the room to hear both the question and the answer.

"Now lads, let's have tea first, then we can talk".

She threw meaningful glances at Joseph, but he failed to understand. However, Elizabeth had successfully taken the sting out of the meeting. The three of them sat at the kitchen table and tucked into chicken slices, a quarter of pork pie, hot boiled potatoes and a side salad. A plate of homemade bread slices accompanied the meal. Joseph used the golden butter generously on his slices. His family were very fond of butter.

Elizabeth swept away the plates and cutlery, and all other remnants of the meal. Joseph and John removed to the sitting room. Joseph was well over six feet tall, but his manner was completely non-threatening. Nevertheless, John felt unhappy and not ready to talk about it with him. There followed an awkward silence that was only broken by the return of Elizabeth.

"Right, let's talk".

She sat down close to John and patted his arm.

"Are you ready, John? Start at the beginning".

John felt comfortable with his sister, and began to tell his story for Joseph to hear.

When he had finished, Elizabeth turned to Joseph,

"Isn't this awful? Whatever is she playing at I'd like to know. Poor John, this must be so terrible for you".

Joseph nodded in agreement. The situation seemed so alien to him, he did not understand it at all. He did understand the knocking they all heard. He went to the front door.

"Hello Joe, everything alright, me' duck?"

It was Carrie Moon, their neighbour, who felt particularly close because she had grown up with the Brown kids in Scalford. Joseph let her into the sitting room.

"Carrie, whatever's the matter?" asked Elizabeth.

Carrie cast her eyes around the room, knowing full well they had a visitor,

"Hello Jack. I'm sure I've seen your brother today", she said with a leering smile about her lips. "Gave me quite a strange feeling, but I'm positive it's 'im. It's like seeing a ghost after all these years", she again paused for effect. "I think it was Billy, and he was with some woman. I saw him close by the station, just walking into the hotel next door".

TWENTY FIVE

The morning air in Quorndon was bright and clear. On such a morning, the dog fox and his mate rest in their lair, shunning the brightness of the sunshine. After a night's hunting and a hearty breakfast, they feed the litter of cubs, five of them, that gambol around their paws and play games. Billy and Ann took breakfast in their room, shunning the gaze of other guests for the while. By the hour of ten they were ready to move on. They retraced their steps to the rail station and soon got a train for Derby. They spent just the morning in that place, Billy walking on air with Ann on his arm – a proud couple. By lunch they were in Belper and in mid-afternoon took a carriage to Nottingham. Billy had the intention of sharing his happiness with his sister and Joseph. The idea was still strong in his mind when they alighted in the Beast Market. Ferguson Street was not far off and they started to walk. Billy didn't know what baulked him, but he suddenly held back and his frame shuddered against Ann. He had broken with his brother, what would his sister say or do? Ann clasped Billy to her, caring, warm, noble. He realised how much he loved her. She was stronger in her character than Billy. She took charge, said the visit was ill advised, and Ann and Billy turned round. They found a hansom back to the station, and walking out into the street, Billy suddenly thought he had seen a familiar person across the road. He thought no more of it and turned on his heel. Billy pointed out the hotel next door, so they took a room for the night.

The room that night was heaven, or so it seemed. Ann, as proud as she was, was pliant. They were not immodest - they turned down the lamp. They were not giddy youngsters either. They undressed slowly, carefully. It was a warm evening, so no discomfort felt. The bed was lightly covered and welcoming. Ann kissed his afflicted eye, as if to say she noticed it, but it did not deter her feelings for him. She stroked his hair as Billy stroked hers. He pulled her gently towards him, covering her face and arms and ripe breasts in kisses. She breathed deeply and stretched her arm to his groin, and her strong fingers found his manhood. It was quickened and erect for the first time in many months. Billy stretched his back in pleasure, and found Ann climbing over him, legs athwart, so that her fingers could guide his cock into her soft, moist body. Like a stag at rutting, he began to thrust, gently at first, but the excitement grew stronger. Ann moaned. They were ecstatic. As the dam breaks and the waters rush, so they reached a climax that was as *silver fired in a furnace, purified seven times*. The calm returned. Ann's tears dampened his chest. Ann turned her face away. She was clearly troubled but it was an unspoken darkness. Billy's loins were hot again, but discretion bid him nought. *'And the mountain burned with fire into the midst of heaven, with darkness, clouds and thick darkness'*. There was no small voice that night. They slept.

As Billy and Ann took a simple and satisfying breakfasting, they had no idea that the fight, that which they were prepared to 'take to the upper reaches of the Empire', would imminently present itself at their doorstep. As they made move to leave the hotel, at the very door, the dark clouds broke about them. Two figures, menacing and urgent, approached them quickly. Billy's sister Elizabeth and her husband Joseph had found them. God knows how, but their words were arrows, quick, darting, squibs – finding their mark. Ann grasped Billy tightly in alarm.

Joseph's face contorted with anger,

"What the hell are you doing?"

"You've wounded John!" said Elizabeth emphatically.

Joseph again,

"Ann, think again!"

"Come with us, for pity's sake!" said Elizabeth, as she tried to take Ann's arm, now gently and pleading. Ann rebuffed the move.

Neither of them were actually manhandled, though all the time it seemed they might be torn apart. Billy's blusterings in the face of this family quarrel were useless, as ineffective a moment as any in his eventful life, either this side of the world or the other. All was mayhem and bustle, until the small voice, strong and getting stronger, commands attention. Ann swept aside the squibs with a withering,

"Wait! What of my feelings? Tell John I'm sorry, but I love Will – and that's all there is to it. Go on, tell him!"

Elizabeth and Joseph were pulled up short by Ann's firm words; they were nonplussed. Again, in a noble moment, Ann had taken charge. In the face of family feuding, she had thrown down the gauntlet and established the primacy of her own feelings, her own happiness. In a sweep she had her Will pick up the bags, and they walked away from the fracas. Elizabeth looked dejected and broken; Joseph was gormless. On the street corner, Billy saw the figure that he had seen just the other day and knew instantly who it was – Carrie Moon, their old neighbour from Scalford! Whatever was she doing here? In the same instant, he noticed that she was leering at him - he now understood how Elizabeth and Joseph had found them. He said nothing to Carrie, or to Ann, and they were soon out of sight as they turned into the railway station.

There was a train due to leave and wishing to put distance between themselves and their unhappy experience, they hurried for the train getting ready to depart – for Newark.. Newark was inconsequential, but they judged that they could easily be followed on a later train, so spent just an hour or two there, got some lunch of pork pie and fried potatoes and then switched lines and took the train to Grantham.

Billy and Ann found themselves in Spittlegate as they emerged from the station. Mid-afternoon in Grantham was quiet, but the air was smoky with a pungent smell, and sooty; the effects of the many ironworks and a brewery were clearly felt. They were both deep in thought, Ann clearly troubled. Billy's heart reached out to her, he had asked a great deal of her. A short distance down Wharf Road, they found the Blue Boat Hotel that was able to offer them a room for one or two nights.

"Mr and Mrs Brown, is it?" said Milner, the publican as he swung the register round for a signature. Billy signed it where indicated without reply. Their room was at the back of the hotel, and they were not disturbed. Billy gently began to speak,

"We need to put more miles between my family and the two of us", he explained. He mentioned Yorkshire and a new life they could build together; how they could take this chance and make a go of it. Ann was not replying, and soon her shoulders were shaking. Billy embraced her and pulled her close, her warm tears through his shirt. He encouraged her to lie down and she slept soundly – probably exhausted. He got to thinking of their next move, the northern rail line through Grantham – goes to Doncaster via Retford, skirting the edge of Sherwood Forest as it plunges towards Yorkshire – away from Melton.

He did not know when it fixed in his mind to seek that revenge – the revenge he had sailed round the world for. The idea grew as Ann slept. It would be relatively easy to get to the Melton area from Grantham – passing through Waltham and Thorpe Arnold to the Toll Gate. Billy was still turning these ideas over and over in his mind as he ordered a light supper for them both. When Ann roused a little, he carefully offered her a drink, and she wakened further to enjoy a bite to eat. Beneath the honey coloured moon, the dog fox licks and grooms the vixen; Billy told Ann how much he loved her. Again, Billy spoke of the need to go north – something she seemed to have accepted. Then, curse it, he told her he

151

had unfinished business in Melton. The look on her face told him she did not understand this – it seemed to frighten her. He decided to leave the subject. They retired to bed.

Wednesday morning was warm and sunny. They did not take advantage of it – ordered a breakfast for their room. Cosy that way, and out of the gaze of nosey parkers! Ann straightway wanted to know what the 'unfinished business' was about. Of course, Billy could not tell her straight. He simply said he had a score to settle from the time of the trial, and with one of the witnesses – truthfully it was the chairman of the jurors, Woodcock. Ann, bless her, was puzzled. On the one hand, she recognised the need to travel north away from trouble with the family. On the other, here was Billy talking of a different sort of trouble that would keep them both in Grantham for a few days until it was sorted. His mumbling made her cross, but she could see he was determined. To their surprise, most of the morning was gone. They decided to walk out to the canal and perhaps find some lunch near the towpath. Out for a stroll, the couple looked further down Wharf Road and found the canal basin with a couple of day boats only. This was perhaps the happiest moment in their lives.

"Mr and Mrs Brown – sounds lovely, Ann".

"Don't forget, Billy – I'm already 'Mrs Brown'".

"I haven't forgotten", he replied bitterly.

There was one boatman in sight, seated and puffing at a pipe. Billy and Ann approached him.

"Good day, Boatman! Are you busy?"

"No, things are pretty quiet – as you can see!"

Billy pulled out his favourite pipe, looked questioningly at Ann, found approval and sat down with the Boatman. Ann wandered off a little way, watching the water.

"Why are things so quiet?" Billy got a light from the old man and tamped down the bit o' baccy with the handsome stopper he had brought from Van Diemans Land. They began to gossip.

"It's the railways that 'ave done it".

"Has the rail company bought the canal then?"

"Aye, acquired the canals and replaced 'em with railway. Took a lot of men off the land as well, promising higher wages".

"That's a mighty big change, isn't it?"

"Whether 'tis for good or ill, only time will tell".

Boatman Robinson knocked his pipe on an edge and made to return to work. Billy thanked him. Indeed, they both enjoyed the gossip. Ann drew alongside and smiled. Heavenly smile, thought Billy. Billy and Ann walked on.

"I could 'ave been back at Campbell Town. I used to sit on the verandah with old George and smoke. That's where I got this pipe stopper".

Ann handled the warm bowl of the pipe, admired the markings on the stopper, and then handed them back carefully.

A bright June day, the water plashing against the canal edge as barges glided by, pulled by magnificent horses on long harnesses. Ann seemed happy. After the conversation with Boatman Robinson, they noticed all the signboards now bore the name of a railway company. They lunched at a wayside inn, bread, pork pie and beer. Their chatter did not include the burning questions. Neither were they referred to in the afternoon as they enjoyed each other's company, once more in their hotel room. It was the act of throwing off their coats that aroused something in their minds.

Ann moved forward and began to pick at the belt around his middle. Billy stood and let her. She fumbled with the buttons on the fly, then, as his swelling piece appeared she fell to her knees and buried her face in his groin. Straightway he felt the immense pleasure of her warm mouth around his cock. He leaned forward to remove her cotton top, tearing at it in his ecstasy. They moved to the bed shedding more clothing. Billy was atop of Ann, finding her firm breasts in his palms, crushing her warm lips with his. His damp, erect cock slid easily into her loins and excitement grew. His thrusts were strong and deep.

Ann looked deep into his eyes, softly whispering his name, "Will".

The rush began and he groaned her name with pleasure; "Ann".

They were both oblivious with the stolen liquid emotions of the moment. In an instant, the calm appeared and they lay panting. They lay still in each other's arms for a long time.

Over a light supper Billy felt compelled to say again that the business over at Melton was important, but he recognised the need to go north very soon. For a moment, Ann had the look of immolation and he almost choked for fear of loosing her. Ann put her fingers to his lips, gently, firmly,

"Surely", she said, "the business at Melton can wait?"

Reason might say it could. But by now, he was unreason personified. He concurred, knowing full well that the Melton business could not wait. They slept, both of them fitful, fighting the demons until exhausted.

Surprisingly, they ate a hearty breakfast. Ann tucked into her bacon and eggs with relish. She may have thought it would sustain her on the journey north. Billy knew it would sustain his purposes.

"That is lovely," she said as she pushed her plate away from her. "Thanks, Will, that'll keep me settled".

"I'm not sure where we shall have some dinner," replied Billy, keeping his eyes lowered. Ann immediately sensed that Billy had a lot on his mind. The short walk to the station was made in quiet chitchat, Ann nudging Will's arm.

"Where to, then Will? North you said".

"It's right to go north. We can make a new start in Yorkshire", he repeated.

"It might be right, Will", she hesitated and looked him straight in the eye, "but that doesn't mean you're going to do it, does it?"

Billy blustered a little without commitment, and as he bought two tickets for Doncaster, Ann visibly relaxed. The train was at ten, about twenty minutes to wait. It was a fine morning, so they walked along the platform and found an empty bench. Billy sat down and pulled Ann close to him, taking her hand,

"I've got unfinished business in Melton, Ann, and I must spend a little time bringing it to a conclusion", Billy explained. He confessed as a penitent, but Ann clearly did not trust those *hollow and deceptive* words. She knew she could never trust him to do the right thing. Nevertheless, Billy was insistent,

"I can get off at the first stop, Retford I think, and from there get easily to Melton".

"Ann broke her own silence and insisted,

"I shall leave the train with you", her voice faltering, "I shall go to my brother George. It'll be over Will".

The words seared Billy's heart and his brain, as the train thundered in, mirroring his turmoil. A guard helped Ann with her luggage – one case. The guard offered Billy an arm but this Billy spurned. He was still stumbling through the enormity of Ann's decision, so that by that time the two of them were close to blubbing. They must have made a sorry sight. Indeed, there was one gentleman in the carriage compartment who looked at them and hurriedly vacated to another. So they had the seats to

Death By Peppermint

themselves. Billy sat beside her, but straightway moved to the seat opposite to be able to look at her face.

"I could collect you at George's", he said, fighting to keep the links with her family open.

"No, Will, I've told you it's over if you go to Melton to do this thing".

"I love you", he interrupted, and quick as a flash she said,

"You've a funny way of showing it".

"Look, you mean the world to me, and when I've finished the job at Melton, I want to carry you off and spend the rest of my life with you".

"It's no use, Will. When you go off, it will be the end of us. How often must I say this? Will, it is the end".

The train rattled into Retford station, its wheels crushing his hopes beneath their iron. They got off, with Ann grim faced and striding, *as iron sharpens iron,* towards the exit. Billy followed, his mind racing, with revenge to the fore and the culmination of all his efforts so far. He approached the exit in a sheepish manner, and offered the tickets to the gatekeeper, who looked at them with surprise – they were for the full journey to Doncaster – but made no comment.

"These passengers must know what they are doing", he mused.

Billy raced on through the forecourt, mercifully empty but for Ann's clip clop. Panic was setting in; he could not convince her.

"Ann! Ann!" he pleaded.

She stopped momentarily, and he fell on his knees in front of her.

"Please Ann, please let me collect you at your brother's house".

Ann took a step back, Billy shuffled after her,

"Ann", he choked.

Ann stepped aside, and turned to him,

"Will, bye. Bye, Will", she said softly, chucking him under the chin and bending low to kiss his forehead. Billy was overcome by the familiar scent, the closeness, but Ann was moving away towards a line of carriages.

"Ann, darling!"

The carriage carried her away. It turned out of the station yard and was gone. No words were possible. His heart rose up his throat; he sobbed heavily. He had lost her. She had slipped through his fingers; warm, noble Ann – gone.

TWENTY SIX

Billy was a crumpled shape in the station yard for what seemed a long, empty time, with only a black void in his mind, but her smell lingered to torment him.

"Ann! I'm so sorry!"

He called her name in vain; he pummelled the ground with his fists. She had gone. Unreason made him lay this mess at the door of Woodcock, earned or not.

"That villain's going to pay for this!" he heard himself shout to the empty yard. There was no answer save the draughty station yard and its dust tormenting him. He stood up and dusted himself down. Slowly, he began to reason again and to dwell on his purpose – his reason for turning back to Melton to deal with his archenemy. If he needed to seek payment, this was a job he needn't rush. So he determined to return to Nottingham first and lie low for a while, to think it out. His feet were like lead as he re-entered the station.

Within the hour Billy was back in the city and he moved away from Ferguson Street, to find a hostel on, perhaps, the Derby Road – other side of town. This done, he got to exploring the busy city centre, because he had plenty of time – and thinking of time, he considered taking his watch to be repaired. The shop he thought of was Cooke's, where he lingered awhile outside. The window display was mildly interesting, with a cased grandfather clock taking a prominent position. Billy was thinking it was a nicely crafted case that used a distinctive grain of oak, which would enhance any hallway in a big house. Billy always had a liking for the big house!

His reveries, however, were suddenly and urgently assaulted by a terrific noise. He swung round to observe a coal higgler's dray veering first one way and then another, all the time throwing sacks of coal about while drifting towards the crowds in the market square. The driver had clearly lost control, and the horse in its panic was causing mayhem. Billy moved instinctively forward to try to grab the trailing traces. Even these were whipping about, but the dray had stopped and the horse was rearing up with flailing forelegs, causing many folk in the crowd to scatter in alarm. Billy managed to hold on to a rein and pulled hard. At the same time, he used the whiffling noises in his cheeks to try to calm the horse. He remembered this, because his brother Dick used the same method with his horses – and he was so much better at it than Billy. However, the horse recognised the pull and the blowing noise. Its wild eyes lit on Billy and the wild kicking immediately began to bate. Within five minutes, the horse was calm and Billy could stroke its forehead. The shaken driver was not much more than a lad. His features reminded Billy of Dick – his warm smile and questioning looks. The lad thanked him,

"Are you alright? That was a good job you did. Look how obedient the horse is now!".

"That's alright, it was nowt really".

There was a murmur in the gathered crowd of onlookers, and they began to applaud. Billy beamed with pleasure, and took his leave to walk back towards Cooke's, the watch repair shop. Billy entered the shop to be greeted as a hero,

"That was a splendid job you did to calm that horse!" said the proprietor.

"Oh, it was nothing really", he repeated.

"How may we help you, sir?"

"Could you please look at my watch? I think it may need a clean as well as a repair".

"Your watch is Australian, isn't it?" questioned Cooke, peering at him through owlish spectacles, whist turning it over in his hands.

"I believe it is," replied Billy.

"There was an inscription at the back of a kangaroo and the words "Launceston VDU""

Billy was non-commital, but knew this was the very reason that he was attracted to the watch in the first place. It was meant to be practical and not just a gewgaw. Cooke found the workings clogged up with grease – dark, viscous stuff.

"I can get it working quite quickly, now I've cleaned it."

"Thanks. It hasn't worked since I bought it."

"Well, you have a bargain here, sir, the back plate is gold."

Billy accepted the watch and paid the bill without further words and left. He had no idea that that conversation, as brief as it was, would one day condemn him to death.

In the few hours he had in Nottingham, Billy made three big decisions. Firstly, he made himself a promise – to deliver the sad news of young Richard to his family in Derbyshire. Secondly, he felt completely at ease with his mission to seek revenge – revenge he had crossed the

157

world's oceans to achieve. Thirdly, he thought he should try to patch up his quarrel with his brother John. *"What causes fights and quarrels?"*

So it came about that Billy made enquiries at the railway station for links to Derby. He found it convenient to travel one day and return the next. He had a particularly sad duty to perform. Ever since the loss of young Richard Pratt, during that fateful journey from Deptford to Van Dieman's Land, Billy had treasured the papers found in the boy's trunk. They simply stated his name and those of his parents, Lemuel and Sarah Pratt, of Parish Row, Kirk Hallam, in Derbyshire. He had no way of knowing whether the boy's parents were still alive, or whether he had brothers and sisters. Nevertheless, he felt bound to seek out the boy's family and to extend his condolences. Whatever family was there now, they probably did not know what became of Richard. Who would tell them? Billy saw himself as the messenger, and duly took the ten o'clock train that reached Derby at eleven in the morning.

Outside the station at Derby, Billy approached a rank of carriages and spoke to the first man,

"Can you take me to Kirk Hallam, please?"

"Immediately, if you so wish".

"That I do, thank you".

The carriage first crossed the St Mary's Bridge, then took the road to Chaddesden, later swinging round the grounds of Dale Abbey, reaching Kirk Hallam by midday. The driver asked a local resident for Parish Row and moved on. Billy alighted and approached an old lady sitting knitting at her door.

"Excuse me, madam, the Pratt family?"

"The Pratts?"

"Yes, are they still here?"

"Yes sir, I'm number twelve and she lives at number twenty".

"I'm obliged, madam".

Billy and the driver walked together along the row,

"She lives here?" mused Billy.

"Sounds like she's alone, sir" said the driver.

They reached number twenty and Billy walked up the tiny garden path and knocked firmly but not too sharply. There was a sound of movement within and of a bolt being drawn. An old woman in a dark cardigan opened the door. She wore a dark dress. She peered at him through strong eyeglasses.

"Yes? Do I know you?"

"Hello, madam, you don't know me, but I was a friend of your Richard's".

The old lady put her hand to her throat and gripped the door tightly,

"Of my Richard? Dear Lord, what of my Richard?"

Billy asked,

"Do you think I could come in to speak to you?"

"Of course, if you have news, come in and sit down".

Billy entered the cottage. It was neat and tidy and sepia photographs were on the dresser. Billy could see the young Richard very clearly, standing with an older man in waistcoat and trousers. That must have been his father.

"Is Mr Pratt around?"

"I've been a widow for eleven years, sir".

"Oh, I'm so sorry. He would not have heard of Richard then?"

"No, he went to his grave not knowing anything".

"Well, I'm afraid it's sad news, especially after all these years. Richard looked after the horses on the convict ship bound for Van Dieman's Land thirteen years ago. I'm afraid he was ill-used…"

Billy stopped speaking and asked Mrs Pratt if there was anyone who could come and sit with her. The old lady demurred,

"You carry on, sir, after all this time I'd rather know".

"I say he was ill-used. He was very young and there were evil men on board who preyed on him then murdered him".

"Oh Lord, murdered you say? But he was a harmless strip of a boy when he left Hose – where we used to live, where he grew up".

"I can tell you, he was a harmless boy who liked nothing better than to look after his horses".

"He was always good with animals, and yes, he was fond of horses. But you said he was murdered. Murdered, Oh my Lord", she cried using her handkerchief to stifle her mouth.

"I'm afraid he was murdered by some ruffians out to satisfy their gross lusts", Billy stood up, tears afflicting his eyes, "I'm sorry to have to bring you such news, madam".

Sarah held out her hand to Billy, who accepted it and bent down to kiss it gently. He sat down again. Sarah Pratt was agitated,

"May I offer you some tea, Mr ..er?"

"Call me Billy, please, and can I put the kettle on for you?"

"No, I wouldn't dream of it. You sit there, I won't be long".

Billy wiped his eyes and looked around the poorly furnished room. He had already noticed how neat and tidy it was, because there was good light from the rear window of the cottage; so the cottages must have an east-west aspect, he thought. Sarah returned with a tray bearing teapot, two cups and two saucers, milk jug and a sugar bowl, which she placed on the low table in front of the cold grate. She stirred the pot and replaced the knitted cosy.

"Tell me, Billy, did Richard have a proper funeral?"

"I'm not sure you can call it 'proper', you see he was cast overboard when the ship was travelling at high speed. So with no body, we asked the Chaplain to pray for him".

"Oh dear, the more you tell me, the more awful it sounds. Would he have known much about it?"

"I think not, madam, he was possibly bemused enough by his treatment that he didn't know what was happening when he was picked up and thrown overboard. He would have died instantly in the cold water", Billy stopped, as Sarah was again upset.

"I'll pour the tea, Mrs Pratt", Billy set about the cosy and poured two cups. He milked one and put two spoons of sugar in it, and settled back. Sarah recovered and milked her cup, but declined the sugar.

"So he had no Christian burial?"

"I'm afraid not, only Christian prayers spoken over him in absence so to speak. His grave is the sea", and added, "*And the sea shall give up its dead*".

The lady cried quietly into her lace, and then,

"Thank you, sir for taking the time and trouble to bring me news of my dear son. He was our only son. May God bless you for this act of kindness".

Billy finished drinking, placed the cup and saucer on the tray and stood up. Sarah stood and stepped forward to shake his hand.

"I'm pleased I visited you. It was right and proper to do, especially as I had respect and admiration for young Richard. Good day to you, madam".

"Thank you, Billy, you've settled my mind now. At last, I have news of my son and I can pray for him properly".

They walked to the door, Sarah holding Billy's arm. The carriage was waiting for him, so he climbed aboard. The driver urged the horses forward and Billy waved to the old lady standing at her door. She acknowledged him with a raised arm and then went indoors to her private grief.

The carriage drive back to Derby was achieved within the hour, so that they reached the station at two in the afternoon. After a quick enquiry within, Billy realised that there was no link to Nottingham until the morning. This meant finding a temporary berth, so he walked over to the Station Hotel where he was able to book into a single room for the night. Whilst waiting for the room to be prepared, he ordered a sandwich and a pot of tea for his late lunch. It was a light, airy room with strong sunlight flooding in. Billy settled back in his armchair feeling good with himself – a Christian duty fulfilled, *'We have only done our duty'*. He looked around, observing the comings and goings of a very busy room. The tea he had taken was a bit stronger than he was used to. He felt around his mouth with his tongue; he licked his teeth and found them furry. Catching the eye of a waiter, he ordered a Clary Water, both to aid his digestion and to refresh his mouth. Feeling much better, he judged it was time to go upstairs. He settled down with a newspaper he had brought with him, the *Melton Times*, in which he read a report with great interest. It concerned the church at Scalford – the Parish Church. Apparently, and to Billy's disgust, the Duke of Rutland had promised financial help to thoroughly restore it and to add an organ. The Duke had already paid for the rebuilding of the chancel in 1845, and this latest venture of restoration was not expected to be completed until 1859. Billy was cross,

"Well! Bogger me! 'is Grace 'as nowt better to do with 'is money!"

Billy rifled through the pages, ignoring Melton Parish news and the births, marriages and deaths entries. He did find more Scalford titbits. He learned that the Post Office in the village received letters from Melton at 7.30 in the morning, and that the post boxes were cleared by 8.45 in the morning and again at 2.45 in the afternoon, but that this arrangement only applied to weekdays. Billy was ruminating on the worthlessness of such information when an article on the development of the rail connections through the Midlands caught his eye. The railway was an absolute miracle to Billy who had been out of the country for more than a decade. He was just thinking to himself that here was an article worth reading, when there was a light 'tap-tap' on his bedroom door. He folded the newspaper and walked to the door still clutching it in his left hand.

He asked,
"Who is it?"
But there was no reply. Curious, he opened the door to find a figure standing there in the darkness of the landing.
"Billy, me' old mate, how are yer?"
The speaker stepped forward into the light thrown out by the bedroom door. Billy saw that he was dressed in a fustian jacket, but the red necktie was so recognisable that he had never forgotten it,
"It's Tommy isn't it?"
"That's right, Billy, Tommy Beattie".
Even after such a long absence, Billy remembered Tommy, one of Heathlighter's generals and a character.
"Let's go down to the bar for a beer, Tommy", said Billy, closing the bedroom door behind him. The two men parked themselves in the snug – they had this to themselves, as it was late in the evening. The beer from a local brewery was acceptable and they settled down.
"How on earth did you know I was here, Tommy?"
Tommy tapped the side of his nose conspiratorially,
"We've kept the same system in place all these years, Billy, so your movements across the Vale and into Nottingham were noticed and reported. I live in Derby, so this bit was easy!"
"Is Heathlighter still active, then? Only, he was an older man when I knew him"
"No, Heathlighter is retired, along with three or four of his gang, but his intelligence system is still in working order".
Billy noticed that Tommy had the ends of two fingers on his left hand missing, and was instantly curious,
"What happened, Tommy, your hand?" he said, pointing.
"A refill first, Billy, if you please?"
Billy arranged the refill of their tankards and Tommy took a quick couple of gulps,
"It happened about seven years ago, on a job through Waltham that went wrong. We made our escape through Scalford", Billy nodded at the mention of his home village, "and on to Holwell and the Broughtons. I'm afraid at Holwell I was unhorsed. At full stretch I grabbed for the trailing leads with my left hand, and they must have wrapped around the two fingers because they ripped the ends away. I must have rolled into a ditch, because the following riders just passed me by. I remember

nothing more except that Heathlighter managed to return to look for me. He'd given the chasers the slip at Ab Kettleby".

"That was good of him – to come and find you".

"Yes, he always looks out for his men; that's what I respect him for. He got me onto the back of his horse and rode home with me. His doctor came and dressed my hand, and it was healed and healthy in five weeks".

"It must be awkward though", mused Billy.

"Not really, I'm right-handed for most things anyway".

"It allows you to lift your glass!" Billy laughed.

"Well, Billy, it's good to have met up with you after all this time, but it's late and I have to be going".

"Alright, Tommy thanks for your company. I was so surprised!"

Tommy rose and made towards the door. Billy walked to the door himself and they shook hands and bid each other 'goodnight'. Billy thanked the landlord at the bar,

"I'm obliged, sir, sorry if it was late".

"No problem at all, I'll lock up now though".

The landlord locked and bolted the front door, and turned back to Billy,

"You'll be leaving tomorrow, sir?"

"Yes, landlord. I have a train at ten in the morning".

"You'll settle up then in the morning?"

"Yes, if that's alright?"

"It'll be fine, sir".

The two men retired and unseen hands extinguished the lamps in the bar. Billy was tired, but he was uneasy, thinking of the visit of Tommy Beattie, and the intelligence gathering that went on even then throughout the East Midlands. His mind turned over the embers of their meeting, repeating the images on his brain *ad infinitum*. At last, Billy was exhausted, and he fell into a light sleep that soon developed into a deep slumber.

TWENTY SEVEN

It was a bright morning, and Billy settled his bill after breakfast and left in ample time for his train. He was in a surprisingly good humour. Billy thought of his visit to Sarah Pratt the day before and again smiled with pleasure at a mission accomplished. He thought of the surprise visit from Tommy Beattie. He thought also, as he walked to the railway station, of his promise to try to settle his differences with his brother, John and his father. Billy purchased a ticket for Leicester, and was directed to the correct platform. Within a few minutes, the engine steamed in, pulling five carriages. Ten minutes later, it pulled away under full steam and whistled as it emerged from the station. It was an enjoyable ride, in full sunshine, that lulled him into a false sense of well-being. He pulled down the window of the carriage, and leant out so that his hair was blown by the strong wind. The occasional coal smut spoiled this interlude, so he withdrew and closed up the window. If he was to heal the rift between himself, his brother John, and their father, Jack, then he was to garner all his strength of character. So, he still felt good as he arrived at Leicester station, and it was only a few roads walk to Bedford Street. Billy took a deep breath, checked his appearance, brushed himself down and knocked at the door. His Dad opened the door to him, and it was immediately obvious that he was shocked. His reception showed Billy that his father was in a right strop with him. His Dad's tone was biting,

"You're playing with fire, son! You've come between a man and his missus, and mark my word; only ill shall come of it. Your Mam would have taken her tongue to you!" He raised an arm in Billy's direction, "John's a stricken man. Where's Ann now, not with her husband, that's for sure! And it's your doing!"

Billy countered this intended blow as vigorously as he could, but the barb about his Mam cut him up something rotten. He sobbed,

"I miss her so".

Billy was upset – indeed, in a blind rage. He began to back into the street and John, who was by now trembling, followed him. Billy raised his pistol and found John in his sights,

"I'll protect my sister, and this is loaded. God strike me dead if I wouldn't shoot the first man dead that meddled with her!"

This was Billy's quick anger and bitterness shining through; John stood transfixed. Billy strutted two paces forward and shook the pistol, then backed away again. His brother still stood trembling. A neighbour from three doors away was standing on his doorstep, leering at this fraternal spat. Billy noticed the neighbour, so his display was directed to him and his brother; both to frighten and to threaten his brother, but also to impress the neighbour. In both respects, Billy succeeded, as the neighbour disappeared inside very quickly, and John reacted badly to the jibe and began to shake.

Their father, Jack, appeared in the doorway and immediately exerted his authority by his calmer composure. He told them,

"Hey! Come in, both of you. Get off this street!"

Jack abhorred any kind of public exhibition, and he held the door for them, gesturing that they must enter. The two brothers obeyed their father without question, despite the highly charged atmosphere. Once inside, Billy was again much affected and he began to shake himself with pent up emotion. His father stepped inside, having carefully closed the door behind him. Seeing Billy so affected, he enfolded him in his arms, the very arms that previously had been raised to strike him. The two were close, warm; hearts beating as one, in a loving embrace. It was this sight that greeted John as he returned from the kitchen where he had gone to wipe his face. John was not the same strong character as his brother, remember he shakes. *"Mountains shake!"* Visibly moved himself, he hugged them both, forever preferring harmony to strife.

With some difficulty, John attempted reconciliation,

"It's alright, Billy. Everything's alright now. I forgive you".

Billy heard his brother's plea whilst still in the arms of his father. He waved his hand in acknowledgement, hoping his response was not too disdainful; more the awkward feelings between two brothers. Billy stood away from his father and offered his hand to his brother – a gesture that John understood immediately, and grasped the proffered hand eagerly. Their father went to put the kettle on the fire. The tea was a welcome precursor to a meal, at which all three sat down at the table exchanging glances and smiles, but saying nothing. The silence was awkward. Billy used the silence well,

"Can I really say", he thought, "I'm in the bosom of my family?"

Answer came there none, but of one thing he could be sure; he could not tell them of his dark intentions, and what foul reasoning of revenge drove him on to his own destruction. His thoughts were cut short, as the impasse was broken. John finally let rip. He shook,

"Why Billy, why? You must know how cut up I've been!"

"I'm sorry, John. It was a foolish, selfish thing to do, and I'm sorry".

John leapt to his feet, threateningly, pointing,

"I hope you'll burn in hell for what you've done!"

Jack was on the point of intervening, when a knocking at the door interrupted matters. Jack moved to answer this summons, and opened the front door to find Mary Ann from two doors away,

"Is everything alright?" she enquired as she noticed John shaking.

Jack tried to bar her way, but Mary Ann was curious,

"What's the trouble, then?"

Mary Ann tapped John on the shoulder as though to emphasise her point, and John was offended,

"Oh dear! Don't tap me, I'm so bad!"

Mary Ann noticed Billy sitting there,

"Oh, it's you, isn't it? The family Romeo?"

Jack was hearing too much,

"That's enough, Mary Ann. You're only here to make trouble, so come on – out of it!"

"Oh Jack, I'm only trying to be a good neighbour, that's all. We all have trouble with our kids".

"Then you should be trying to sort them out, not ours", said Jack, loathe to place hands on the woman.

Mary Ann was not moved easily, she was portly and well-upholstered. She turned to John again,

"There, there me' duck, how's your wife?"

John was no match for this termagant, and his shaking increased. He sat down suddenly, thinking this would help, but the chair and table creaked. Billy could stand it no longer. He got up from his place on the small settee, and faced Mary Ann squarely, pulling the pistol from his pocket,

"You have a scold's tongue in your face, and my advice to you is to shut up!"

"Well, I never, are you threatening me?"

"You'd better leave now", said Jack, ushering her towards the door.

"He's dangerous, he is, waving that pistol about".

Billy walked over to the dresser, and placed the gun in the drawer. Mary Ann flounced out of the front door, and went immediately to gossip with the coal higgler who lived further along Bedford Street.

Mary Ann had departed at last, leaving troubled waters in her wake! John was shaking; Billy was walking up and down, supposing he was walking the plank! Their father, Jack was in his armchair wringing his hands and moaning,

"No good will come of it. No good, I tell yer".

The mantelpiece clock, in a quiet, hesitant voice struck the hour of ten. A rainstorm could now be heard beating against the windows, and Billy thought he was tired,

"I'm off to bed. Perhaps we should all try to get some sleep, it'll do us good".

Billy moved to the stairwell, and John joined him. The two brothers went upstairs; their father could be heard raking the embers of the grate, and blowing out the candles. The house quietened, and the rainstorm slackened. But the next morning it was just as bad. Jack told Billy, as he put a pan of bacon on the newly stoked fire,

"I hope you can settle matters, lad. I mean with John and Ann".

"I hope so, Dad", said Billy, watching the bacon sizzling.

John cried and shook a little,

"I do love her, y'know. I'd 'ave 'er back like a shot".

Billy coped with the toasting of bread slices and the long handled toasting fork that usually sat on a nail at the side of the hearth. It was not long before all three were tucking in to their toast and bacon. Billy sensed that the breakfast had calmed the atmosphere after the storm. The morning was bright and cheerful. *The Lord answered Job out of the storm.* Indeed, Billy washed the plates and John dried them. That done, Billy said,

"I'm going to spend the day in Melton, and might get as far as Scalford".

So it was that Billy took his leave of his Dad and John after breakfast. He walked to the city centre through St Margaret's and found a stand of carriages. He made his way back to Melton and in the Market Square got a carriage bound for his old home, Scalford. There were still some details he needed to find, such as if old man Woodcock worked alone; whether he had live-in help. He called in at the local grocery store when it was quiet, and spoke to the manager,

"I want to call on the Toll Gate keeper, Woodcock. Do you happen to know if he lives alone?"

The shopkeeper was puzzled,

"The Toll Gate? Do you mean the one at Melton?"

"Yes, I do. Do you know it?"

"Well, I've had occasion to travel along that road, but I'm afraid I don't know the Keeper's circumstances".

"No matter", said Billy, dismissing the idea calmly.

He examined the shelves of goods before leaving and quietly closing the door behind him. The village was beginning to wake up; there were a few more people about. He walked slowly up the street reading the signs of twitching curtains, or people turning away and stepping indoors rather quickly. This was of no concern, for he walked and thought things through. He crossed the street to the cobblers, where the proprietor was working on his last in the porch. Billy stood and watched the artist at work, applying his skills to a pair of fine, black boots. He was soon joined by a couple of passers-by, one of which recognised him for Scalford-born,

"You're back again, then," said the bewhiskered man.

"In trouble again are you?" enquired the other, taking his cue from the first.

Billy did not like the questions, and at first he ignored them. But a few more onlookers had gathered, and their voices began to mix with the cobbler's hammering on his last. He quickly became confused. In an effort to quell them, or impress them, or both, Billy raised his own voice, noticing the village constable out of his good eye,

"I'll not be transported for nothing next time, whatever I do, it'll be something to be talked about".

The constable made no show of having heard his comments, and quietly moved on and down Town Street. The small crowd also dispersed, so that Billy could speak to the cobbler,

"Do you know the Toll Gate at Melton?"

"Aye, I do", answered the cobbler, tersely.

"Do you happen to know the keeper and whether he lives alone?"

"The Keeper? Let me see. You mean Woodcock. Well, he's an old man and I have heard that his grandson lives with him, but I don't know how true that is".

"I'm obliged, sir. Thank you for your time".

Billy felt he had achieved something by his visit. He almost crowed with pleasure - he being so cocksure. He now felt emboldened – but was he bold enough to make his first challenge of old Woodcock?

Billy noticed a carriage waiting by *"The Plough"*, and made his way back to Leicester, only to find his Dad and John still in a foul, distressed state. Ann was still at her brother's house. By evening he needed a breath of fresh air and walked out into the street. Will, a neighbour, was out there and they chatted. Will asked Billy right out why he had run away with his brother's wife. This Billy immediately rebutted,

"I only went with her for her protection, and any man who molested her, I'd blow his brains out!"

To emphasise the point, he showed Will the pistol and said it was loaded.

Will observed,

"I see that the cap's still on".

So by this time, half the street knew Billy had returned from overseas, that he'd spent time away with Ann, and that he looked a fearsome sight when wielding a pistol. Billy had no idea then that this vivid picture would be part of his downfall, or that Will had got rather a better look at the pistol so that he remembered its dark barrel and lock. It wouldn't have mattered, except that Billy foolishly lost the pistol, in circumstances that shall be described. Remorselessly, all was falling into place. The old man had no live-in help, only a young grandson for company. Billy now had a reasonable grievance against him, though only Billy and his conscience knew the real, deeper reason why he was out to get him! Billy spent a further day with his Dad and John, then on the Friday he explained he was "going north", that he'd caused them both enough trouble and heartache, and wanted to make a fresh start, perhaps in Yorkshire. His Dad said little; John even seemed to cheer up. Billy made to leave; there was no demonstration of affection, for which he was thankful. He walked away in the direction of the Melton road. As usual, he found a carriage and driver at St Margaret's prepared to take him to Melton. Fortunately, this same cart was making for Scalford, so he had words with the fellow and he was agreeable to Billy staying on. It was evening when they arrived and he straightway booked into the *Plough Inn*.

*

In Market Overton, Leicestershire, Ann, wife of John Brown, who always trembled when stressed, was at the house of her brother, George.

"Billy is hell-bent on some feud or other", she complained.

"Yes, me' duck, and why are you not supporting 'im?"

"I would have done, George, but he could only think of revenge or something worse. If he truly loved me as he said he did, then he would have run away with me. I would have willingly gone with him. He threw the chance of happiness in my face"; she faltered, sat down sharply and sobbed. George was at once the careful brother, put his arm around her,

"Sorry, sis. I didn't mean to press you so hard. There, there me' duck".

"It's alright, George, thanks".

"So what now, sis? What about John?"

The question dug deeper still, deeper than Ann could bear, and she cried again, holding her brother's arm to her face. George bent over her and patted her shoulder. At last, he volunteered to go and put the kettle on.

"A cuppa will cheer you up, sis".

"Thanks, George".

Indeed, Ann perked up after her cup of hot tea, and was soon her old smiling self.

"It's a big question, George".

"What is, sis?"

"Whether John will have me back".

"I expect he'll waste no time in telling you".

Ann was surprised,

"Do you think so? Will he let me know?"

"Of course he will, if he's not such a fool".

*

In Bedford Street, Leicester, John trembled as he put pen to paper. He was writing to his wife, Ann, presently with her brother George, at his house in Market Overton. He loved her still. He wanted her to come home. He wrote,

"My darling Ann,

My life is empty without you. You make my life worthwhile. Please come home. If you must spend a while longer with your brother, then do so, but please – not too long. We must put the folly of the last two weeks behind us. For my part, I forgive you – I hope you will forgive me. Please come home. Write, or get George to bring me news.

I love you,
Your anxious husband,
John"

TWENTY EIGHT

Billy was in the *Plough Inn* at Scalford for the weekend. He was within striking distance of the Toll Gate House. He spent his time rehearsing his revenge in his pub room. He cleaned his pistol and checked the time on his watch. Just as he play-acted the knock on the door of the Toll Gate, he had a sudden thought. He was going to need to confirm the precise information about the Toll Gate keeper, but was not certain how to do this. He imagined there would be few in Melton that knew this man. Perhaps there was an old man in Thorpe Arnold that might know of Woodcock and the Toll Gate. It would have to be an older man, he thought; the young folk of today were all flibberty gibbets!

He smiled inwardly, 'Look at yourself Billy, it's you that are growing old!' He stretched out on the bed to look at the tarnished ceiling – a water stain in the corner indicated some problem with the roof. Billy turned his attention to the immediate problem - the fields around the Toll Gate needed to be considered, both for ease of access but also for the escape route afterwards. He could picture those on the Melton side perfectly, and was confident they could provide cover for the nighttime; they might also help his escape. Then he thought about the north side of the Toll Gate. Perhaps that would be better – say around the Doctors Lane fields. At least these would give direct access to the Vale of Belvoir, and from there to all destinations north! Billy warmed to this idea. Perhaps a chat with his old school friend, Moore the baker, might make everything clear.

On the Saturday, Billy had his breakfast and then spent time in the lounge. He worked out that the best day to make a move would be Tuesday – market day in Melton and a magnet for the farmers and their folk for miles around. It might also, he thought, be quiet around the Toll Gate. His thoughts were interrupted by the arrival of the baker's rounds man – just a slip of a lad, delivering the landlord's usual order. The clattering of the pie trays and the breadbaskets lasted a good quarter of an hour, with the boy traipsing in and out. At last, Billy heard him taking his leave of the landlord, so on his way out, Billy accosted him,

"You from Moore's of Timber Hill?"

"Aye, sir".

"Then do you think you could take a message for your master, and bring me an answer on Monday?"

"I can do that for you, sir. What's your message?"

"Ask him if it's alright for Billy Brown to have supper with him and his family on Tuesday evening".

"I'll do that, sir and bring you a reply on Monday".

The boy acknowledged the stranger, and left the pub.

Billy returned to his room for the rest of the day. Indeed, he made arrangements to eat in his room, so that he had no reason to move on the Sunday. On Monday morning at about ten a.m., Billy was sitting in the same place as on Friday, so that the baker's boy could find him without trouble. Sure enough, the lad who looked twelve years old walked in dusting himself down and clapping his hands together to disperse the flour,

"Mr Billy, sir? My master asks me to tell you that you will be welcome at the house on Tuesday evening for supper".

"I'm obliged, lad. Here's something for your trouble", and handed him a florin.

"Thanks, Mr Billy, no trouble".

The lad left; Billy was able to smell warm flour for ages. The rest of Monday was quiet; Billy wasn't bothered in his room.

Tuesday dawned bright and cheerful, but the western skies looked a little overcast; perhaps they heralded a shower or two. The village was coming to life, there were a few people beginning to stir. Wagons rattled through, followed by a herd of cows being shepherded along the way, by a pair of dogs and a young lad. There were anxious moments when the leading cow turned into the Vicarage gateway, but the young lad was equal to the task, and the dogs made short work of guiding it out onto the lane again. Billy heard the noise of happy chatter, as friends and family met for their weekly rendezvous,

"Hello, Florrie, how are you?"

"Mustn't grumble, Elsie. Cup of tea, shall we?"

There were knots of people here and there who seemed to be making up their minds whether to head for the Melton Market,

"There's a carriage at eleven for Melton, should we get that?"

"Aye, if you've change for this trip, and I'll pay on our return".

Billy watched this procession of daily and weekly business from his window seat. With the midday sun beating in, Billy had great difficulty keeping busy, going over and over the plan, such as it was. Indeed, this repetitive pattern induced heavy breathing so that Billy was soon in the middle of forty winks!

Billy's forty winks lasted about an hour. He washed in his room to refresh himself, and then, in the afternoon around four o'clock, he left the *Plough Inn*. Billy stepped into the lane, and was almost swept away as the procession of newly-bought cows were followed by a flock of newly-acquired sheep – all returning after a hectic day at Melton Market. Billy could remember the Beast market at Melton, held every Tuesday to coincide with the street market. He stood awhile and watched the skilled drovers and their dogs working the familiar streets of the village with expert eyes. As the beasts and their minders passed through, the village folk went about their business. Billy had moved only a street or two before he felt the first spits of rain. He pulled his collar up and looked for shelter.

Old Kathy's walking stick goes 'tap' 'tap' as she reached the tree at the end of the road. She pulled the little Scottie dog to her side and they both sought the shelter of the branches in the gathering shower. Old Kathy was a familiar figure in the village, especially since she was widowed by a rogue accident on the farm a couple of years earlier. Her now dead husband, John, had worked on the land for most of his sixty years – like his father before him. Of course, he had slowed down, so that when the shire horse reared up in the traces, John was not quick enough to avoid the whiplash that threw him beneath the animal where the beast trampled him to death. Old Kathy fussed with the only dog left of, perhaps, half a dozen in the past; she adjusted the walking stick to better bear her weight.

Billy saw her from afar as he walked along the lane, so ambled to the tree for shelter at the same time. He nodded in a polite address to the old lady, and she returned it with a warm smile. Billy shook off the water from his shoulders, now grateful for the shelter offered by the tree.

"Good afternoon", he said.

"Good afternoon", she replied.

"It'll blow over soon enough".

"I expect it will", she said, leaning down to settle the dog, "You from these parts?"

"I'm from Frisby, but I was born in Scalford, so I've been looking up old friends".

"I know you!" she peered at him closely, "You're one of Peppermint Jack's boys".

"No, madam, you're mistaken; never heard of him. My name's Smith, William Smith".

"You're no William Smith, but never mind that. Where are you off to in this?" She indicated the rain, now a heavy shower.

"I'm visiting friends in Thorpe Arnold and then paying my respects to the Tollgate keeper at the bottom of the hill".

Old Kathy laughed,

"Respects? Is that what you call it? To old man Woodcock?" She cackled, "At the bottom of the hill?"

"You know him, then?" enquired Billy.

"Know him? He was bailiff for years and my husband had a run in with him often. He was a stubborn bogger, and he's a man who still does not understand the meaning of fair".

Billy did not need her life history, or her husband's, so he observed,

"It's clearing up now. I'll make a move, take care of yourself and good day!"

He didn't understand what Old Kathy chuntered on about then. She was still cursing and waving her stick as he descended into a hollow of the hill that led down to Thorpe.

The cross-country walk to Thorpe Arnold was easy enough in the warm sunshine that took a firm hold and even began to turn the standing water into steam. He felt strangely calm as the wispy warm ringlets rose up and were swept away in the breeze. When he thought of the happenings on the other side of the world, and especially what befell poor Bob; he found it difficult to believe how calm he was! When he reached the Grantham Road, he turned towards the cottages on the Thorpe side of the Toll Gate – there being only two hundred yards between them. As he walked towards them, the old man Joseph passed him by but didn't recognise him after all this time. It was his house Billy made to enter, quiet, silent but for the heavy ticking of a clock on the mantelpiece. The old'un virtually followed him in.

"Where are you from? he said, What's your name?"

Billy told him straight he was from Scalford and his name was Brown. Immediately he began to talk in a general way about Woodcock at the Toll Gate, fishing for some information.

"Does he live by himself, then?"

He replied,

"No, hardly," and ushered Billy into the garden. Billy had a look in another of his windows, then nodded his farewell and began to walk towards the Toll Gate.

He'd rehearsed what he would say. He found his hands trembling as he approached. He had watched others do the same, reaching the gate and shouting to the old man,

"Gate!"

This time, on foot, no wagon waiting, he shouted,

"Gate!" and the old man appeared and looked at him closely.

"Water? Can I have a drink of water?"

His reaction was instant,

"Be off with you, you'll get no water here!"

His roughness seemed to Billy to be typical of the Woodcocks. This man's son or nephew, in Van Diemans Land, administered roughness. The old man was a snot-pot and he told him so to his face. He turned away,

"Bah!" he scorned.

This frosty attitude sealed the man's fate. This would be the last time that Billy was spurned by a Woodcock. The noise had brought the young boy to the door as well – Billy reckoned him to be about nine, maybe ten. Feeling mildly angry, he walked quickly on. In the fields close by, a fellow was working – so he wandered over to him.

He was the first to speak,

"What do you want?" he enquired.

Billy dissembled that he was from London, come to see acquaintances in Melton on Timber Hill, but spent an hour or two with old man Woodcock at the Toll Gate. Billy told the fellow that Woodcock had reckoned he had neither wife nor housekeeper. He was fishing again for information. Sure enough, the fellow confirmed that only the little boy lived there with Woodcock.

"It's a lonely place," Billy said suggestively, "a dangerous place on your own. If I had not a wife, I should have a housekeeper for company like."

Billy asked the fellow if Woodcock went to bed or sat up all night.

He considered this, then replied,

"I don't know, but if anyone went to the Gate, he'd have to get up to let them through."

The fellow made to move off towards Melton, so Billy accompanied him, making more observations of this, that and the other. He told him that there were many people about on the Thorpe Road, as was usual on a market day. The fellow agreed politely, so Billy told him he was a clock and watchmaker from London. He repeated his own opinion that old man Woodcock must be very lonely at the Toll Gate house, before turning away in the direction of Timber Hill, first crossing the Longate Lane and then the Scalford Brook. He stopped to look at the Corn Hill mill, with its sails revolving majestically in the gathering dusk. The heady smell of new made flour clung to everything around. All was reflected in the waters of the brook, giving an eerie darkened image, as though its walls were dressed about with black tourmaline. Was this a sign? Did some Great Hand make a signal? It was with some foreboding that Billy walked on along to Timber Hill and found the home of his friend William Moore, the baker. It was late evening when they sat down to a supper of hand-raised pork pie, with a delicate crust of new pastry fresh from William's own ovens. They jawed about their almost forgotten schooldays in Scalford. They both laughed when Billy mentioned Old Kathy whom he had left chuntering to herself that afternoon. She was well known to William Moore. It was a jolly occasion, considering the sober work Billy had to do anon. He chatted to William's wife Frances, and made a fuss with the young baby, Tom. He chatted with the servant. Billy was not used to being waited upon, or to using a man as some sort of inferior. To be fair, Moore didn't seem to use him as a lackey. All was jovial, and Billy left late between ten and eleven of the clock.

Billy slipped down to the Sage Cross and worked his way along Sherrard Street towards the market place – now quiet, swept clean after that day's melee. A large house loomed on his right with railings right down to the footpath. You know his liking for big houses; never lost it. He was the only figure moving as far as he could see. A side gate was ajar. Despite his shuffle, Billy moved quietly and crept through the brick arched gateway adjoining the house. There were a few elegant lime trees in the gardens. But what he had just entered was, he realised, the kitchen garden. It felt sheltered and comfortable. He was fortunate to find sacking in the lea of the walls. Before long he was drowsy. A sudden noise stirred him, until he realised it was only a cat rattling a bucket as it jumped – as surprised to see Billy. Now his mind was racing. His thoughts focused on the image of a woman, Ann, his brother's wife.

Desire welled up, warmer than any fire. A choking spasm he half stifled. The thought of warm, noble Ann caught him by the throat and shook him. He listened intently, but no other soul stirred. Blessed sleep settled down with him. *"He grants sleep to those he loves"*.

Billy woke early. The garden was silent in the burgeoning dawn. Diamonds of dew bedecked the spiders' webs all around him as the sun rose. The detail in the garden wall became clear. A craftsman bricklayer had made them, no doubt. The walls of the garden had hollow channels and were beset by fires in the autumn to afford a bland and protected area for green vegetables and soft fruit. That summer, it was offering similar protection for a vagrant such as himself. He was suddenly alert. Was that a light lit within? Was the big house stirring? He thought it prudent to move on, so he shuffled cautiously towards the kitchen door and slipped out another gate and headed for Moore's on Timber Hill. A wash and a breakfast later, Moore and his servant and Billy walked off to his fields alongside Doctors Lane. The servant – his name was Harry – was a likeable fellow and a willing worker. Harry and Billy set to as Moore directed, to clean out a ditch. Summer weeds were choking the rain gullies, but their hard work made a big difference. Billy had learned to work hard overseas, where the convicts had to make an effort or get lashed for it. That morning, Harry and Billy set up quite a rhythm and worked well together during the morning. Billy shared his opinion of old Woodcock with Will, called him a snot-pot for not giving him water as he needed. But, as much as Billy bent down to clear the ditch, he kept an eye on a rough looking hovel on the side of Moore's field, near the gate. He was thinking that it lay within striking distance of the Toll Gate – say two hundred yards or so. It could suit his purpose very well, he thought. So, after some dinner at Moore's, Billy bid him farewell and thanked him. Billy returned to his field later in the afternoon. As he walked along Doctors Lane he passed a workman by. Billy thought the workman took little notice of him, but was corrected later. Soon, he settled for the coming night within the hovel. Just two interruptions, the first quite early in the evening. Billy froze stock still as a black cocker spaniel surprised him in the doorway of the hovel. The animal greeted him with a slobbering wet lick. In a wild moment of joy, he believed it to be Jock, returned from the afterworld of all canines, but then he heard a voice,

"Acre, here boy, here!"

The dog lifted its head and sniffed. It was obedient; it bid a sort of farewell, barked once and went bounding off to his mistress. Old Kathy made a fuss of him, played with his woolly ears. She had no idea that Acre had found a human being, let alone that wild lad of Peppermint Jack's.

In the hovel, Billy sighed in relief. The dog had not been the cause of his discovery. The second interruption came just as he was getting his shoes off – an old bloke burst in to demand what he was doing there.

"I'm resting", Billy replied.

"Oh, so you'll lodge here tonight, will you?" he offered.

"No, I shan't; would if I was drunk, but not tonight".

Billy's reply seemed to satisfy him and he left. Billy settled down, checked his pistol again, that it be loaded and his knife sharp. He slept fitfully, mindful of the time. He dozed; he smiled, thinking of those pleasant romps with Jock, the black cocker spaniel, over the Thorpe Hills. The Thorpe Hills? They were just over the way, he realised. The pictures in his mind tumbled over, just as Jock did in the bales of hay. Billy was warm and happy. He knew when it was ten, and something started to niggle at his mind. The picture of Jock being led by the rifle-toting Jack and into the barn, poked Billy into half sleep, troubled him and he tossed about, inwardly and silently angry. He thought he heard the bells of Melton.

TWENTY NINE

As the bells of Melton indicated eleven in the evening, Billy was already asleep in the hovel. The day ahead was the culmination of all his struggles with the Woodcock family. His body was at rest, but his mind was still working; still providing visions of the most important people in his short life. He had lost all three of them; his dear Mam – now with her Maker, his dear Ann – gone to ground at her brother's house, and Bob, his staunchest friend – murdered in a desperate struggle with the crazed albino lackey of the Woodcocks'. Memories of the happiness he had, and lost, again disturbed his sleep; then he wrestled in the grip of a clammy nightmare. Billy thought he heard the banshee cry; that witches rode his sweaty brow. It lasted for seconds, Billy might have said for an hour He turned and pulled his coat over him. The warmth and close smells of earth encouraged him to sleep. He didn't hear the midnight bells, or the hooting of the hunting owl. All was quiet, as Billy dreamt again. He fought the phantoms of his young life, the rides with Jim and young Dick, the bailiff's men giving chase. His brow was beaded as he sweated through the fights on board ship, the clash of the *Montagues* and *Capulets*. His lips formed a silent smile as he remembered Ann, noble Ann, the quiet times they had together, the laughter. Billy saw a curious figure in his sleep, that crept towards him, looking this way and that, then raised a bell and prepared to ring it.

One single bell rang across the fields, grazed the damp grass and reached the hovel. Billy was awake and aware that he was but a short spell of time from his destiny. A fox, confident of his own destiny, loped past, its tongue lazily lolling to his left. It was surprised to see Billy, but did not check its pace. Reynard had the scent of chickens. The bell's sonorous tone was ebbing away as Billy stirred, rubbed down his aching limbs, checked his weapons and rehearsed more than once the sequence of his attack. He was fully alert as he set off to follow the short path that led to the Toll Gate House. As quickly and decisively as Reynard, Billy could see the tangle of damaged feathers strewn around the entrance to a covert to his left. Reynard had his prize. Billy was about to find his. He had his scent; his purpose was firm. It was not that he was *raised for this very purpose*; the feud that had damaged his family and his own life was now close to its terrible settlement. This fight, after all, was for Bob and for himself – this man snatched Billy from his family and sent him around the world to the other side. This man presided over their ejection from Scalford; he organised the sundering of Billy's links with Leicestershire, and harried him with evil minions wherever he travelled. These thoughts provided Billy with an armour of justification that encouraged him to think,

"Tonight, *it is mine to avenge!*"

His mood was black as he stepped on to the silvery road; he intended to act quickly and decisively. He made the best shift that he could, practising the leg swing that dear old George had taught him in Van Dieman's Land, and soon the house and gate loomed through the pungent darkness. As he walked, his memories flooded in as though to divert him from his purpose. He remembered Bob's wise counsel,

"Be alert, and be careful". Old George, the storyteller, and his *"Simba, bwana!"* spoke now to Billy as clear as if Old George himself were present. Billy stopped and listened; noticed the Reynard bark and an answering bark, the only sounds in the oasis of the Toll Gate House. The unlit windows gleamed as though the house was alive and watching him. The gate creaked even though it was closed. The door was in shadow, waiting demurely for a knock. In the dead of night, Billy knocked at the door and shouted,

"Gate!"

There was the distant noise of someone stirring and then the sharp withdrawal of the bolts top and bottom. There was the creaking of the hinges and the heavy breathing of the gatekeeper. As the old man opened the house door, Billy surprised him and pushed him back inside, brandishing his pistol in a threatening manoeuvre. He splayed his fist across the old man's chest, raising the muzzle and fired twice in quick succession. The gatekeeper staggered back but did not fall. Imagine Billy's amazement when the bullets failed to stop the old man. On the contrary, the old fella seemed galvanised into action; drawing strength from God knows where, he grappled with Billy.In the ensuing struggle, Billy was so caught up with controlling the old man; he failed to notice that he had dropped his pistol. Old Woodcock momentarily let fall his arms, suddenly winded by his exertions. Billy's hand was suddenly free; he seized the opportunity to draw out his knife and slashed at the old man's ear.

"Your son's dead, old man!" he gloated as he drew the blade across his cheek and down to his chin. Woodcock was clearly shocked; his old eyes blazed at Billy, his face reddened and his demeanour grew furious. Billy's blade played with his nose and baldhead. Locked together in a deadly embrace, they stumbled wildly around the room. Crashing into table, then the chair, Billy expected his foe to fall. Fall! Why don't you? Suddenly Billy's arm was slashing at the man's neck as though one was felling an ox.

As *"the thief comes only to steal and kill"*, Billy was no thief. This man represented his personal plague – his family had mocked and taunted Billy around the world. This was his dark revenge. Billy's arm dropped and he drove the knife in firmly and sharply, straight to the gatekeeper's manhood. Now he stumbled and began to fall, scraping his forehead on the point of Billy's blade as he did so. He coughed blood and spittle. The ox finally collapsed, and died.

Billy thought the house was deathly silent – but no! He heard the unmistakeable sounds of whimpering, and suddenly remembered the young boy who kept the old fella company, his grandson. The boy was in the bedroom and already his voice betrayed rising alarm. He must be silenced - even though the gatehouse was fairly isolated on the Thorpe Road – but any passing traveller might hear. Billy threw open the bedroom door; was greeted with the warm smell of blanket and pee. The boy was sitting up in the bed, already wet through by anxiety. The boy trembled as he tried to shield himself with his counterpane. Billy avoided the piteous eyes and the innocent mouth. He raised the blade in his right hand up to his left and swiftly, but silently, brought it slashing down upon the boy's trembling neck. He gurgled as he slumped across the reddening bedclothes. Billy's rage was not quite satisfied; he stabbed at the boy's loins and scraped the knife across his stomach. He was already dead. Let *"the dogs come and lick his sores"*. Billy did not notice that he had also dropped the pipe stopper. The house was now quiet. Could anyone have heard this commotion? Billy looked around, saw nothing but redness. It was a house of blood – blood everywhere, the redness of anger.

Billy's mind raced, the actual finish of his feud with old Woodcock shocked him by its ferocity. That he had to kill the boy saddened him greatly. He told himself, this was no time for tears. He rallied and felt the urge to open his lungs and defiantly bayed, as does the dog fox in triumph. His yell echoed around the house of death. He told Bob, wherever his ghost might be, that his death was avenged. Amongst all the jumbled ideas he had, the need to escape this carnage pressed in urgently upon his mind.

THIRTY

Billy sat among the scattered and bloody debris of the Toll Gate House. He held his head, downcast, in his bloody hands. His achievement was horrific, but triumphant. The enemy, that tried to reach him across the world, was dead. Billy cared not a jot for him. What did grieve him sorely was the death of the young boy in the bedroom. This thought brought him to tears, if only for a few minutes that stretched out, feeling much longer. Billy was shaking with emotion when he at last realised the urgency of his departure. His movements then were almost automatic.

He changed his appearance with fresh clothes, the dark trousers and a brown cloth coat, and he left the house of death.

All was darkness beneath a weak moon as he, in common with the hunting fox, set his mask for the hamlet of Clawson, cutting across the fields. But as he hastened, he felt his coat lighter than it should have been. He knew what was wrong! Where was the pistol? It was not there; he must have dropped it in the house. He could not return to that horrific scene. He must press on. He was late. It was after five in the morning, and it began to rain – just a drizzle. He reached sleepy Scalford village along the lane, where he got rid of the cord trousers, the waistcoat, a shirt and a hat, all stained with blood; so he cut them up and threw them in the ditch. His pace quickened along the back lane to the stout Stathern windmill, where the drizzle had stopped. A workman walking towards him said,

"Good morning", so Billy asked him if it looked likely to rain.

He pulled his hat down and his coat closer and carried on towards the village of Stathern, and on through another two miles or so to Harby. The time now was about six in the morning. Another workman walked along the road to Nottingham. Billy fell in with him and asked how far to Nottingham.

He answered,

"About fourteen miles. Are you going to Nottingham?"

Billy told him he didn't think so. He turned off towards a farm and Billy followed the Nottingham Road to Cropwell Bishop. It was nine o'clock and he found *The Wheatsheaf* - an inn by the side of the road and called the landlord to see if he could have a pint of ale at the door. He answered very kindly,

"Why don't you come inside and rest awhile?"

Death By Peppermint

The pint of ale was satisfactory and Billy thanked the landlord.

After about half an hour, Billy emerged into the road in time to see the postman on his rounds just knocking on a door. He watched for a moment and saw the man answer the knocking. Within a few moments a lad appeared at the entry leading a horse; he accepted a note from the postman and mounted up and cantered off down the road. Billy saw the horse break into a gallop as it reached the edge of the village. Billy thought no more of this incident and left in the opposite direction, again heading for Nottingham, and soon met a labourer with a lad that looked like his son, obviously – from their clothes – on their way to work at the brick and plaster works. Billy told them he'd had nothing to eat that morning, and they offered him bread and cheese. It tasted wonderful. Billy was spinning a yarn now,

" I had a gold ring on every finger and a gold watch, but I had to sell the lot for something to eat. Would you buy my clothes in exchange for the your frock coat?"

But the man would have none of it, especially as the frockcoat in question was daubed with plaster and smeared with brick dust. Billy lingered a little while at the roving bridge, before he asked the way to Nottingham and set off.

*

In Market Overton, Ann, wife of John Brown, who always trembled at times of stress, had packed her bags. She was preparing to leave her brother George's house. Her husband had sent her a note to say she was welcome in his house, just as soon as she was ready to return.

She was ready. The carriage arrived. Brother and sister embraced and Ann climbed aboard. With a cheery wave, she was gone – returning happily to her husband.

By late afternoon, Ann was arriving at Bedford Street where her husband and father in law lived. It was a quiet street, with few people walking about. There were some silent witnesses to the return of this errant wife. One in particular, Mary Ann, lived only two doors away, and she was already twitching her curtains. She had a grandstand view as John stepped out of his house to greet Ann. He trembled as he bent to kiss her extended hand.

"You're very welcome, Ann".

"Thank you, John".

He helped her with her luggage, and led her into the house. His father was standing in the kitchen where the last rays of a strong sun were sinking into the evening. He heard John and Ann coming to the front door, so he emerged to meet them. He greeted Ann with a smile and an embrace.

"Come in, luv, and sit yourself down".

"Thank you".

Ann was mightily relieved at this warm welcome. She took off her coat, and John took it to hang by the door, then found an armchair and sank into its welcoming lap. John and his father sat down and all seemed well. But it was not a normal afternoon; it was not every day that a wayward wife was welcomed back into the bosom of her family. John was the first to speak,

"I missed you, Ann. It was a difficult time".

"I know John, I'm sorry it was difficult – silly me, I know it was difficult for you".

"Do you feel settled now, more settled than you were?"

"Of course, John. Thanks for your note – that was sweet of you. I realised then that I do love you, and I've got over my light-headedness".

"Light-headedness! Is that what you called it?" John's father exploded.

"Leave it, Father, please leave it!" said John, agitated.

"Was it light-headed to hurt your husband so?"

It was at this critical moment that their neighbour saw fit to interrupt. Mary Ann, from two doors away, could contain her interest no longer. She was rapping on the front door.

Jack opened the front door roughly; he was still angry. Mary Ann was in full sail. Solicitously, she pushed in,

"Oh Jack! Whatever's the matter, me' duck?"

She needed no reply, as she floated into the sitting room to confront the trembling husband and his wife. She assessed the situation in seconds,

"You've returned then?"

Ann said nothing but looked away.

"Are you having her back", Mary Ann addressed John.

Jack, more composed, was now in the room, but Mary Ann was standing arms akimbo, so that he could not reach his favourite chair by the fire. John was trembling, but valiantly tried to reply,

"Leave my wife alone! You're pushing your nose into matters that do not concern you!"

"Alone! Your wife is never alone. She's always got a man in tow", said Mary Ann with broadside guns blazing.

Jack was aghast at this jibe,

"C'mon Mary Ann, out of it. You're not wanted here, if you're going to stir up more trouble".

Jack's anger gave him the strength to grab Mary Ann's arm to pull her round,

"Will you leave, or do I have to turn nasty?"

"But Jack, you know I'm only trying to be a good neighbour. Are you really going to accept this trollop back into your family?"

"Out, y'bogger, get out of it now!"

Jack pulled Mary Ann towards the door; John moved quickly forward to lend a hand, so that between them they expelled this man-of-war into the street. Mary Ann set her jib and sailed off into the sunset.

John slammed the door shut and leaned back against the coats hanging there. Jack stood puffing. Their eyes met, and the next second they were in an embrace, and Jack began to laugh uncontrollably. The house was filled with merriment, as the three of them dealt with this crisis with fun.

"She's a sight, when she gets going!" said Jack.

"She's got a mouth on her as big as the southern ocean", said John.

"You've never seen the southern ocean", said Jack, and there was another round of merriment.

"But I've read about it", complained John, sitting down beside Ann.

Ann took John's still trembling hands in hers, and spoke,

"John, dear, there's something I must say".

John was at once attentive, while Jack excused himself,

"I'll go and put the kettle on. We all need a good cup of char".

Ann continued,

"Your brother bowled me over, what with him being a world travelled man with flattering talk. I'm sorry it was difficult for you, but it quickly became difficult for me. Billy had only one thing on his mind – his revenge. I thought I loved him", Ann caught her breath, and John squeezed her hand encouragingly, "but I loved a phantom, not a man. I..."

John put his finger to her lips and hugged her,

"It's alright, gel. I understand. You're home and that's all that matters now".

Jack returned to the sitting room with a tray of cups, saucers, and milk jug and sugar bowl. He placed it on the table,

"I'll just go and fetch the pot".

They drank their tea quietly. Jack was settled in his favourite chair by the fire.

*

The streets of Nottingham were very familiar, very busy; Billy made his way up into the centre of the city. He passed a wheelwright's and a blacksmith where the heat and flames occasionally spewed forth into the thoroughfare. He skirted around the ever-present audience of local children. He found himself opposite a carpenter's shop, and the sweet smell of new turned wood was obvious. Billy had a sudden thought and slapped his sides, slapped the pockets. Where was his tobacco pipe stop? - the beautiful pipe stop that was fashioned on the verandah at Flo Whittle's hostel in the growing port of Hobart. Old George had made it for him, now it was gone. Where could he have dropped it? He knew, of course. He must have dropped it during the struggle with his archenemy in the Toll Gate House. Billy resigned himself to the loss; there was no way he could go back for it. From the centre, he headed towards the Station Street area, and Ferguson Street where his sister and her husband, Joseph, occupied the old brick works. Billy stepped into the yard and was surprised how much the noise of the city was lessened within those walls. He found Elizabeth on her own,

"Billy, how lovely to see you!"

"Where's Joseph, is he in?"

"Joseph's working in the north of the city at present. He won't be back until late evening. Have you eaten, Billy, can I get you something?"

Billy was hungry, so Elizabeth found him a bite to eat, a late lunch of pork pie, salad and chips. She cooked enough for the both of them, and joined Billy adding a slice of pork pie and a little salad to her own plate. They settled at the table and began to tuck in.She stopped eating, so Billy stopped also,

"Do you want some bread and butter, Billy?"

"Oh, yes please, that would be fine".

Elizabeth efficiently and quickly sliced the loaf and buttered a couple of rounds for each of them. These were placed on the table, so that they were within easy reach. The meal was enjoyable for both brother and sister, but Elizabeth took the opportunity to study his face, his general demeanour as he ate. She knew straight off that something was wrong – something was disturbing him. She could always tell if Billy was upset, or in the wars; as when he was bullied by an older boy who pestered him, sometimes winded him with a punch in the midriff. Elizabeth remembered teaching him to stick up for himself; remembered with satisfaction that Billy then taught the bully a lesson he'd not forget in a hurry. She knew him so well, understood his feelings.

"Talk to me, Billy" she said softly, "What's wrong?"

Her question stung him, he stiffened momentarily but then his shoulders fell and he trembled with the enormity of what he had done. Elizabeth folded him in her arms, brushed his hair, and kissed his face.

"Tell me, Billy," she whispered.

"I've killed my enemy. I've travelled across the world to get him. He was the cause of my exile, and for the death of my closest, staunchest friend".

Elizabeth's eyes grew wider and wider. She put the back of her hand to her mouth in shock. She quickly understood that he had to leave, and nodded as he explained,

"I'm thinking of going north".

"Why north?" she asked.

"I have friends in Yorkshire. It's a wide, empty county where I can get 'lost'".

Billy was reassuring her. She could ask, 'What friends?' and he would be at a loss to tell her. This made the leaving hard but manageable. He stroked her hair and held her tightly before opening the door. She cried quietly and told him,

"You be careful. Do you hear?"

She thrust some cash into his hand and turned away, upset as Billy walked out across the brickyard, already wet from a brief shower, and into the street. As he reached the street, Billy noticed the postman on the opposite corner, making notes on a pad of paper. The postman put this in his sack as he noticed Billy. Billy walked on to the station.

*

In Melton Mowbray, the Inquest on the bodies of Edward Woodcock and the young James Woodcock, found that morning in the Toll Gate house on Thorpe Road, was opened with formal identifications. The evening meeting was a sad one, and brief. The evidence from the baker, Alfred Routen of Asfordby, was both harrowing and effective – how on his rounds, at three in the morning, he was on his way to Grantham, and getting no answer at the toll gate, he entered the house and found the carnage within. No other verdict was possible, murdered!

The next day, the funeral procession wound its way to the Thorpe Road cemetery, a stone's throw from the Toll Gate house itself. The cortege included the two sons of Edward Woodcock. Samuel and Helen had travelled home from Swindon, where Sam was an engineer on the railway. They had brought their three young sons with them. Philip was home from London, where he was an artist, together with Jake his friend, and another artist – a Royal Academician. The people of Melton lined the route, making their own sad vigil a poignant protest at the crime. Close by the house of death – the Toll Gate House – the cortege stopped in quiet salute to the murdered pair at the point of their living and dying. Men, horses and hounds were milling about. No red coats in evidence, no foxhounds, these were bloodhounds. Goodyer was there astride a bay mare, directing the men and hounds to follow the scent from the very door of the house, and leading towards the back lane to Scalford. The pack was about twenty strong hounds, with a dozen or so men; half of these were policemen. They drew up to attention at a signal and waited for the funeral procession to move on. As it moved down the road, the hounds received the scent from a bundle of clothing found earlier in a ditch close by the Scalford back lane. This done, the hounds were given their heads,

"Off! Off!"

and the men and riders moved away down the lane, gathering pace, hounds straining at their leashes, eager and expectant. Goodyer was equally excited – this was serious work. The killer must be found and brought to justice. Runners moved ahead to ensure the gates that were set at intervals along the back lane were open.

The hounds bayed – Lord knows what they've found!

"Could be anything", shouted his deputy.

"Bah! Bloody bloodhounds!" betraying his lack of confidence!

The men rode on, uncertain whether following fox or fugitive. Along back lane, the riders had spread out either flank of the lane. Every once in a while, riders and horses suddenly took to the air and sailed over brook, or fence, or hedge.

This procession swept up to Scalford Village and beyond into the Vale of Belvoir. At Stathern Mill, the throng was augmented by half a dozen of the horses and riders in the service of his Grace. Gossips after the event were sure his Grace was one of the riders, but this was unlikely. At Harby, the men were revived by a tot of whisky at the wayside pub before heltering, skeltering down the scarp of Belvoir near Stathern, and on towards Cropwell Bishop. A short stop there, and a line of heads above the hedgerow signified the comfort of a pee by eighteen or so men and boys. One boy in particular achieved instant recognition by peeing right over the hedge. Into the sixth hour, and men and horses were close to the outskirts of Nottingham. The bloodhounds had stopped; they were milling around. The men agreed the trail was cold. They did not know that Billy, in fact, had already caught a train at Radcliffe and headed north.

Goodyer was vehement,

"Is this it?"

"Yes sir", observed his deputy.

"So we are empty-handed – bloody bloodhounds!"

They turned their mounts towards Melton, and the hounds and keepers were left behind to await their expected transport. Goodyer had been only half convinced that the whole expedition was worthwhile, but now was grumpy and inconsolable. The scent was cold; the fox went hungry, Goodyer was hungry.

The following day, Goodyer was heartened by a telegram announcing the arrest of a man reputed to be Peppermint Billy. There was elation amongst Goodyer and his officers, but it was short-lived. The prisoner had perfect eyesight – Peppermint Billy had a definite blink, a squint that had afflicted him since birth. The prisoner with perfect eyesight was released.

THIRTY ONE

Billy settled in a corner of the carriage, trying to look inconspicuous as the train rattled on towards Nottingham, beating rhythmic and sonorous music. The familiar countryside did not interest him, and he was just beginning to doze with the gentle pattern of the iron rails, when a squat, ruddy-faced man entered the compartment and sat down opposite. Billy looked and recognised him at once, so that as the man began to utter,

"It's B ..."

"Mr Heathlighter, sir!" Billy interrupted him, a finger to his lips.

Surprised, Heathlighter smiled broadly,

"Folks'll wonder. Two strangers on a train, where have they come from, where are they going?"

Billy laughed,

"Why am I not surprised to see you?"

"I don't know, Billy, why do you think?"

"I expect it was Tommy, Tommy Beattie, with another snippet of information".

"Ah, yes. That would be the reason. Tommy is very efficient at passing on information".

Billy acknowledged this, but wanted to know how he had received information since he left the Toll Gate House,

"So, when did you know I'd be on this train?"

"I assumed you'd be on this train after you left your sister's".

"Really, who could have said?"

"Do you remember the postman at Ferguson Street, or the postman in Cropwell Bishop? And his lad haring off on his horse with a note?"

Billy's eyes widened and he blinked more rapidly as recognition of the methods used sank in,

"Tommy thinks the world of you, but you're not active any longer, are you?"

"Yes, I know Tommy is loyal and effective. I'm retired and respectable now, y'know!"

"Yes. Tommy said as much. I liked him!"

Time seemed to have treated the one-time gang leader very well.

"I'm off to see my grandchildren other side of Nottingham, how about you?"

Billy deflected the question for the time being,

"Tell me about Tommy's accident – when he lost the ends of two of his fingers".

"Oh that! Well, all I can say is that it was a freak accident. Just one of those things really".

"Yes, it was surprising. I'm going to see friends in Yorkshire".

"I remember now, I know you've been away a good number of years. Your brother, Jim, is he still away?"

"Yes, as far as I know he is".

"It was a real pity you both went away. The two of you together were as good as four of the others - really good workers".

"That's nice of you to say so".

The train was noticeably slowing down.

"This'll be my stop", said Heathlighter, as he rose to leave, "I am very happy to meet you again. I wish you well".

He took a step towards the carriage door and turned back to Billy and asked,

"Are you comfortable for travelling, do you need any cash?"

Billy was embarrassed and did not answer. Heathlighter assumed that he could do with some assistance, by looking at Billy's rather unkempt appearance, and thrust a couple of florins into his hand before leaving abruptly.

A while after, Billy reflected on the encounter with his former gang leader. Even retired, he received accurate intelligence, so it was hardly a chance meeting. Moreover, even after all these years, he was looking out for his own men, making sure they were well taken care of. Billy fingered the two florins in his pocket and reckoned Heathlighter to be an honourable man. The rattling of the iron rail increased as the train sped on towards Yorkshire. Billy dozed. The train reached Wetherby, Yorkshire, early afternoon. Billy was on a slippery slope. He had followed his instincts and travelled north. By this time the story of the murders was abroad. National and local newspapers and journals were carrying the oft-elaborated story – and, more importantly, Billy's picture. He was exhausted as he descended into the station, ignoring what seemed to be an official, staring without really noticing. It was a busy scene; there must have been dozens in and out the place. Perhaps the official's idle brain was busy recollecting the morning news, even trying to remember the face staring at him from the print. Billy walked the anonymous streets, tired and hungry and fighting thirst. He was no stranger to thirst; chain gangs were mostly dry. He needed to find a room, a kind landlady; which he did and settled down after supper to a fitful sleep. The next morning, he walked out into Wetherby and enjoyed a walk in the bright sun and fresh air. These helped to clear away the foul odours of the hovel and the house of blood. On the Sunday morning, Billy found a Methodist Chapel. His old habits were well engrained; he thought a lot of his dear mother, and joined the Sunday service. Afterwards he thought to return to his lodgings, but first felt the need for a drink. The tavern, *Blacksmith's Arms,* was inviting, so inviting! Indeed, it looked warm and cosy. It was pretty busy as he stepped into the Tap Room and ordered a beer. It was a misjudgement, a massive misjudgement. The *Leeds Mercury* lay on the bar table, with a passable likeness of him for all to see. It felt like drowning, lost and helpless. Where was Heathlighter now? He could certainly have used his help. In that same second, the publican, James Mason, cried out,

"It's 'im!" like a man possessed.

The hubbub in the smoke-filled bar momentarily stopped, and a dozen pairs of eyes were fixed on Billy. Where he found the strength to sup his beer, he did not know. But he raised the glass to his lips, just noticing through the haze a lad slipping away behind the bar, where the publican was now so red in the face Billy feared he'd have apoplexy. His eyes met those of the publican's. This was a tight corner? He needed a ready wit – and coolness in this hostile atmosphere.

There were raised voices outside the tavern.

"What's that you say?"

"Murderer? What murderer?"

"Eee, lad! You be sackless!"

Evidently, the boy had reported it first to a mostly sceptical audience sitting on the stone steps. Out of breath and pale through his freckles, he told them, with no leading up to it, that he, Peppermint Billy, was in the beer house.

"He's never!" said one and another, together.

"Can't be!" - another.

Not all the onlookers were sceptical.

"We must do sommat!"

"By gum, after 'im!"

Almost immediately, William Eccles, the Parish Constable, and a well-built policeman joined them! He'd read the *Yorkshire Post* and had this villain's picture. Hearing the shouts on the steps, he urged the policeman forward, who drew his truncheon and made for the door. Billy made as if to walk out. As Billy gained the doorframe, he was swept up in the arms of this burly policeman who shouted an oath that sounded more like an obscenity than a cry of triumph. The Constable crashed into the bar after him and drew himself up to his full height.

"Your name?" he prodded, making it clear that it would be foolhardy, nay impossible, to take to one's heels.

The circle had narrowed. In as firm a voice as he could muster, Billy replied,

"I'm from Bedford, I'm William Parker".

The policeman seemed unconvinced and charged him with being the man who committed the murders at Melton, and his superior agreed. Within a few moments, the Parish Constable returned to the police station and caused a telegram to be sent to Goodyer in Leicestershire. He returned to the *Blacksmith's Arms*. It was four days since the murders were discovered. The manhunt, that involved the use of bloodhounds from Barkby Hall, was effectively over. The Parish Constable and the policeman then escorted him to the Wetherby lock-up. The Constable found out where he was lodging, so sent a constable to gather up his belongings. These were brought back to the police station where the Constable had ordered a search of Billy's clothing and person. An attractive watch was found together with a small bundle of letters addressed to one, Elizabeth Scott, of Nottingham. These items were all confiscated.

*

In Melton Mowbray, the Superintendent of Police, William Condon arrived in his office in an expectant mood. Surely an arrest could not be far off? Within an hour of arriving, he was in conversation with a County Police Constable, Edward Bishop,

"Brown's under arrest then!"

"Yes sir, we have notice from Wetherby that a man answering his description is under arrest".

"That's good work then!"

"Yes, very good and very speedy. Brown was arrested at four in the afternoon, and in Wetherby lock-up by half past the hour".

"OK, we need to get him returned to us – can you meet Goodyer at Normanton and help bring the prisoner to Leicester?"

"Yes sir, I will leave immediately".

*

The questioning at Wetherby resumed,

"I'm a gentleman's servant,' he protested, 'a watchmaker and can garden and groom and wash up dishes".

Clearly, the state of his hands gave a lie to all this. The Constable insisted,

"You're a weather-beaten man and never been employed at in-door services".

He asked,

"Have you ever been out of England?"

Billy emphatically denied it, adding,

"I found the envelopes addressed to Elizabeth Scott on the road, and I bought my watch at Nottingham for two pounds. I arrived from Nottingham on Thursday and before that I have been at Leeds, Ottley and Bradford".

Billy told him,

"I am a native of Bedford Town but have lived with Mr Johns at Greenwich and Mr Johns has gone into a foreign country".

The story seemed believable, and he was left alone for a short time. He could see through the glass partition that the office was buzzing with people, some uniformed. Suddenly, a fresh-faced young bobby arrived with a note that he handed to his superior. The Parish Constable then told Billy that an officer was coming from Leicester. He could squirm no more. He shook off all semblance and confessed,

"My name is Brown and it is no use telling any lies about it", he said, "the reason I denied being a convict was that I thought if it was known I should not get any work in the neighbourhood. I am Brown of Scalford and I slept in that hovel a couple of nights before, and I passed through the Tollgate, but never molested the old man".

Billy was put under lock and key, and a guard was posted at his door.

Within the confines of his cell, Billy was distraught,

"I've run my last race; cried my last tears. The world should know how easy it is to sink to the very depths of depravity. I've been there! It cost me the support of a very dear friend and broke my family. I sought revenge, and revenge is blind with false sweetness. Goaded by vicious men throughout my life, and one in particular provoked my unreason. I became a terrible behemoth to serve one purpose – cruel murder".

Above all, he recognised nobility too late,

"Bob was noble, but his life was cut short by evil. The lovely Ann showed nobility in her every waking moment, and in the choices she was forced to make. I forced her. What we briefly had was very precious".

Warm memories flooded his mind and disturbed his manhood, so that he turned away from his guard making a sharp intake of breath. The guard was alerted and rushed in to check his condition. He found him, kneeling, as if in prayer. He immediately withdrew.

*

Police Constable Edward Bishop and his boss, Goodyer arrived at Wetherby. They lost no time before reaching the Police Station and introducing themselves.

"Welcome, sir", said the duty officer, "Buckland! Take these gentlemen down to the cells to see prisoner Brown".

"This way", said Buckland, and walked to the far door and entered the corridor that led to the cellblock.

Goodyer approached the cell with something approaching exultation. The murderer was within his grasp! He spoke to the guard,

"What state is the prisoner in?"

"He's quiet, sir", the guard unlocked the cell door, "the last time I looked".

The four men walked in to find Billy flat on his back on the cell floor, his trouser flies were unbuttoned and the surrounding clothing was wet. The guard moved forward to pull him to his feet,

"Sort yourself out! Do those buttons up! You've got visitors".

Billy shuffled to comply, fumbling with his flies but getting exasperated that he couldn't manage them. He stood a forlorn figure, head cocked to one side, listening.

"William Brown, you are under arrest for the double murder of Edward and James Woodcock in the Toll Gate House, Melton Mowbray", said PC Bishop.

"We are here to escort you back to Leicester, where you shall stand trial", added Goodyer. He turned to the guard, "Get him cleaned up and ready to leave by one o'clock".

"Yes, sir", replied the guard, "There will be lunch for you, gentlemen, in the meantime".

Buckland found the scene distasteful,

"This way, gentlemen, let's go and find lunch". He led Goodyer and PC Bishop back along the corridor to the main desk. Lunch was being served in the Superintendent's office, so Buckland delivered them to that room.

Meanwhile, Billy was taken to the washrooms and stripped. Buckets of cold water were thrown over him and his clothing was wrung out in the laundry and dried over a warm steamer. Billy yelled, more for the indignity that he felt than for anything uncomfortable. Within half an hour, Billy was dressed in warm clothing and returned to his cell, where his own lunch was served. He picked at the indescribable mess, found a piece of meat and chewed it. He pushed the plate away and grabbed the apple. He enjoyed the fruit. At ten minutes to one, the guard returned and got him ready to leave. At five minutes to one, the guard led him out to the main desk, where Goodyer and Bishop were now waiting. The Superintendent was there for the formal handing over. This done, the prisoner was escorted to the train for his journey back to Leicester.

THIRTY TWO

Welford Road prison stood austere and forbidding about half a mile from the city centre of Leicester, at the junction of the road opposite the *Turks Head* Public House. The prison resembled an impressive and strong mediaeval castle, the sort you might see in the Welsh border country. It was unwelcoming to prisoners. Turret played a rondo with turret; battlements danced a gavotte with battlements. Prisoners were deposited without ceremony, just the turn of a key! Peppermint Billy was locked up, awaiting trial. The windows of his cell were set high in the wall, so that light slanted down like knives through butter, or arrows through the soul. Billy's thoughts were in turmoil, fresh from interrogation and confession. He agonised over the death of the young boy – an innocent in all this trouble. The old man paid the price of his interference in Billy's life, indeed in the whole family's business. As Bailiff he could have exercised some benevolence, but none was in evidence.

"Woodcock's done for, Mam", Billy addressed the memory of his lovely Mother, "He's paid back for Jim, Dick and me!"

It was an emotional moment, and tears welled up and brimmed over. Billy cried quietly; he had no wish to alert the guard, but the memory of his mother had a powerful pull. Almost as strongly, came the feeling of pride – yes, pride; to have known a warrior like Bob, Billy's best friend. Pride in meeting the challenge from Woodcock and his cronies, and winning through. Billy wins! He was receiving the champion's trophy, but Ann dashed it to the ground. Ann, his dear love, was angry. She wanted to know,

"Billy! Why did you leave me?"

"My noble Ann, I am so sorry!"

Billy responded to her anger all over again, and cried softly for a while. His whole humour changed as he thought of his older brother, Jim – presently in Van Dieman's Land. His memories were warm; they wrapped him in a shawl of sensitive, fraternal love. Billy particularly remembered the brotherly care he showed, in the Battle of Colston for example, or in the raid on Harby. Billy's smiles returned.

He was in cheerful mood, when he received a visitor. The Governor made his introductions,

"Good evening, William Brown. Are you ready for your trial tomorrow?"

"Good evening, sir, I feel quite prepared".

"You do realise, I hope, that there is no defence. This is because of your confession. So the trial is a formality to allow the jury to come to a decision on your guilt. The law will then mete out punishment".

"I am aware, sir, that I am now in the hands of the jury".

"God bless you, William Brown".

"Thank you, sir"

*

The smell of the courtroom on this fourteenth day of July in the Year of Our Lord 1856 was heavy with wax polish. The wooden bowl of justice gleamed. Atop this bowl, the Lord Chief Justice Jervis was a towering figure with a fine aquiline nose and piercing blue eyes. These scanned the courtroom below with precision and something approaching bombast, as the effect on those beneath his gaze is immediate and very salutary, as when a child was admonished or a junior clerk upbraided by the accountant. Thus, Peppermint Billy in the dock counted for very little in the panoply of red, black and gold ranged before and above him. The lion and the unicorn squared up against each other, their limbs balanced the royal shield precariously between them; as Billy's life was similarly balanced delicately between the prosecution and the defence. Another lion lurked around the regal ermine and crimson cap atop the crown. As he smelt the polished, panelled walls and seats, Billy knew that there were legal dangers lying in wait for him!

The work of the court was gearing up for the start of testimonies; first hearing from the prosecution. The defendant's attention was on the Scottish lion, lurching fiercely against his red tressured fence; Billy's knuckles tightened on the rail of his box. The Irish harp was silent, brooding, and mysterious; the courtroom was hushed and expectant as Mr Mellor opened the case for the prosecution. Billy's fingers drummed; they clutched the polished rail, just as the three playful leopards of England gambolled across their scarlet field, glistening in the sunlight that suddenly filled the courtroom. Mellor's words did not gambol; he spoke with calm confidence. His pronunciation was crisp and sharp, spitting out the words rather than rolling them. As the harpist then strummed and stroked, Mellor spoke gently through a litany of truths that seemed to him so self-evident that this trial might be deemed unnecessary. He was of the 'take him out and hang him!' school. Even so, he was confidently going through the procedures laid down in Her Majesty's laws. Everything in its place for Lord Chief Justice Jervis!

Every word reached Billy's comprehension. He listened carefully to Alfred Routen, the baker from Asfordby, who discovered the two bodies at the Toll Gate House on 19 June.

"I got out of the cart and observed the door of the Toll House a little open and I saw the body of a man lying on the floor in a pool of blood, dead".

The baker apparently ran to the first house and then to the Parish Constable Clayton to tell them what he had seen. John Clayton, the Parish Constable of Thorpe Arnold testified that the Baker had called him up about half past four o'clock in the early morning of 19 June.

"The Toll Bar is situate about a quarter of a mile from my house. I immediately went to the Toll Bar and found the Door partly open and Edward Woodcock lying dead in a pool of blood on the House floor. His face and neck were all over blood and several cuts upon him, there was also what appeared to be a pistol-shot wound in his breast".

Billy looked down at his feet, as the Parish Constable continued,

"I went into the adjoining Room and saw the body of a little boy named James Woodcock who resided with old Woodcock at the Toll-Bar - he was dead and lying upon his face on the Bed. I observed his throat was cut and his head nearly severed from his body and there were also two cuts on his loins. I found a pistol lying on the floor of the House close to the body of the old Man. There was a quantity of Blood on the Pistol. I also found a Tobacco-stopper on the House floor near the door. I gave the same Pistol and Tobacco-stopper to Condon the Police Constable".

Billy chose not to listen to the description of the two bodies found in that house. He had as clear a picture in his mind as anyone in the courtroom. So the testimony of Surgeon Barwis passed right over him with no obvious effect. Billy listened mostly with his head cocked on one side, probably because of his squint, possibly to avoid the glare of the sunlight. This led to Mellor repeating or emphasising a point here and there, in the belief that the prisoner might not have heard the proceedings. Mellor introduced the witness William Condon, who was not just a 'constable', but the Superintendent of Police who lived in Melton Mowbray. He confirmed the receipt of the pistol and the tobacco stopper. This caused Billy to cuss silently as he remembered his folly at dropping them in the Toll Gate House. Condon had shown the tobacco stopper to Cooke, the watchmaker at Nottingham. He'd also received a leaden bullet from the Surgeon Barwis, and on testing it with the pistol found it rolled down the barrel. It was Condon who had visited the hovel near Doctors Lane. Inexorably, the trial wound on. It was now the turn of two neighbours of Bedford Street, Leicester – William Asher, a coal higgler, and William Moulding, a framework knitter. Both of these remembered Billy visiting home, going away with his brother's wife and the disturbance he made when he returned alone. Billy smiled at the manner in which they gave evidence, one hesitant and the other loud. He continued to smile as they described Billy waving his pistol around in the street and threatening,

"God strike me dead if I would not shoot the first man dead that meddled with her".

He remembered defending his beloved Ann, and would do so even then if he were free to do so.

The next witness caused some astonishment to Billy. John Carpendale owned two fields off Doctors lane and remembered Billy quizzing him about old Woodcock,

"He asked me whether the old man went to bed or sat up all night. I said "I did not know, but if any body went to the Gate at night he must get up to let them through"".

The old pensioner Joseph was called next. He lived in a cottage not far from the Toll Gate, and he remembered Billy talking about Woodcock and whether he lived alone or not. Billy sat up straight to listen to his old school friend, William Moore, who then identified the clothing found by the police as matching what Billy wore when he was working with him. He also remembered that Billy had worked for him in Doctors Lane cleaning out the ditches, and that he had gone to look at the hovel that the prisoner apparently slept in. Indeed, William could see the stubble marks; that the Toll Gate could be seen from the front of the hovel; that the hovel was only three hundred yards from the Toll Gate. Nothing in Billy's demeanour changed. Did he feel betrayed by his old friend? Rather – he felt satisfied that a true version of events had been delivered to the court.

The next witness was the man who interrupted Billy in the hovel to ask if he was going to sleep in it,

"I said, "Hello, old Boy, what are you doing here?" He said, "I am resting a bit". I said, "Then you mean taking your lodging here tonight". He said "No, I don't, I might do so, if I was drunk, But I sha'nt tonight". I then went away".

Thomas Roberts, one of the constables at Scalford, about three miles from the Toll Gate, gave his evidence relating to the discovery of bloodstained clothes,

"I got into the ditch amongst the weeds which were very high and a very deep ditch. I set my foot upon a black silk handkerchief and in the same ditch a few yards from each other I found a pair of corduroy trousers, waistcoat and shirt. The trousers, shirt, and waistcoat were torn up and in a wet state as though they had been recently washed. I gave all the same articles to Police Constable Fox, and Fox and I afterwards searched and found a hat".

At that point, Mr Mellor cross-examined the witness, wanting to know if the constable knew the prisoner,

"I know the prisoner has been transported some years ago. I first saw him again on Monday the 9th June last in Scalford Town Street, and there were many people around him, I heard him say, "I will not be transported for nothing next time, I will do something to be talked about". This distance from Scalford Village to where I found the clothes is about a mile, and there is a road leading from the place where I found the clothes to Stathern, and it does not pass through any Village on the way there".

The witness, William Fox, confirmed he had received the clothes, but had passed them on to Superintendent Burdett. Superintendent Burdett confirmed he had received the clothes, but after finding spots of shoemaker's wax on the trousers he gave a portion of them to the surgeon Barwis. The Scalford Blacksmith, John Hewerdine, gave evidence of those clothes being worn by the prisoner in his shop on 16th June,

"I was present on Monday the 16th June when the prisoner was at our Shop, when my Father said to the prisoner, "Billy, you must mind, if they get hold of you again you will go for life". The prisoner said, "I should not like to be transported any more, I'd sooner be hung, and maybe I shall be yet".

The evidence of Ann, his brother's wife, had a marked effect on Billy. He found it almost too much to bear. He had lost her love utterly, and here she was telling the court that the clothes were very like those given to Billy by her husband. Billy recognised the nobility of Ann's statement. She was in staunch support of her husband. Billy's face was calm and his pulse raced a little fast. He kept his eyes lowered rather than to look at his lovely Ann disowning him. He wanted to tell her how sorry he was, but of course this was impossible in the courtroom. John, his own brother was called next and Billy was mortified, thinking that he had done such wrong to his brother. It was his brother's testimony that clearly identified Billy's trousers and his hat. John did not look at his brother in the dock the whole time. He trembled a great deal, as he usually did at times of stress.

The clock and watchmaker from Nottingham, John Cooke was there. He wore owlish spectacles, and stooped a little, as if he was at his workbench. He remembered Billy well, his awkward squint and his shamble. He recalled Billy's rough hands – never meant for careful work, not 'bookish'. He particularly remembered the tobacco stopper, hand-fashioned and 'colonial', mixed up in the small change that Billy proffered for payment,

"He pulled out his money three or four shillings in silver, some coppers, a knife, some string and a tobacco stopper which he held with his money in his hand until he had paid me. The tobacco stopper now produced by Condon I make no doubt is the same although I am unable positively to swear to it".

Billy heard this part of John Cooke's testimony and was reminded of the kindness of old George – a simple gift that now served to condemn him. Moreover, the Parish Constable of Wetherby, Henry Crossley testified to finding paper in Billy's watch. This, the watch recovered from where it had been dropped in the Toll Gate House. This, the watch printed with a picture of a kangaroo and the legend 'Launceston VDL'. This, the watch that certainly nailed him as lately returning from his transportation to Van Diemans Land. Billy wondered why he had dropped it? Why had he found the watch so interesting? The very features that encouraged him to steal it, from the sleeping man at Ma Whittle's Boarding House, now condemned him. He nodded as Brian Farah, the ship's carpenter gave his evidence – the prisoner's clear intention revealed twice – to take revenge.

There were other witnesses, but it was in the third hour that Mr Mellor began his summing up. For this most heinous crime, he demanded the death penalty. The jury agreed and the prisoner was asked if he had anything to say. In the packed courthouse, Peppermint Billy defiantly said,

"It's all false, it's all spite and malice and nothing else!"

Lord Chief Justice Jervis received a square of black cloth. Billy stood as upright as he could and fixed his gaze on the bewigged and powdered figure above him, mesmerised by the actions of an aide who placed the black square of silk over the wig of the Lord Chief Justice. Everything in the correct fashion for Lord Chief Justice Jervis!

Jervis intoned the sentence,

"...that you be taken to a place of lawful execution and there to be hung by the neck until dead".

This was rock bottom, Billy!

"...and may God have mercy on your soul".

*

Billy wrote this in his prison cell, the condemned man.

"This is a grim place. I've seen better in this land and over the seas. What a difference now! Payment is due, my life for the toll. My heart breaks for Ann, her love, her warmth. But I guess it's no use supposing now. It cannot be and that's a fact. Or just suppose that my beginnings were elsewhere but Scalford, not in that place where, with three brothers and a sister, I learnt to take milk from the parlour, race snails up a neighbour's door; or later rustle a horse, and fire a hayrick when the farmer pressed his anger too far. My brothers were my teachers and I a star pupil. I'm beginning to think that a different upbringing in another place could have determined my present fate differently. Or perhaps, my lovely Mother were not mine but another's; then darling Ann were not my brother's! Such thoughts, such longings tear me to pieces. *Let the day perish wherein I was born*, I young Billy, to 'Peppermint Jack' and Mother. My brother John I wronged utterly, and yet he cries and trembles, too cut up to be with Father".

Elizabeth, his sister, was a powerful comfort to Billy, with Dick and Jim still overseas for all he knew. Hanging tomorrow, the Lord's vengeance would take him from the earth. They were a world away from those heady days of childhood, three tearaways, as when Billy took a plump duck from a farm with help from Jim, cooked it in clay and they enjoyed it. Farmers were enraged and the boys chuckled. The upshot was, villagers came that day, shouting and cussing, with cudgels and rakes, and pulled down the cottage around their ears so that his Mam and Dad took the family off to Frisby, towards Leicester, where life continued to have its ups and downs. His widowed father Jack stood then at the Turk's Head opposite in sight of the gallows. Ann had thought long and hard about her relationship with Billy, realising that her love for John was supreme – a decision that was respected by Billy as a noble decision. Yet, she had sent in a precious note with golden words as sweet as honey, the words of her forgiveness.

Epilogue

William Brown, also known as 'Peppermint Billy', was hung at 8am on the morning of Friday 25 July 1856 at the Leicester Prison on Welford Road. It was the last public execution in Leicester. A crowd of 25,000 gave little trouble to the 150-strong squad of Goodyer's police. Jack, Billy's father, watched the proceedings from the vantage point of the *Turks Head* public house across the road. As Billy swung on the gallows, his father was heard to say,
"Well done Billy. Tha's died a brick".

Billy made no confession; gave no reason for his actions. It is the contention of this storyteller that the guiding statement by Billy, given twice to the witness Thomas Sarah, is the *raison d'etre*,
"Thank God we are getting pretty near home – I will have my revenge and then be off again, and I will murder the person who sent me".

There was toll money in the house that fateful night. It was not touched. The police story of simple theft is too simple. If Billy's revenge was indeed to be perpetrated on Edward Woodcock, the Toll Gate Keeper, then the reason behind it has to concern the 1843 Assizes when Billy was sentenced to transportation for ten years. Edward Woodcock may well have been a jury member, even the Chairman of the Jury, so that his position on the jury was significant enough for Billy to remember and to later seek revenge.

*

When my Grandfather, William Thomas Randle, died in 1957 aged 84, local newspapers claimed him to be distantly related to the murdered Toll Gate Keeper and his grandson. Whilst Grandfather's sister, Mary Ann witnessed the marriage of his stepsister Ellen Radford to Thomas B Woodcock in 1899, the family tree research conducted by me indicates no relationship to the murdered man and boy, or to their families. Edward Woodcock, and his sons were born in Dudley, Staffordshire. The father of Thomas B Woodcock was born in Rutland. My Radford cousins concur with these findings.

Tim Randle

About the Author

Tim Randle was born in Melton Mowbray in 1942. His grandfather, William Thomas Randle was born in the Toll Gate House at Melton – the scene of the Peppermint Billy double murders.

He is a retired Headteacher and School Inspector who now works as a genealogical researcher. He is married with two grown sons and two grandchildren. He now lives in Surrey.

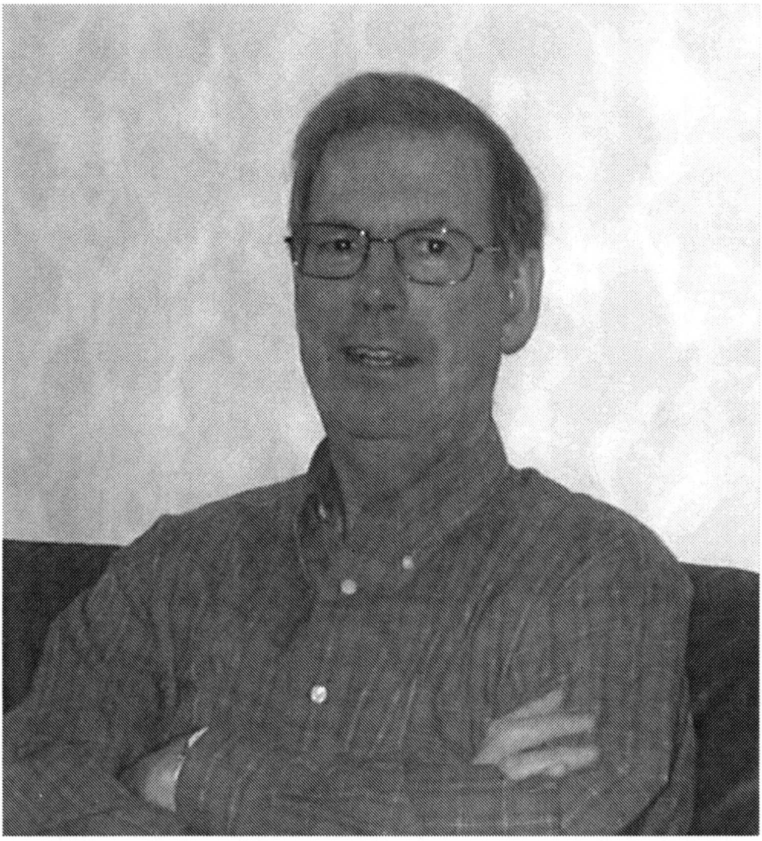